A THIN SHARP BLADE

FRAN SMITH

I

Professor Legrand's tabby cat, a sweet-faced friendly animal, especially beloved of the children in Eden Street, liked to sit between the railings on the knee-high wall and stand on her toes, rubbing a cheek against the black uprights, purring to be stroked.

That morning little George Goodman spotted Minmou from across the street and before his nursemaid could prevent it, he hurried over, paying no attention to the dairyman's horse waiting outside number eleven. The two-year-old's chubby hands were held aloft, ready to feel soft fur. 'Pus-stat!' he called.

It was only Vita and the nursemaid who saw what happened next.

The horse, who wore blinkers, turned its head and must have caught a glimpse of a flapping shape rushing towards its hindquarters. It bucked violently, causing the dairy cart to rock, rattling crates of milk bottles, tossing one or two out to smash on the road. Its right rear hoof caught George, so that he was lifted, spinning, into the air. His hat flew off. His sailor collar flapped. Vita had the image in her mind for weeks afterwards; a plump body, arms wide, legs pedalling, seeming to hang aloft a moment, then beginning to fall towards the elegant row of cast iron arrowheads pointing upwards along the top of the railings.

There was a long silence as the child landed, jerking as his trajectory was interrupted by the sudden catch of a spike. Vita, throwing aside an armful of books, reached him first, and stepped between the boy and his shrieking nursemaid, instinctively wanting to spare her the sight. The sharpness of the upturned spikes, the undefended softness of George's little body, the swift momentum of his fall - it seemed to Vita, as her mind struggled to take everything in, that the most terrible injuries were inevitable. And she was there first. What should she do?

The nursemaid staggered and fell wailing to her knees, leaving Vita to take the weight of the boy's hanging body and lift it to release the pressure. George was at shoulder height and limp, his face a little blue. She called to the dairyman, now running towards her, to help. As she did so, George shuddered and came to life, uttering a short roar of outrage. His face reddened as Vita watched because his clothes were tight at the neck, where she now saw the sharp black point protruding close to his left ear.

'Hold him up,' Vita called, and climbed onto the wall to fumble at George's neck. Finding three tiny buttons, she struggled them clear of their finely crocheted loops. It seemed to take far too long. The boy was now making a gurgling sound, flailing his arms and kicking his small buttoned boots. In the background the terrified cries of his nursemaid echoed around the street. Neighbours ran to their windows in alarm. At last the square blue collar came away from the jacket. The boy drew a long breath. His cheek was pressed against the sharp black arrowhead.

'We must lift him up and away,' Vita told the dairyman.

'You take him under the arms. I shall push from underneath.'

She so feared the child's injuries that she quailed and felt like closing her eyes, but the dairyman did not notice and followed her instructions. Between them they raised the boy clear of the spikes and set him on the pavement. He lay there silent and rigid, his eyes tightly shut, his hands in fists, the golden curls that his sisters so admired a tangle on the muddy flagstones.

Vita pulled off her shawl and set the boy upon it. Turning him over, pulling his clothing aside, dreading the sight of ripped flesh, the spread of scarlet blood into the crisp pleated undershirt, she found only a long reddening line running down his spine. It had barely even broken the skin. The arrowhead had missed George entirely. Instead of being skewered – the injuries too catastrophic to imagine – he had been hung like a coat on a hook by his sailor collar. Later examination found that apart from this long graze his most serious injury was a curved bruise on one hip, presumed to be the first impact of the horse's hoof.

Most of the railings in Eden Street had their arrowheads removed soon afterwards. Professor Legrand kept his; a single man and a mathematician, he declared the probability of a similar accident in Eden Street to be infinitesimally remote. Neighbours thought him a cold fish, even if he happened to be right.

Mrs Goodman, George's mother, had seen her baby son hanging from the railings out of her drawing room window. Once recovered from the shock, she declared Vita a heroine and told her husband and all her friends about the girl's admirable presence of mind. The sailor collar was framed and hung in the hall, its ragged hole forever reminding children to be more careful than Georgie as they crossed the street. The nursemaid left and went to work in Newmarket, in a street without railings.

Another consequence was that Vita, even while the little boy was being marvelled over and a small crowd had gathered to tut and re-tell the tale – he was already being tossed higher and further with each telling – Vita decided that she must know more. She never again wanted to feel the helplessness she had felt as she ran towards the little body hanging from the railings. What if the spike had not missed him?

Georgie's father, Dr Goodman, a short, intense Welshman, called that evening. 'I believe my little son owes you his life, Miss Carew,' he declared, shaking her hand vigorously. 'My wife tells me you ran to help without hesitation. It was most courageous. I assume you have some medical knowledge?'

'No, none at all!' Vita told him. 'I have never felt so wretchedly ignorant.'

'Why then you must attend my First Aid classes!' he boomed, his thick fist encircling the tiny sherry glass Aunt Louisa had offered. 'Thursdays at the Emmanuel Hall.'

'Are these *ladies'* classes?' Aunt Louisa wondered.

'If Fate arranged for a qualified *gentleman* to be present at every accident, first aid would hardly be necessary,' Dr Goodman declared, swallowing his sherry in a single gulp. 'Until that day, I shall welcome both ladies and gentlemen to my classes, and both will be trained to save lives! I firmly believe that the skills of rescue and resuscitation are essential learning for everyone, Mrs Brocklehurst. Today's incident proves my point, I'm sure you'll agree.'

It was difficult to disagree with the booming vigour of Dr Goodman.

'I should like very much to come, if my aunt permits it,' Vita told him.

Dr Goodman winked in conspiracy. 'Don't worry. I shall persuade her,' he boomed, as if her aunt were not there, standing next to him.

2

The First Aid class was full of unfamiliar anxieties for Vita. What should she take? Would a notebook and pencil seem too presumptuous or would it be the barest minimum? What should she wear? Would there be strenuous activity? Her aunt watched her dither in the hall, fiddling with her hat, picking up and then putting down her notebook, and could stand it no more.

'Are you ever going to leave, dear? You have stood there for half an hour.'

'I am suddenly unsure. I have never attended a class. Not in anything. How am I to behave?'

Aunt Vita looked the girl up and down and decided now was not the moment to mention the lace trim that had ripped along one sleeve, or the dab of mud on her skirt.

'Your manners are excellent, Vita. Your natural instincts will tell you what to do.'

'The others are all policemen, Dr Goodman says.'

'Yes. That is unfortunate, but they will at least be well-behaved, one imagines, even if they are not, strictly speaking, gentlemen.' Louisa opened the front door and stood expectantly beside it. 'You know the way. And Vita, if it becomes...uncomfortable, thank them politely and come home. You need not subject yourself to First Aid classes if they include unpleasantness.'

It was the word 'unpleasantness' that set Vita's feet in motion. She hurried down Eden Street towards the Church Hall, clutching her notebook. It was not that she wanted to hurry towards unpleasantness, or hungered for it, but she passed the now blunted railings where Georgie had once hung and was reminded what had led to this.

Twelve young police officers, in full uniform, were already standing in a group when she peered round the arched wooden door. Clustered, they reminded Vita of a set of comic skittles in a child's bowling alley. Dr Goodman's voice rang out from a dim corner of the hall, 'Come in, Miss Carew. Gentlemen, please join me in welcoming our newest recruit. Now, this evening's subject is How to Stop Bleeding. Charlie here,' he indicated a boy of about ten standing to one side, 'is our patient, and we are going to practise the main methods of preventing severe loss of blood after an injury. We will begin with injuries to the limbs and then move on to wounds to the torso and head. Well, class? Don't just stand there, I want you in groups of three or four! Let's get to it!'

It was a chilly hall. The chairs were not comfortable and the tea they brewed half way through the lesson was not particularly good either, but Vita remembered that lesson for the rest of her life. She learnt to raise bleeding limbs above the heart and apply pressure to wounds on the torso and head. She came away with a booklet and a pile of bandages to practise with before the next class, but more importantly she left with a sense of purpose so powerful that it made her charge like a bolting pony all the way home.

Dr Goodman called a fortnight later to report to Aunt Louisa.

'The girl is a natural first aider, Mrs Brocklehurst. She is calm, deft, and quick to learn. She leaves my police constables far behind in every class. You say she shows an interest in science?'

'She reads her brother's college books. He is in the second year of Natural Sciences at Trinity.'

'Does Vita think of studying herself? If so, I should like to encourage her.'

'It would offer false hope, I'm afraid.'

'Why do you say so?'

'Frankly, there are insufficient funds in the family for the education of both my brother's children.'

'That is regrettable. She shows a marked aptitude, as I say. Will you allow me to pursue the matter on her behalf?'

Louisa looked doubtful. 'Vita has not been well-educated. She nursed her mother for several years and before that relied on a rather eccentric German governess. Practical first aid is one thing, but any sort of academic study of science would far outstrip her capacities. Besides, where can it lead?'

'To the advancement of a promising young mind; to the expansion of intellect...'

'To what end? Only frustration, surely, if she threw herself into studying only to find her learning could have no outlet. I have seen women made miserable by being thwarted in such a way.'

Dr Goodman was not so easily shifted. 'Indeed,' he said. 'But I have also seen them made miserable for the opposite reason: the restriction and confinement of a good mind can lead to a lifetime of bitterness.' Goodwin's tone, bantering and jovial at first, had now become so serious that the room seemed to darken around them.

'Dr Goodwin, I mean only to do the best for my niece. She has few advantages in life.'

'Then let her develop her God-given gift – let her try her

hand at least at studying science. She can continue to read her brother's books, and she can attend some of the lectures – they are public, young women are seen there. It may be that she tires of the project, or develops some other interest, but for the time being, why not allow it?'

It was in the face of this tidal wave of Welsh persuasion that Louisa Brocklehurst let her niece lose on the world of academic science – to the extent of allowing her to read her brother's books and spend at least some of her days at a little desk in her room in uninterrupted study. But she could not remain inside the confines of her room forever, especially after Dr Goodman had given her a printed copy of the lecture list.

3

It took Vita several attempts to attend a lecture. At first she was too afraid to do more than watch from the street as boisterous crowds of young men surged into the lecture buildings, their gowns waving behind them. 'Don't block the door, there's a good girl,' one of them said when she dared to approach a lecture room, 'this is Physics, it isn't for you.'

Vita could, by arriving early, find a seat right at the back, where the young men were less likely to stare, and where there might even be one or two college ladies to keep her company. If she was late she could not bear to go in; it would mean opening the heavy double doors and walking to wherever a seat was free in full and hostile view of everyone already sitting in the raked seats of the lecture hall – a fate too awful to be contemplated.

So generally, arriving breathless to find the doors closed and the lecture under way, Vita sat outside on the stairs. In many ways this was not such a penalty. The lecture was quite audible and she could spread her papers out and sit comfortably taking notes on her knee, but there was the major disadvantage that the diagrams on the chalkboard could not be seen. Once or twice already this had meant that her notes, when she re-read them, made very little sense.

'As you will see *here*, and *here*,' she would hear the lecturer say, 'there are clear differences...' but they were frustratingly not clear to her. She waited until everyone had left at the end and crept in to see if anything was left on the board. It usually was. Lecturers rarely stooped so low (or rather stretched so high) as to clean their own blackboards.

Cambridge was lovely that morning. Autumn was turning the leaves and a high wind the night before had tossed them into orderly golden puddles at the foot of each chestnut tree in the gardens of Downing College. Clutching the music case she used to carry her books, Vita hurried on, the chill in the air catching her breath and the tailwind of the previous night's storm snatching at her hat, making the hatpins tug at her hair. The clocks chimed twelve while she was still only half way there, so she was resigned to another lecture spent on the stairs, but when she reached them she found another young woman already settled in her place, writing.

The girl was leaning intently forward, her ear turned to the double doors, trying to hear the lecture. Without interrupting, Vita sat beside her, taking her notebook out as quietly as she could. Together they listened to Mr Montgomery's description of the process of titration for the duration of his lecture, then with practised efficiency, the moment he finished with, 'Thank, you gentlemen, until next week, then,' both stuffed books and pens back into bags and slipped off the stairs, out onto the street and into a doorway, before the jostling crowd of young men elbowed their way out and dispersed on foot or bicycle, heading hungrily back to their colleges for luncheon.

It was only then that the two young women had a chance to speak.

'I usually go inside and copy the diagrams once they've all left,' the other young woman told Vita .

They went into the lecture room and quickly began to copy Montgomery's diagrams into their notebooks.

'I'm Clara Benn, by the way,' the other young woman said, offering her hand.

'Vita Carew.' They shook hands, smiling, and would have said more, except that the doors burst open and a pair of young men strode in.

'I swear I left the damned thing on the bench...' one was saying, but they fell silent when the saw the girls and sauntered over, looking over their shoulders at what they were doing.

'Ah, copying things down, ladies?' one said, 'this is Science, you understand. *Science. Titration.*'

'Oh, come on Tubby, leave them to play at being bluestockings, I want my lunch,' said the other, clambering up the bank of seats and finding his pen where he had left it.

'They always scribble away,' Tubby went on, speaking as if the ladies were not there at all, despite being close enough for them to smell the tobacco on his breath as he leaned between them. 'I have a whole row of them in my elementary Anatomy lecture and they take the most painstaking notes. I don't believe they understand a single word. I swear they've come to the wrong room and think they're studying Divinity!'

'They'll soon realise their mistake when they reach certain parts of the anatomy, I dare say!' said one, slapping his friend's shoulder.

'Food! Come on!' said the other, and they clattered out of the lecture hall again, their roar of laughter echoing after them.

'Well,' said Vita, 'I'm glad I did not have to face those two alone.'

'They're harmless enough,' Clara told her. 'You'll meet a lot worse. One thing they said made perfect sense, though, lunch is a very good idea. Would you join me for something? There is a tearoom nearby.'

4

'Good for you,' Clara said, over mushrooms on toast in the steamy tearoom.

It was the first time anyone had ever reacted to Vita's tentative plan to study with spontaneous warm encouragement. The shock made Vita blink hard and fumble with her knife. 'It's Anatomy for me,' Clara went on, 'I've always been fascinated. My father was a vet – a horse doctor. I assisted him in his practice for years.'

'Have you been attending lectures here for long?'

'This is my second year. I'm at Newton College. There are nine of us scientists there altogether. And you?'

'I've only attended a few. I read my brother's notes occasionally. He is at Trinity.'

'Do you plan to study yourself?'

'There isn't much chance,' Vita said, 'I am not well educated, and the expense...'

'There are numerous scholarships, had you thought of that?'

'For women?'

'Yes.'

'I'm not sure I would be eligible – or clever enough.'

'I'll make some enquiries, if you would like,' Clara said. 'And if you could study more formally, would it be Natural Sciences? Perhaps you are interested in Medicine?'

Vita found it difficult to reply. The idea had been hidden inside her own head for so long that she was shocked to hear it spoken aloud.

'You can't graduate or gain a medical certification,' Clara continued, 'but I know some women who have travelled to Switzerland or Paris, you can qualify there.'

'Switzerland?'

'Lucerne, to be precise.'

'And they go alone? They study alone?'

'They do. The expense is considerable, obviously. And one must learn the language to a high standard. I have known several ladies who have done so. And one who went to Paris. I have a friend at the Women's School of Medicine in London, too. She can't qualify formally, but she is content to work without it.'

'I fear the expense. My father would fear it, anyway.'

'I understand,' Clara said, 'but you should not allow that on its own to prevent you from pursuing your calling, if it is a genuine calling.' She set her knife and fork together on her plate and touched her napkin to her lips, smiling.

Vita sighed, 'I may not be able to make the choice myself,' she said.

'I don't know your personal situation, of course, but I do know that an element of determination is usually necessary. That's something we all have to learn. It was a pleasure to share the stairs - and lunch - with you, but now I must be getting along, I have work to do this afternoon. No doubt we shall meet either in or outside a lecture again. Here...' she pulled a crumpled document from her bag and put it on the table. 'You can keep this, but do not part with it. It is a private newsletter circulated only among women students. We try to keep it to ourselves.'

5

Eden Street in Cambridge in October 1903 was generally a peaceful enough place at half past seven on a Wednesday morning. Maids were about their work, early deliveries of food and coal were beginning, but on the whole you were more likely to hear the song of blackbirds or the boots of passing workmen on the cobblestones than a loud scream.

A passer-by might have analysed this scream as a short, shocked cry - more a bellow than a wail - expressing outrage rather than fear. If the same passer-by had waited a short time (not passed-by, in other words, but lingered) he or she would have heard a slammed door followed by raised voices and within the half-hour, the same loiterer would have seen a large and angry woman carrying a bulging Gladstone bag flounce down the front steps and march determinedly off towards the city centre.

'Mrs Teague gone?' Aunt Louisa asked, over breakfast. 'Dear me. Why would that be?'

Vita looked down at her plate. 'It was my doing, I'm afraid. It was a dissection. I thought I'd covered it. She screamed when she saw it in my study and said she could not stay in the house if that sort of thing was going on.' She buttered a piece of toast and reached for the honey. Her aunt stirred her tea carefully before replying,

'A dissection, Vita?'

'Yes, Aunt. It's when you...examine something in order to study what's inside it. Dissection is essential in the study of...'

'What sort of thing were you examining?'

'An amphibian,' Vita said, 'the breathing organs of an amphibian. I shall go on to the blood vessels and nerves after that.'

'Do you keep the creature in a tank?' asked her aunt. 'Where did you procure this amphibian?'

Vita feeling uncomfortable with the line of questioning, concentrated on pouring her aunt a cup of tea.

'What do you feed it?' her aunt went on, frowning into her teacup.

'I do not...It does not need food, Aunt. It is dead.'

'A dead frog? In your bedroom? This is what Mrs Teague disliked so heartily, I suppose. What good to you is a dead frog?'

'Well, as I said, I need to examine it.'

'How? How can one...? Wait. Are you cutting it up?'

'Yes. You see in order to...'

'You are splitting dead frogs open in your bedroom? Small wonder a perfectly good maid has just marched out of the house.'

'It is a very neat and inoffensive procedure, Aunt. I am following exactly the same process the students of Biology follow. Edward would have dissected frogs, birds and probably small mammals last year before he was able to go on to human anatomy.'

'But your brother did not do this in his bedroom, Vita .'

'No, the students have laboratories. Even the women's colleges have them.'

'Does it not smell? Is it not unwholesome, contaminating? Does it not putrefy?'

'Not at all, I assure you,' her niece replied. 'I have followed the directions to the letter. I used formaldehyde, Aunt, it really doesn't smell unpleasant. Not once you're accustomed to it.'

Her aunt, whose own work frequently filled the house with the smell of turpentine or linseed oil, took a sip of her tea, raising an eyebrow. 'I won't allow anything that smells unpleasant, Vita. It isn't fair to the servants or the neighbours. '

'Edward's professor says animal dissection is the crucial first step in the study of anatomy.'

'But aren't there books?'

'Of course, but one must learn the practical skills as well. It's very delicate work. The blood vessels and the nerves are tiny. It takes great precision.'

'I'm sure it does, but if it frightens the staff away we shall be in great difficulty.'

'I regret that, but who could have predicted that Mrs Teague would be so sensitive? She looks as if she could wrestle a bullock, frankly, and my frog is nothing horrifying. In its own way, it is in fact very beautiful.' Vita glanced up, caught her aunt's eye, and quickly added, 'I apologise, Aunt. It was inconsiderate to leave a dissection uncovered. Perhaps I could help you find a new maid?'

'It is not easy to find good servants, Vita, especially in a city like Cambridge, where they can so readily find work at the colleges. We must take care not to offend any more of them. I must insist that you lock your study door in future.'

'I will, Aunt, and I regret causing Mrs Teague to leave so dramatically.'

Louisa Brocklehurst sipped her tea. She was a neat woman, mostly dressed in black, but with a white lace cap on silvering fair hair. Her hands, holding the decorated bone china teacup, were delicate, but often paint-stained. There was a piercing quality to her light blue eyes, which even now, whilst expressing concern, if not actual irritation, shone with a steady enjoyment of life. She was fond of her niece, and pleased to see Vita's energies renewed by the course of studies she had assigned herself, even if science and Biology in particular seemed an eccentric choice.

Losing a maid was certainly inconvenient, but Louisa's greatest domestic fear was that she might lose Monsieur Picard, her French chef. Monsieur's cooking was superb. No guest ever left a dinner at Louisa Brocklehurst's hungry or unimpressed. Maids came and went, but nothing must ever offend Monsieur, for his *boef bourgignon* and *crepes suzettes* attracted the great and the good to Mrs Brocklehurst's table, and an excellent French dinner frequently encouraged them to commission the portraits that supported the household.

6

The crash of a bicycle thrown to the ground outside and footsteps bounding up the steps to the door alerted the ladies to the arrival of a tall young man, who swept into the room and began immediately to butter a piece of toast.

'Good morning, Edward dear,' said Aunt Louisa, unconcerned by this ravenous raid on her breakfast table.

Edward leaned over and hastily kissed the cheeks of his aunt and his sister before taking another huge bite of toast. His aunt handed him a cup of tea which he drank in one gulp.

'Morning ladies,' he said, 'I must hurry to my 9 o'clock lecture, it's Professor Rusbridge and he's a stickler. I need my Anatomy books, Sis. And the diagram. The hand, wasn't it?'

'Yes. The tendons drawn and labelled. They're ready on the table in the hall,' Vita told him.

'I hope you have been accurate. And not too pretty. Last time he said it looked pretty enough to be the work of a lady. The chaps all laughed merrily at that one.'

Vita frowned. 'Pretty? I simply used coloured pencils for the labels for the sake of clarity.'

'Yes, well, don't do it again. Nothing wrong with getting a bit of help with diagrams and so on, but one needs a certain discretion. I can't have Rusbridge thinking I delegate all the donkey work to my little sister.'

'Is that what you do, Edward?' asked Louisa, passing her nephew the toast rack.

'Not at all,' he said, 'I simply allow Vita to read my notes and lend her my textbooks. In return she provides a few drawings, preferably without any girlish flourishes. Isn't that so, Vee?'

'What will Rusbridge be lecturing on this morning?' Vita asked.

'*Professor* Rusbridge to you. Osteology of the cranium, I think it is. Something of the sort, anyway.'

'Are you well-prepared?'

'Well, obviously not, as you have had my books.' He crammed the last of the toast into his mouth and reached for another slice, which he carried in his teeth into the hall.

'Will you come for tea, Edward?' called his aunt after him. 'I've ordered a few cakes from Fitzbillies.'

The name of the famous cake shop was enough to halt Edward's rushing feet. 'Is it a special occasion?' he asked, leaning back round the dining room door, with several large textbooks under an arm.

'I have invited Professor Rusbridge,' his aunt replied.

'Rusbridge? Whose lecture I am almost late for?'

'Yes. I thought you might want to be introduced socially. He is a very influential man, and I wanted to present you to him, now that you are in your second year.'

'Aunt! Are you pulling strings on my behalf?'

'I am simply inviting a friend to tea and hoping my nephew will join us. Will you?'

'How can I refuse?'

The door slammed and the ladies watched Edward leap onto his bike and pedal off, the books bouncing in his basket.

'The cranium,' Vita said, wistfully.

'Is the cranium an interesting topic?' asked Aunt Louisa.

'Very.'

'Do they feed them at Trinity College? The way Edward eats when he visits suggests to me they are not generous. He is always hungry.'

'Edward has been hungry since he was born, Aunt Louisa. I'm surprised you hadn't observed that before. Besides, he does physical training every day and the exercise makes him even worse. His trainer told him to eat raw eggs. A dozen a day, I think it was.'

Her aunt was silent for a moment, imagining the impact on her modest domestic budget of a dozen eggs a day. 'Do you have plans today?'

'We are resuscitating the drowned in First Aid this afternoon. Until then I shall continue with my frog.'

'Don't frown, Vita, dear, you'll get lines on your brow. My committee is raising funds for the poor children of East London this morning, you would be most welcome. It is not healthy to be always at your desk. Will you be here for tea? I have ordered quite a generous number of cakes.'

'I'd give all the cakes in Fitzbillies for a chance to examine a cranium.'

'What is a cranium, exactly, dear?'

'A head.'

'I see.' Aunt Louisa set down her tea cup and rose from the table, 'Well, I hope you won't be tempted to dissect any heads in your room, Vita, that really would frighten the servants away. Which reminds me: I rely on you to call at Pearson's Agency in Regent Street and set about finding a new maid. Mrs Pearson scrutinises the references of all her applicants most carefully. One hears such terrible stories of maids gone bad. If the newspapers are to be believed it is an epidemic. If they are not stealing the silverware, they are setting fire to the curtains with their careless candles – or worse, *far* worse sometimes. The ladies of the Church Welfare Committee have stories that would make your hair stand on end. Oh, and Vita, do write to your Papa, he asks after you.'

7

'Cornwall?' said Vita. 'You are a long way from home.'

'I am, Miss, I grew up on a farm but I worked as a housemaid after I left school. I set my heart on seeing something of the world. Mr Meeks is a distant relation, he said I could stay until I found a position. He said he'd have me in the shop – I can do figures – but his wife does not care for my country way of speaking. I don't sound right to the ladies and gentlemen. They don't want to buy their ribbons or their French lace from someone who sounds like a milkmaid straight off the farm, do they?'

'I suppose not,' Vita agreed, feeling that this was probably unfair, but nonetheless true.

'So, I hope to find a position as a housemaid. I done the work before, at the Reverend Harcombe's house in Plymouth. They were always satisfied with me there. I have a reference.'

It was while waiting to buy stamps in the Post Office that Vita's attention had been drawn by the Situations Wanted advertisements. There were a dozen cards on the noticeboard but the one that took Vita's eye was written in a bold, curly hand, with flourishes top and bottom, as though the writer had given some thought to its presentation as well as its contents. *Experienced General Maid*, it said, *new to the city, seeks position. Very good references. Please apply to Meeks' Haberdashers, during shop hours.*

Meeks was nearby, so on impulse Vita called there immediately. Once she had explained her mission, she found herself being scrutinised from both sides of the shop by Mr and Mrs Meeks, who were serving customers, but who ordered a small boy apprentice to go and find someone they called 'Tabs'. He disappeared down a tiny twisting wooden staircase in a corner. When he re-emerged, panting, he told Vita that Miss Tabs would be with her shortly and would meet her out the front.

The young woman who came round the corner and curtseyed politely to Vita was about her own age, with dark hair and eyes and the colouring of someone who had grown up in fresh country air. She looked, however, anxious and tired, with dark shadows under her eyes and a generally downcast look. She was, she said, Tabitha Miriam Hindcote, from Cawsand, Cornwall.

'My father is rector of a parish not far from Plymouth,' Vita told her.

'Then he will most probably know Reverend Harcombe,' the girl said. 'He and Mrs Harcombe will always give me a good character. They were full of regret when I had to leave their employment before, but my mother took ill and I had to help on the farm for a time.'

'Would you be willing to come and meet my aunt later today?'

'If you don't mind my asking, Miss, how many are there in your household?'

'Only my aunt and I.'

'Oh! Only two ladies.'

'Yes. We keep a cook, a French gentleman, but no other servants.'

Miss Hindcote looked up sharply. 'I never met a Frenchman before.'

'He is elderly, and not very sociable,' Vita said, 'but his food is most acceptable.'

'I never tasted French food, either,' said Tabitha. 'It would be fancy, I suppose.'

'My aunt's guests vie for an invitation. Will you come to us this afternoon?'

'Yes. But, Miss, there is one thing...' Tabitha began to say something, but Vita was distracted by the bells of Great St Mary's chiming the half hour, reminding her of her First Aid class. She handed Tabitha one of her aunt's cards.

'Come this afternoon at two o'clock and my aunt will speak to you,' Vita said and hurried off towards the church hall which was a good twenty minutes' brisk walk away.

Tabitha frowned briefly and read the card before tucking it into her apron pocket and following another customer back into Meeks'.

BEHIND THE LONG MAHOGANY COUNTER WHERE BOLTS OF fabric were spread and measured, Mr and Mrs Meeks watched this encounter with keen interest.

'She'd better not ask too many questions,' Mr Meeks murmured to his wife. They always spoke in low tones in the shop to avoid the staff overhearing.

'They can be very dozy, the academic people around here,' said his wife. 'They'd forget their own heads if they weren't screwed on. Not practical. Heads in the clouds. They'd trust anybody.'

'She's not a bad girl, I suppose,' said her husband.

'She's a liar. I don't believe a word she says. I want her gone.'

'Isn't it our duty to tell? Tell the new employer, I mean?'

'Duty? Our duty is to keep our family by running this shop. No lady would shop here if they knew we employed that sort.'

When she returned, Tabitha hurried across the shop floor and let herself into the back room where she had been folding offcuts out of sight of the public. The dim store room was three steps down from the polished mahogany counters and glass-fronted display cases that the public saw.

Mrs Meeks, came to find her. 'Well? Did she offer you a position?' she asked, looking over Tabitha's shoulder to inspect her work.

'I am to go and meet the mistress of the house this afternoon.'

'Did you mention your reason for leaving?'

'I said I did not speak in the ladylike way that was expected.'

Mrs Meeks pursed her lips. Her busy hands straightened the pile of offcuts. 'That is true. Did you mention the other matter?'

'No.' Tabitha said, 'I meant to, but the lady hurried off.'

'It is my duty to inform another employer, if you do not,' Mrs Meeks told her, sharply. 'There is the reputation of the shop to consider.' Mrs Meeks did not look at the girl directly. She reached a pile of paper bags from a shelf nearby. 'You were deceitful, Tabitha. It is not what we expected of you. I shall have to tell her myself, if you do not.'

A tiny bell rang, summoning Mrs Meeks to a customer. She smoothed her apron and, adding a professional smile of greeting to her face, stepped back up into the shop.

8

Louisa Brocklehurst was completing the portrait of a professor of Philology that afternoon and so immersed in the complexities of his generous beard that she did not hear the knock on the door and had to be reminded of the interview. She carried the smell of oil paints into the drawing room with her.

'My niece tells me you are from Cornwall,' she told the girl, who was sitting on the very edge of her chair, a small purse clasped with both hands on her lap.

'I am, Madam. I came to Cambridge only two weeks ago.'

'And what do you make of the city?'

'I have not been out a great deal, as I work in the shop and the hours are long. The parks I've seen are pleasant for walking.'

'You'd miss the sea and the hills, I imagine. So, you are looking for a maid's position? And you have references from your last employer in Plymouth, my niece says.'

'Yes, Madam.' From her small handbag, Tabitha produced a folded letter and handed it over. Louisa read it with care.

'This is a very good reference, but it is nearly three years old, have you none more recent?'

'I had to leave that position at the vicarage and go home. I was needed to look after my brothers and sisters and help on the farm. I am the oldest of seven.'

Louisa looked searchingly at the girl. 'And who is caring for your brothers and sisters now that you have left?'

'My younger sister is sixteen now.'

'You chose to move a very long way away.'

'I have relations here: the Meeks at Meeks' Haberdashery.'

'But you do not want to stay there in the shop?'

'They do not care for my country way of speaking.'

Louisa looked down at her hands and rubbed at a spot of brown paint. 'And when you worked for Rev and Mrs Harcombe, Tabitha, what sort of household did they keep?'

'They had four children, a nursery maid and a gardener.'

'And they were clearly most content with your work. Their reference is excellent.'

'Yes, Madam.'

There was a reserve about Tabitha that made Louisa hesitate and want to ask more, but there seemed little else to ask, so she switched to informing her instead. 'We are a small household here, as you see. My niece and I are the only residents, although my nephew is a frequent visitor, especially at mealtimes. I keep a cook. I believe my niece has mentioned him, but no other servants. I undertake portrait commissions, and I have a studio, which I will not ask you to clean. You will rarely need to enter it. My niece is pursuing an interest in science in her room upstairs. She carries out... procedures occasionally in connection with her studies. She would prefer it if you did not move anything in that room either.'

'Yes, Madam, I understand.'

'The other consideration, and it is very important, is that my chef, Monsieur Picard,'

'...the Frenchman?'

'Yes. He is absolutely in charge of the kitchen. His standards are high. He can, perhaps, seem a little brisk or even impatient from time to time. Or so the other maids have told me.'

Louisa was watching the girl closely to see her reaction and was pleased to see that Tabitha remained steady in the face of this description.

'It is not that he is unpleasant to work with, or unkind. If he takes to you, you can learn a great deal from Monsieur. He does not live in, he has his own apartment. Your room would be in the attic, it is a pleasant room with a fire and a good view, and there is a small room in the basement you can use to store your trunk.' Tabitha seemed to relax at this. Her hands clutched her bag less rigidly, though she still did not look up or smile.

'So, Tabitha, would you like to think the position over for a day or two?'

'No, Madam, I would be happy to accept the position if you offer it to me.'

'And you are happy with the terms? £20 salary, Sunday evenings and a half day a week off by arrangement?'

'Yes, Madam.'

'And the usual three months' trial?'

'Yes, Madam.'

'In that case, I am happy to welcome you to the household. You may move into your room at your earliest convenience.'

'Would this afternoon be too soon Madam? I should be glad to begin my duties. Mr Meeks will send my trunk round on a trolley with one of his storeroom boys.'

'I don't see why not. He can bring it round to the back

gate and through the garden most easily. Vita will show you out that way. I have guests for tea at four o'clock, would you be able to help with that? Monsieur Picard – we always call him Monsieur - does not begin work until five, but I have ordered cakes from the bakery.'

'Yes, Madam. I shall start work as soon as ever my trunk can be brought round.'

As the newly-appointed maid left, Louisa remarked how efficient Mrs Pearson's agency had been to find her so swiftly. Vita, about to explain that it was she who had found Tabitha, not the agency, was interrupted by the prompt arrival of her aunt's next client, a flamboyant professor of Italian whose elaborate greetings overwhelmed all thought of maids and references, at least for the moment.

9

Tabitha's first duty was to help re-arrange furniture in the sitting room to allow the afternoon's special guest to sit on the small sofa and still be within easy reach of the pastries. Louisa found the new maid usefully strong - lifting chairs and sofa with little effort - but her manner was stiff and unsmiling. Finding ways to accommodate the Professor's considerable person without damage to her best chairs soon distracted her from the thought, however.

On previous visits, Professor Rusbridge's bulk had indeed loosened the jointed arms on her favourite stick-backed Windsor chair, but that was because he was sitting for his portrait, which meant a longer period of stillness with all twenty-three stones of him bearing upon the narrow spindles. The Professor had been pleased with his portrait and his recommendations had kept Aunt Louisa in commissions for several years.

Professors loved having their portraits made almost as much as Mayors and Masters, and Louisa Brocklehurst's way of capturing their air of authority, whilst managing also to imply generosity of nature, good humour and profound wisdom, meant she had a waiting list eager to pay her unashamedly high fees.

Professor Rusbridge was a single man, his life having been devoted entirely to Science. Most of the gentlemen whose portraits formed Louisa Rusbridge's commissions were single. She had a theory about this, which was that the hours spent being scrutinised, captured and immortalised in oils in her studio acted as a sort of compensation for the lack of female attention these gentlemen received in their private lives, but naturally this was not a theory she cared to share, or even to examine in any great detail in her own thoughts for fear of unpleasant implications.

Under instruction Tabitha laid the table using the best lace cloth and the household's finest china and silverware but on her own initiative she added a small vase of late roses from the garden, which pleased her new mistress. Having been instructed not to lay out all the cakes at once, but to keep some back and produce them as a second helping, she went to the kitchen to boil the kettles.

Professor Rusbridge, expected at four, arrived by cab at half past three, though it was at least ten minutes later when he finally eased himself with a sigh onto the little sofa. There had been a great deal of manoeuvring needed to extract himself from the cab – both the driver and his young groom were needed to assist him down the small steps to the street, even after he had passed sideways through the narrow cab door. Then there was the single step of the pavement and three more, rests taken on each, up to the front door, where he rang the bell with such a flourish that Tabitha, in the kitchen below, jumped and almost dropped a plate of cucumber sandwiches.

'Professor! How good of you to come,' Aunt Louisa offered her hand and it was taken in a plump ringed one and brought to the Professor's prominent lips. Having painted his portrait, his hostess recognised each of his features like a group of old friends; the small grey eyes, the substantial down-pointed nose, the chins overlapping the high stiff collar – she knew each individually and could recall the colours she had needed to capture the way the light fell across them in the studio. The mouth, she remembered, had taken a lot of work, needing plenty of blue. It had been a challenge to suggest the way the lips seemed to reach forward from his face. Smiling at him now, she was still not sure she had done it justice. She had seen an etching in the Fitzwilliam Museum of a rhinoceros recently, its top lip reaching for a branch, and been reminded of the struggle.

'Delighted, my dear Mrs Brocklehurst, always a pleasure!'

'Come and make yourself comfortable,' Louisa led the way and indicated the carefully placed sofa. She rang for tea. 'We will be joined by my niece and nephew,' she said. 'My nephew, Edward, I think I may have mentioned, is in his second year at Trinity.'

'Ah yes, I remember,' said the Professor, who had not remembered, and whose attention was now directed towards the cake stand.

'And my niece, Vita, whom you have not met, is staying with me here for a while.'

'Ah,' said the Professor, 'a young woman who has followed her brother to Cambridge! She is not the first young woman to do so, Louisa, nor will she be the last. Young ladies are drawn to Cambridge like bees to the honeypot. We can hardly blame them. Just as long as they do not keep the young gentlemen from their academic work, eh?' The professor beamed at his own playfulness.

A slight rigidity crept into Louisa's smile, but she overcame it by passing her guest a tea plate.

'My niece is developing an interest in Science herself, as a matter of fact,' she told him.

'Dear me,' interrupted the Professor, with a grunt of laughter, 'I do not think that should be encouraged.'

Louisa decided to redirect his attention. 'How has your health been, Professor? I do hope the damp summer did not disagree with you. Did you take your usual vacation in Yorkshire?'

'I did indeed. The most agreeable month at Whitby. I have been working for some time on bivalves, as you know, and made several very useful observations there in my laboratory. The bivalve anatomical structures are particularly promising as an avenue for further study. Your nephew would be interested in this work, no doubt.'

'I'm sure he would,' Louisa said.

Tabitha arrived with the tea tray and set it on the table, leaving swiftly to answer the door to Edward and Vita, who both entered breathlessly, having cycled in one case and run in the other.

10

The Professor lumbered to his feet and the introductions were made.

'I was just telling your Aunt about my most recent work on molluscs, young man,' continued the Professor, once the formalities were over. Edward's name had already slipped his mind; Vita's had never lodged there at all.

'A fascinating field of research, I am told,' Edward replied, taking the plate his Aunt offered and looking searchingly toward the cakes.

'I never fail to return from a field trip renewed and eager to continue my research,' continued the Professor, 'there is nothing so stimulating or so engrossing as daily observations, painstakingly recorded. They are the source and the essential basis of all science. I am sure you will agree.'

'Oh certainly,' said Edward, 'absolutely, yes indeed.'

'Your nephew will make a fine scientist, I see, Louisa,' remarked the Professor, accepting a cup of tea.

The sandwiches were offered. The professor nimbly took three, noting in passing that they were rather small and that he had eaten only a very meagre lunch. Edward and Vita took one each. In Edward's case this required enormous self-control.

'And tell me, young man, what field do you intend to pursue? Have you set your life's course? Perhaps you are too early in your studies to have discovered your academic intentions.'

Edward finished a mouthful and was about to answer when his questioner continued, 'I, of course, would urge you to aim for research in the biological sciences above all. Get a fellowship; make your mark. There is new work under way of the most promising kind here at Cambridge. Why, my own department is constantly in need of talented young men.'

'I was considering Medicine,' said Edward.

'Medicine?' The disclosure made the Professor blink and cough slightly. 'An unusual choice. Perhaps it runs in the family. Is your father a medical man?'

'Not at all. He is rector of a parish in Devon,' Edward said.

'And yet you mean to practice medicine? How very unusual. If you fancy yourself a country doctor I must tell you it is dirty, menial work, ill-rewarded and wearing to both body and soul. I have seen it ruin many a promising young man's prospects. Most country doctors are worn out by the age of forty. You would be turning your back on the excellent opportunities that a fine education can offer you.'

'I would simply like to put my training to use in some beneficial way,' Edward told him.

The professor smiled, causing a particle of salmon paste in his moustache to bob. 'You surely do not mean to suggest that it is only in general medicine that science is beneficial?' he asked and reached for a few more sandwiches.

'More tea?' asked Louisa.

'Not at all,' Edward replied, 'I am well aware that the benefits of scientific research are subtle, interconnected and often only obvious long into the future. I have simply always longed to do active work. Being out of doors suits me.'

The Professor was mollified by this at first, but then a tiny moment of suspicion clouded his expression. 'Oh well,' he said, 'at least you do not profess to have a *calling*. I dread meeting a young man who decides he has a *calling*, don't you, Mrs Brocklehurst?'

'Do take a cake, Professor, the Florentines at Fitzbillies are particularly well-regarded.'

'Thank you. I will,' he said.

There was a moment's lull, interrupted by the sound of more water being added to the teapot.

'And how are you enjoying Cambridge, Miss...'

'Carew. Vita,' her aunt murmured, quickly supplying the missing name.

'I have been taking First Aid classes with Doctor Goodman. Perhaps you know him,' Vita said.

The Professor chuckled. 'First Aid? Goodman is teaching First Aid, is he?' He turned his gaze to her for the first time. 'First aid is very popular. Though I for one have walked this earth for more than half a century without once observing any kind of accident!'

'By law of averages you may see one quite soon, then,' Vita said quietly.

'Personally I believe a qualified physician would be of far greater use than a young person with vague ideas about first aid, however well-intentioned,' the Professor replied. His little finger coiled as he sipped from his teacup.

'There may not be a qualified physician nearby.'

'In Cambridge one can hardly throw a stick without hitting a medical man, so I need not be concerned about that,' said Rusbridge, eyeing the last of the florentines.

'My niece recently witnessed an accident herself and acted very bravely,' Louisa said.

'Well, no doubt that is admirable but, as I say, it is a properly, scientifically qualified medical man one really needs in an emergency.'

'A scientifically trained *woman* might also be passing. There are women studying Medicine too, I believe,' Vita added.

In the background her aunt frowned momentarily.

'Yes. It does happen,' said the professor, with sigh. 'I have even encountered one or two of these ladies in my lectures, though I am sure they didn't understand a great deal, despite the extraordinary rate at which they take notes. I swear they were attempting to write every word!'

He looked to Louisa to share this joke, but she was engaged with the cream jug.

'I have attended one or two very interesting lectures myself, recently,' Vita said.

'I would discourage that, frankly,' the Professor went on, 'there is scarcely enough room in our lecture theatres for the young men. Lectures are not parks where one strolls in order to meet undergraduates. There is serious work to be done.'

❧ 11 ❧

The professor did not look up, so he did not notice the flush of irritation this remark brought to Vita's cheeks. He swallowed a second small cake and continued, 'Even if you were taking a little interest in science, where is the value of struggling your way through a lecture series only to be unable to carry out any serious practical work? The laboratories are too small. They are crowded enough already. Why, my students have to occupy them long into the night, in shifts, already. Where would we be if we had to fit the ladies in too? Women cannot qualify. They do not need this sort of training for the only profession they will be able to pursue – school teaching – I really can't see the point of their getting under the feet of my undergraduates at all.'

'Young women do have to support themselves in life sometimes, though, do they not?' Aunt Louisa asked, smiling and passing the cakes over again.

'Well, only if they do not marry, or if, like yourself, they have the misfortune to be widowed. The young women I have seen at lectures are nearly always the daughters of clergymen.'

'As am I...' Vita added.

'Quite. The daughters of clergymen whose main ambition is to run a little school somewhere in order to subsidise a future husband's stipend in a remote parish. What good is a first class education to such women?'

Vita froze, her teacup hovering.

The Professor paused, chewing audibly and swallowing before addressing his remarks to Louisa. 'I recently read a well-researched paper arguing that the health of young women is badly compromised by intensive study.' He paused and lowered his voice confidentially. 'It re-directs their vital energies. The details are not suitable for the tea table, Mrs Brocklehurst, but I can assure you that the ability of a young woman to fulfil her natural destiny in life: to bear healthy children and remain strong enough to raise them - this essential womanly ability - is at risk when young women choose to go against nature and devote themselves to over-prolonged study. I can think of examples of this among my personal acquaintance, I am sorry to say, and I would certainly counsel your niece to avoid any such course of action.'

Everyone looked at their plate for a moment.

'But you do not oppose the education of women in general?' Louisa said, mildly.

'No indeed! I welcome the inclination some women have to educate themselves so as to be more of a companion to their husbands. An intelligent, cultivated woman is one of life's great joys. And you are a fine example, if I may take the liberty of saying so. No, it is the unhealthy fixation of some young women upon matters unsuitable to the very constitution of the female brain that I so regret. Original research, medical investigation, that sort of thing. No good can come of it.'

He turned at last to Vita and directed his final remarks at her. 'You would be far better, in my considered opinion, to follow the example of your admirable Aunt by acquiring a ladylike accomplishment such as painting. Apply your energies where nature intended; leave Science to the gentlemen.'

A moment's silence settled on the conversation before Louisa rose to her feet, 'Now, Professor, I am hoping for your opinion on my latest commission. Perhaps, if I can tear you away from my niece and nephew, you will accompany me to my studio.'

'I should be delighted,' he agreed, and set about the process of elevating himself from the seated position.

'Do not take the man seriously,' Edward told Vita, after the professor had trundled his way out of room. 'Rusbridge may be a distinguished scholar, but he is famous for his tactlessness, even among the Fellows of Trinity College. There are plenty of girls studying Science. One of them got the top First in Anatomy last year. Quite a scandal. They wanted her marks reconsidered, but even after they were, she still scored well above the nearest man.'

'So she, at least, isn't worried that studying will drive her mad or *redirect her vital energies*?'

'Obviously not. There really is no justice, Vee. You are twice and brainy as I am, and far more disciplined and inclined to study, but the college only offers scholarships to clergymen's sons, not their daughters, so it falls to me to come up to Cambridge and struggle my way through the examinations. You know I'm only doing it to avoid the Church or the Army.'

'Do you really want to be a country doctor?'

'I did not say a *country* doctor,' said her brother, leaning to sweep the last remaining pair of sandwiches onto his plate. 'A city doctor specialising in the hypochondriac rich, is more my style. Somewhere the air is pure and the widows are wealthy.'

At this point his sister threw a cushion at him.

12

After the Professor's visit, the atmosphere in the house darkened. If disappointment could be seen - in the form of a grey ribbon, perhaps - it would have trailed low and limp along the skirting board from under the closed door of Vita's room and wound its gloomy way around the house. The source of this despond was rarely seen, shutting herself up with her books and her attempts at dissection, but finding little energy for either activity, her hopes swatted like a fly against a pan of glass.

Aunt Louisa, as she worked in her studio, was aware of the blow that had been dealt to her niece. She had always been fond of the girl. Picturing visits to Devon over the years, little Vita was always galloping, untidy, over meadows or leading her in muddy boots through woodland paths to point out a special moth or bird's nest. But now the dear creature seemed limp and oppressed. How was an aunt to react? She tried taking Vita with her to one or two of her own social gatherings, but it was clear that the Ladies' Philosophical Circle and the lecture series on Tintoretto were not what was needed. Diversion seemed the answer, but Vita had few friends of her own in Cambridge so far.

What Louisa knew for certain was that Nature had not equipped the girl for handiwork of any sort; her embroidery was a nightmare of knots and a bear cub could probably produce more pleasing flower arrangements. She had no interest in fashion, scarcely remembering the colour of a dress or the pattern of a shawl, and reading even the most elevating novels made her sigh and fidget her feet.

And then there was the troublesome question of the girl's future. She had grown solitary in Devon after her mother's death, and in her aunt's view had spent far too much time cataloguing her father's moth collection and recording bird migrations and the weather. She was such a bookish creature that she seemed destined for an academic life of some kind.

It would all have been so much easier if she had been a boy.

It might perhaps be preferable, Louisa thought, leaning in to perfect the line of a Regius Professor's nose on her canvas, to discourage Vita from her interest in Science, the better to protect her from disappointment. Rationally this was so, but so ardently did some deeper instinct resist this thought that the muscles in Louisa's jaw and arm clenched, adding a painted twitch that took an hour to correct and left the professor with a more distinguished profile than ever he had in the flesh.

Apathy may have blighted certain rooms of number 144 Eden Street, but the kitchen and scullery were enlivened with Tabitha's brisk labours. Even Monsieur, having welcomed her with cool reserve, and tested her with a few unpleasant tasks: cleaning the most fiddly silverware and blacking the kitchen range, for example, found little to condemn. He was secretive about his age, as about most things, but was well into his seventies, and wondered whether he had ever, even in his prime, had Tabitha's vigour; it made him feel elderly. His other observation, if anyone had asked, would have been that, although a hard worker, dutiful and thorough, there was no joy about Tabitha Hindcote. Being watchful and grim-faced were hardly faults that counted, but her face – he thought it might have been pleasant at one time - had forgotten how to smile. A hard life, was his guess.

The ladies only noticed that Tabitha rose at dawn and seemed to be hard at work and running up and down the stairs all day long. Once or twice Vita, who liked to study in the very early morning, was surprised to hear the maid's step on the landing before the sun came up, and once she thought she heard Tabitha let herself out of the back gate, but she always returned in plenty of time to light fires and prepare breakfast.

On this day in particular, a Friday, Tabitha had risen exceptionally early to complete all her duties and now she presented herself, bobbing a curtsey, at Aunt Louisa's studio door.

'I was wondering, Madam, whether I might leave a little early this afternoon. I changed my half day, if you recall?'

Louisa had lost track of the time, as she often did when she was painting.

'I have left a cold luncheon ready. I will be back in time for dinner. I hoped to get to the station to meet a train at noon, Madam. I shouldn't want to miss it.'

'Have you a friend arriving?' asked Louisa.

'A relation,' said the maid, then added, 'from Cornwall. My cousin.'

'Coming to visit you?'

'No, Madam, he is coming to box. He is coming for a fight. Jack Fitzsimmons, the pugilist, perhaps you have heard of him. He is well-known to people who follow boxing.'

There was, as she made this unexpected announcement, a touch of pride in the maid's tone.

'A pugilist for a cousin!' said Louisa, turning her eyes away from the portrait and looking at Tabitha with surprise, 'Goodness!'

The maid seemed to hesitate and weigh up whether she should add any further information.

'He is newly married and his bride is travelling with him, Madam,' she added. She seemed determined to keep her feelings about this to herself, mumbling the words and twisting the hem of her apron as she spoke them.

'Well, if everything is ready, then of course you may leave immediately,' Louisa told her.

13

'I saw a poster outside the Corn Exchange advertising a boxing match,' Vita said, when Tabitha's absence was explained over lunch, 'isn't he called Jack the Cornishman? Perhaps it will be in the newspaper.'

She brought the newspaper from the hall table and they consulted it, finding a notice of the fight on the front page. *Cambridge's Annual Assault-at-Arms. Special engagement of Jack Fitzsimmons, 'The Cornish Wonder', contender for Heavyweight Champion of Great Britain and Sam 'Cockney Boy' Shepherd, former Heavyweight Champion of New Zealand and Australia. Rare visit to Cambridge of these two famous champions. Full programme including sword fencing, bayonet exercises, and drill by members of the Cambridge University Volunteer battalion. Displays of single stick, quarterstaff, Indian clubs and dumb bells. Tug-of-war, vaulting horse, weight-lifting and gymnastics displays including a human pyramid by University, Police and Army teams. Reserved seats may be booked at the Star and Garter, Petty Cury.*

The Cornish Wonder was pictured, fists raised in a boxer's pose. His face was fine featured and apparently undamaged. Cockney Sam Shepherd, pictured beside, was a different matter – he stood, glaring out at the reader with his arms folded and a sneer on his lips. His nose was large and misshapen, his ears stood out like jug handles and his thick dark hair was oiled flat on either side of a forcible central parting.

'What portraits I could make of those faces!' Aunt Louisa said.

'Have you ever seen a boxing match, Aunt?' Vita asked her.

'I have, as a matter of fact. In London. It was some time ago, of course. Your uncle was invited. I expect it was something to do with his work.'

'What was it like?'

Aunt Louisa shrugged and prepared to return to her easel, 'It was a long evening. You do not see only one fight, but a long sequence running up to the most important contest. Perhaps they have changed it nowadays.'

'But weren't you terrified by the brutality of the fighting?'

'Not terrified, no. It did not appeal to me. But many others were obviously enjoying the spectacle. And there were a great many ladies present, as I recall.'

The man who made his way through the throng of enthusiasts at the station was swift in his movements, and sharply suited. He wore a bowler hat, rakishly angled, and the lady on his arm – his new American bride, Kitty Loftus - was far more fashionably dressed than anyone else in the crowd, and possibly anyone else in the whole city that day. Her hat, black and white with a long, waving ostrich feather, marked them out from the crowd at a distance, which was useful as Jack Fitzsimmons, though enormously strong, was rather shorter than average and might otherwise have been difficult to spot. Camera flashes flared on either side as they paused to speak to the waiting reporters.

As she approached, Tabitha could see the spectacle from a

distance. She immediately recognised her cousin and watched as he struck poses for the photographers, laughing with them and pretending to square up to a little boy in the crowd. He was the same cousin, but much changed. She remembered a shy boy, quietly spoken and rather timid among the bolder boys in the family, but here she saw a showman perfectly at home among his admirers.

From the perimeter of the crowd she waved, but he did not see her, until she called. Hearing a familiar accent he glanced over and greeted her across the moving wall of black coats and bowler hats.

'Is that you, cousin Tabitha?'

'Jack!'

'Come here and say hello!'

Somehow the girl pushed through and Jack shook her warmly by the hand. 'How's my little cousin? Grown into a proper lady, I see! Tabitha, here is my wife, Kitty. Kitty, this is my cousin Tabitha from Cornwall, we grew up together. Her family lived along the lane.'

'I swear Jack has a cousin in every city in England! How charming! Good afternoon, Tabitha,' Kitty said, 'Delighted. But, Jack, my dear, we must move along to the hotel now, if there is to be enough time.'

'Come with us, Tabs,' Jack said, taking both ladies' arms, 'we can all have tea at the hotel and you ladies can get better acquainted. All aboard!'

14

Tabitha, not being used either to cab rides or admiring crowds, was quiet on the short journey to the Red Lion Hotel. Kitty, too, said nothing, looking out of the window all the way, the wide brim of her hat hiding her expression. Two powerfully built, dark-suited gentlemen, evidently part of the boxer's training party, sat between them. At the hotel, Kitty, with the air of one well practiced, supervised the unloading of bags and equipment and issued a series of orders to the trainers and hotel staff. Turning abruptly to Tabitha she said in the sweet and unfamiliar tones of an exquisitely mannered American lady, 'I so hope you will excuse me, Miss Hindcote, but there are countless matters that need to be arranged before the contest. I was delighted to meet you. I trust we shall see you at the side of the ring tomorrow? Now don't you be too long, either Jack.'

'I'm sorry she could not stay,' Tabitha said, looking after Kitty's elegant figure as it was escorted up the hotel's grand staircase.

'Kitty is very business-like when we prepare for a fight. Come, we'll have a drink,' Jack said.

Tabitha, awed by her surroundings, chose a table in a corner and sat so that she could take in the lavish decoration of the whole salon. She cut an odd figure in her faded maid's dress among the shining glasses and polished silver. Jack attracted the attention of many other customers, but only smiled and waved a casual greeting when someone caught his eye.

'And what brings you here to Cambridge, Tabs? You are a long way from Cawsand.'

'Do you remember Davey Meeks? Cousin of my mother's? He and his wife have a shop here, and offered me work. I didn't stay though. Now I have a maid's position.'

'You always wanted to travel, I remember you saying that, even when we were children,' Jack said. 'You used to say you'd join the Navy if you were a lad.'

'I thought the sea would be an adventurous life,' she said, smiling. She looked suddenly down at her glass and her face grew serious. 'It was hard at home, I was always planning to get away.'

'I was sorry to hear about your father. They wrote and told me.'

'It was a relief to us, Jack, if I'm honest.'

'He always was a stern man.'

'He was. He sent my sister, Eliza, away when she was expecting. You probably heard.'

'I did hear something of the sort.'

'After father passed on, I went to find her. I thought I could give her some money at least. Maybe bring her back. But when I got there they told me she had died. It was pneumonia. The baby girl was already sent to the orphanage at Devonport.'

'The orphanage? I never knew any of this,' Jack said.

'You were away in America then.'

'What became of the child?'

Tabitha drank her lemonade in one, distracted. Her hand trembled as she set the glass back on the table. 'I went to find her. I meant just to get a look at her, and maybe leave a few shillings, but it was a terrible place, Jack. If you'd seen it you'd have done as I did. I walked away with her. They shouted at me that they would send a policeman, but they did not. They had no care for her. They were glad to have one less mouth to feed. Her ribs all sticking out. She was dirty and hungry.' Tabitha looked away.

Jack frowned across the table at her, 'Where is the poor child now, Tabs?'

'I brought her here to Cambridge. I thought I could pay for her board from my wages at Meeks and visit her now and again. She's a little thing – not strong. There was nobody to look out for her.'

'That's kind of you Tabs,' Jack said. He was alarmed to see that she was in tears.

'The trouble is, I never told the Meeks, but they found out about the child. They didn't believe me. They thought she must be my own child. Mrs Meeks said it would hurt the reputation of the shop, if people thought they had a fallen woman with a child behind the counter, so she put me out.'

Sitting across from her, his shoulders tight in his suit, the boxer took all this in.

Tabitha pulled a handkerchief from her purse and hurriedly dried her eyes. 'My new mistress seems kind enough. Her house is not far from where the child stays –I found a woman who takes in children. I can walk by now and then, and give her a wave. They won't let me talk to her, they say it makes her too upset.'

'You were always kind, Tabs. I remember you bringing

food many a time when my mother was ill.' Jack held his glass and looked into it. 'Is she well now, the little one?'

'She is healthier now. She has the look about her of...' The girl trailed off and concentrated on her own glass for a moment. Jack waited. '...well, she is red-headed and freckled.'

'My brother,' he said, 'she looks like my brother, William. He and Eliza were sweet on each other, I remember that.'

'She does look a lot like him, to be quite honest.'

There was a silence while both studied the patterns in the damask table cloth before them. Laughter and the sound of tea cups on saucers drifted from tables nearby.

'Does my brother know?'

'I doubt it. Eliza never said a word to anyone about the father.'

Jack looked across the salon and out of the window for a few moments. 'Well, I shall call myself her uncle,' he said, drawing himself up, 'and you are her aunt, so the poor little thing is not quite alone in the world.'

'I'm sorry to mention it, Jack, but it is costly, paying for her board. I have only a maid's wages and they pay in arrears.'

'Let me give you...' Jack reached into his pocket, but then said, 'no, I will draw some real money from the bank. Come to the fight tomorrow. See me afterwards and I'll give it to you then.'

'I did not mean to ask you for money, Jack.'

'I want you to have it, but it would be better if Kitty did not know about this, Tabs. I hope you will understand. I will tell her in my own way.'

'Yes. I understand.'

One of the men travelling with the boxer's party approached the table. He said something quietly to Jack, who nodded.

'I am wanted. I must prepare,' he said. 'Here, these are a few tickets for tomorrow. You shall be at ringside with Kitty, right up close. The others are for anyone you might like to bring – good seats they are, mind. Now I must go and get my preparations started.'

The maid looked at the tickets. 'I don't know if I should like to see you hit, Jack. I never saw a boxing match. Only street brawling and that was not something I enjoyed.'

'Boxing to Queensberry Rules is not like rough fighting, my word no,' Jack said, laughing. 'Some ladies do not enjoy it, I daresay, though Kitty always comes to my fights, and watches my training. She knows about fighting.'

'Oh, but she looks so...'

'...so delicate and ladylike?' he said, 'she does, and she *is*, but two of her brothers and her father are all in the boxing line and she knows the fighting world through and through. The Loftus's are a big fighting family in America. They've done well out of it. I shan't take it badly if you give the fight the go-by, but you're welcome if you choose to come. Kitty will bring you to see me after it's over.'

'And do you think you'll win?' she asked, looking sharply into her cousin's blue eyes.

'Win? You can bet your boots on it. Poor old Sam couldn't punch the skin off a custard!'

15

When Tabitha served the soup at dinner that evening, Aunt Louisa asked about her afternoon.

'Did you meet your famous cousin?'

'I did, thank you Madam.'

'And his bride?'

'Yes, Madam.'

Tabitha moved around the table ladling one of Monsieur's pale, fragrant soups. Edward was at the table too, and very interested in the food, as usual.

'My cousin is fighting in the Corn Exchange tomorrow. I should like to attend, Madam, with your permission,' Tabitha added.

'Such an occasion would not be appropriate for a young woman on her own,' said Aunt Louisa.

'I shall go with Mrs Fitzsimmons, Madam. Jack said I could sit with her at the ringside.'

'As it happens, I shall be at the Corn Exchange tomorrow myself,' Edward put in, spreading his napkin on his knee. 'I shall be fencing for the University team.'

'You made no mention of this before, Edward,' Vita said.

'I did not think it would be of any interest.'

Vita turned excitedly to her aunt, 'I should very much like to see the Assault-at-Arms, Aunt, if you will allow it!'

Her aunt looked doubtful. 'Your father would not approve. With all due respect to your cousin's profession, Tabitha, a spectacle such as an Assault-at-Arms and the crowd it attracts is likely to be most unsuitable.'

'Excuse me, Madam, but my cousin gave me tickets for the best seats,' Tabitha told her, 'you will not have to be jostling among the crowd, if you take them.'

Aunt Louisa hesitated, then saw that her niece looked more lively than she had in many days, and sighed. 'Well, I suppose we might go,' she said. 'I should like to see you fencing, Edward, and I happened to hear several of the ladies mention this event in church on Sunday. Now, shall we say Grace before the soup goes cold?'

At about midnight that same night, Vita, reading in her room, heard footsteps climb the stairs. The light of a candle moved beneath her door. She went back to her reading and forgot about this until she was roused at 5am by footsteps passing again.

The Assault-at-Arms in the Corn Exchange drew crowds from all levels of Cambridge society; town as well as gown crowded the raked seats. Vita and her aunt were ushered past jovial queues waiting for the cheaper seats and standing places. Their tickets were for a roped off enclosure right in the middle of the stand, reserved for special guests. Two rows behind sat the Lord Mayor in his full regalia of gown and gold chain of office, as well as several dignitaries from the university, similarly robed.

Aunt Louisa and Vita settled on their cushioned seats - more spacious and comfortable than the plain wooden benches opposite. Very shortly a hush fell, the master of ceremonies strode into the arena, the lights were dimmed and the display began with a demonstration of broadsword fighting. Twelve young men in pairs fought at different stations around the arena. They wore white outfits with armbands, these were light blue, for the university men; red for the men representing the town; green for the army team and dark blue for the police. Each pair's moves were closely followed by an umpire and by the crowd in the nearest seats. Cries and sudden bursts of applause burst forth as particularly daring moves were displayed. The method of scoring was beyond Vita's understanding, but the umpires signalled marks to the scorer after each bout. The young men moved fast, upright and unflinching with one hand behind their backs. Their huge blades whistled around their heads and bodies and the metallic sounds of blade hitting blade rang out. At one end of the hall the points were tallied by numbers on a scoreboard.

When the broadsword fighters had bowed and marched away to cheers from the crowd they were swiftly replaced by the first set of gymnasts. Vaults and leaps then followed, with tumbles and rolls from the height of the shoulders of as many as four men. Again, umpires in the ring awarded marks for each jump, considering its style and the perfection of its execution. Soon the Army and City of Cambridge teams were drawing ahead. The City team of gymnasts stole the hearts of the crowd by making a human pyramid so high that the small boy (the crowd held its breath) who climbed to the top seemed to touch the barrel-vaulted ceiling of the Corn Exchange and look down upon the chandeliers. The men lower in the pyramid trembled and grimaced with exertion as the weight upon their shoulders grew, and ladies were looking through their gloved fingers at the spectacle by the time the boy began his nimble descent and the human pyramid resolved itself once more into a row of men, who bowed, smiling at the cheers. This was followed by bayonet demonstrations using straw-filled dummies. Such was the ferocity shown to these imaginary enemies that most were disembow-eled and several were headless by the end of the display. The first interval came after a military band had led troops of men in full uniform from the local regiments in a display of precision marching. The ladies, half exhausted already with applauding, drew breath and fanned themselves with their programmes as they contemplated the events to follow.

'When is the fencing that Edward will be taking part in?' Aunt Louisa asked.

'It was the épée,' Vita said, consulting her programme. 'He will be coming on soon, I think.'

'When was it that he began fencing, Vita ? Was it an interest he had when he was at home in Devon?'

'No indeed, Aunt, our father is particularly unenthusiastic about any form of combat, as perhaps you remember.'

'Perhaps I do wrong in allowing Edward to pursue these interests,' said her aunt, waving politely at someone in the crowd opposite, 'I had imagined he was free to choose his own pastimes whilst at university.'

'He is, Aunt, truly. Father would not wish to prevent Edward from following his own interests, even though he might wish they were different. Edward boxed at school.'

16

In front of their stand, posts and ropes were being assembled for a display of tight-rope walking. As the lights were lowered again, the university team of rope walkers led the others out and began. One young man, carrying a pole for balance, stepped gracefully out onto the narrow rope ten feet above their heads. The crowd, though, was already distracted by the boxing ring taking shape on the ground below, and although they applauded the tight-rope walkers, there was a distinct feeling that they, and the other demonstrations that would follow, were sideshows to the main event.

Edward's fencing was the last display before the next interval. He marched on with this team and took his fencing stance with his opponent just to their right, so that the ladies had an excellent view. Before they began the Master of Ceremonies explained, as he had done for each of the events, the basic rules of the combat. In épée, he told the crowd, the opponent's whole body from the tips of the toes to the top of the head was a valid target. Each sword had its tip rubbed in soot, so that it would leave a mark if it touched the opponent's white suit. Edward was masked, and only recognisable by his light blue arm band, but as soon as they began their lunge and parry movements, it was clear that a large group of supporters was cheering him on. Although they had little understanding of the rules, the ladies could soon also see that Edward's attacks seemed faster and more effective than those of his opponent. With each burst of activity, the cheering of his supporters grew, until, in a mighty crescendo, the two panting swordsmen took their elegant poses opposite each other and moved in for the final flurry. This time Edward sprang forward with his leading foot so sharply that it was all over in an instant and his fine flexible sword came to rest bent in an arc, with the tip pressed to his defeated opponent's chest, directly above his heart. Both men immediately stepped back, removed their helmets, shook hands, bowed to the crowd and walked away to roars of approval from the university team's supporters as the score on the board was brought level with the army team.

The ladies, who had hardly drawn breath throughout the display, turned to each other in dazzled amazement. 'I believe the dear boy has won!' Aunt Louisa declared. 'How very impressive!'

'He won by several points, I think,' Vita said, looking at the scoreboard. 'I had no idea that he was so good at it.'

'And it was so fast! His reactions were like lightening. One's eye could hardly follow. He is truly welcome to all the breakfasts, dinners and teas he can eat at my table in future!'

There was now a lull in the evening's events as stage hands put finishing touches to the boxing ring. The hum of keen anticipation filled the Corn Exchange hall. While ladies fanned themselves and waved to acquaintances, gentlemen pressed their heads together in groups. Money changed hands in subtle exchanges as they wagered on the outcome of the match. One or two ladies were seen to leave, but most seemed content to stay. The muttering tones of the audience deepened, as though the serious business of the evening were about to begin. Arc lights on posts illuminated the ring so that its canvas seemed to glow. Chairs were set around it for the boxers' corner teams and for the umpires, who sat three in a row with their backs to Vita and her aunt. The hush deepened as the boxers' people filed in and occupied these ringside seats, Tabitha and Kitty Fitzsimmons the only women among them.

All the cheering that had filled the Corn Exchange until now was as nothing to the mighty cheer that erupted when, at last, the announcer sprang into the ring and bid the audience welcome the contender for Heavyweight Champion of the Commonwealth, Mr Jack Fitzsimmons, to the ring. The boxer, in a hooded gown, skipped into the hall followed by a black-suited team of seconds. He trotted towards the ring with one glove raised to acknowledge the crowd, many of whom jumped to their feet and cheered before he had even cast his gown aside. Fitzsimmons was a pale, freckled figure with sandy hair and a lean frame. He wore white shorts and boots laced above the ankle. His finely-featured face was famously unblemished and he was smiling and appeared relaxed and even playful. He turned a slow circle, greeting each side of the hall in turn before saying something to the announcer, who held up a hand to the arena, calling for quiet.

17

'Ladies and Gentlemen,' the Master of Ceremonies began, 'before this evening's demonstration fight, Jack Fitzsimmons would like to issue a Hero's Challenge! He challenges any gentleman here to go three rounds against him. This is an all-comers challenge, just present yourself to the seconds outside the ring.'

There was a deep roar of approval from the crowd at this declaration. A great stirring rustled about the hall, as people looked to and fro to see whether any sportsman would be willing to face the champion.

'Surely it would be madness to do such a thing,' Aunt Louisa said.

Vita agreed, 'Of course it would. Nobody would stand a chance...'

But as she spoke a figure approached the bowler-hatted men in shirtsleeves surrounding the ring and spoke to them. They gathered round and began fitting his hands into boxing gloves. All the ladies could see was that the volunteer was wearing white trousers. He was bare-chested, as was the boxer.

Soon he was climbing into the ring. The seconds were giving him what appeared to be urgent instructions, he was nodding and moving his hands as if to get used to the feel of the gloves.

'Oh Aunt!' Vita gasped and raised her hands to her mouth, 'Oh, Aunt Louisa! It's Edward!'

At a signal the seconds withdrew and the announcer took the young man's hand and holding it aloft declared to the crowd, 'We have a challenger! Ladies and Gentlemen, please welcome Mr Edward Carew of Trinity College!'

A roar of excitement rose up around the two ladies, who sat in frozen silence.

So little had they anticipated this turn of events that they could do little more than stare mutely as the fight began in front of them. A bell rang and the men took their stance and circled one another, eyes locked. The same gang of supporters who had cheered so loudly for Edward as a swordsman now took his side again and began urging him on. At first, the two men in the ring were both smiling. Fitzsimmons, in particular, appeared to be playing a good-natured game with his upstart challenger, darting in, throwing a punch which only just landed, and darting out to wink at the crowd or dance a few playful steps before moving back. Edward responded by stepping forward himself and managing to land a mild touch on Fitzsimmons' jaw. Fitzsimmons, clowning for the crowd, pretended to reel, touching one glove to the supposed injury to his chin, but then sprang back and speedily delivered another jab to the side of Edward's head. It was a light punch, as champion's punches go, but it reminded the crowd, and Edward, what a presumptuous amateur was up against. And so it went on for a few more minutes of the round, with Jack Fitzsimmons springing in to deliver the suggestion of a real blow and Edward receiving one touch after another.

Edward was beginning to pant for breath. His sides were heaving and, tired perhaps from his earlier fencing match, his dancing movements were slower and his attempts at moving forward and landing a punch on Fitzsimmons were fewer. Then suddenly, he summoned a burst of energy and using the footwork the crowd had seen him use as a swordsman, he lunged forward and landed a blow square on Fitzsimmons' left cheekbone. The boxer responded at the half volley, hardly seeming to move. His right arm shot out in a reflex and hit Edward on the side of the head. Edward's knees crumpled, he hit the canvas limp and heavy and did not move.

There was a pause that seemed endless, as the umpire stood over the fallen figure and counted him out, then seconds leapt into the ring from all sides, flapping towels. Fitzsimmons was the first beside the young man, swiftly followed by his wife, who climbed into the ring over the ropes. From then on the crowd could see little but white towels waving and the backs of the bowler-hatted seconds who crowded the ring.

All cheering stopped in the hall as under the bright lights men appeared to be working on the young man, attempting to bring him round. This was not the show that had been intended. A light-hearted display meant only as the overture to the serious fight had gone badly wrong. The entire audience held its breath.

Vita and her aunt, too horrified to speak, could only watch. Louisa's hand was covering her mouth and Vita clung tightly to her aunt's arm with tears standing in her eyes.

A shout rang out and men in the ring began to gesture towards the door from where four men ran carrying a stretcher. Before they could reach the ring, however, there was a movement among the crowd jostling over the fallen figure in the ring. The only female figure among them, Kitty Fitzsimmons, appeared to shout an order, her voice echoing around the hall. Then swiftly she and several of the cornermen backed away and climbed out, and Edward could be seen, standing, head bowed, between two seconds. The umpire took one of Edward's arms and one of Jack Fitzsimmons' and announced, raising Fitzsimmons' gloved fist, that the champion had beaten his challenger by a knock-out. The applause that rang round the hall for the winner was half-hearted but grew louder and followed Edward out of the ring, as, still propped up by two seconds, he was led away, awake, but with his feet stumbling and his head low.

Anxious for his welfare, Louisa and Vita immediately prepared to leave the stand to follow. Just as they were gathering their cloaks about them, however, a young man pushed through the throng and darted across. He addressed them after an elaborate bow.

'Excuse me, ladies, but do I address Mrs Brocklehurst and Miss Carew?'

'You do,' said Aunt Louisa, alarmed in case this messenger brought bad news.

'I have a message from your nephew,' said the young man. 'If I may introduce myself, I am Aloysius Derbyshire, his fencing instructor. I have just left his side. He is recovering, and none the worse for his injuries.'

'How do you do, Mr Derbyshire and thank you,' Aunt Louisa said, 'but we would prefer to come and see Edward for ourselves.'

'That is precisely what he wants to prevent,' Mr Derbyshire told them. 'There is very little room backstage and the doctor has advised him to rest and remain quiet for a short time. He asks me to beg you to stay where you are, and not concern yourselves. He will regain his strength and join you at the door in time to walk you home.'

18

The ladies looked at Mr Derbyshire in confusion, and then at each other. 'Well, if he would prefer us to stay here,' Vita said, 'and it would give him the chance to recover himself a little...'

'That is exactly what he asked,' Derbyshire assured her.

'Then we must remain, I suppose,' Aunt Louisa agreed, 'but Mr Derbyshire, can you reassure us that he was well, and in his right senses when you left his side?'

'He was sitting up and making jokes. Quite his old self, I promise you,' said Derbyshire, 'but I too think he would be well advised to sit where he is for a short time under medical supervision.'

'Well, then, we shall stay here,' Aunt Louisa told him, 'please send Edward our best wishes and tell him we will find him outside the door when the spectacle is over. It seems the most sensible thing. And thank you again.'

The fencing instructor nodded politely and hurried back to the behind-the-scenes area of the arena, leaving the ladies to resume their seats, only partially comforted.

Afterwards Vita's recollection of the night's big fight was

clouded, of course, by these prior events. Even at the time, the roaring crowd and the smell of sweat, damp coats and pipe smoke, along with the brightness of the lights around the roped-off and raised boxing ring, made it pass in a dazzling blur from which only a few tableaux stood out: the men springing out of their corners at the ring of the bell; the umpire counting over a fallen figure, struggling to stand; the crescendo of shouts as one boxer's victorious arm was held aloft.

To Vita's eye, unless one man beat the other to the floor or knocked him out, there was no way of knowing who was winning. But she could see that Fitzsimmons seemed lighter on his feet, more fluid and agile than his opponent. Sam Shepherd's punches, the few he managed to land, seemed punishing - a gentleman on the row behind called him a 'slugger' - but for every punch that made contact with the Cornishman, five or six were ducked or sidestepped. Fitzsimmons seemed reluctant to return blows. More expert spectators than Vita began to notice this and swiftly the air was filled with male voices urging Fitzsimmons forward 'Give him one, Jack!' they called, 'Come on man, land one on him!' but the Cornishman's head was low, his shoulders hunched and he seemed reluctant to do more than jab at the big man swinging at him. Again and again a series of blows ended with the two fighters against the ropes or in a clinch, being separated by the umpire. The crowd was dissatisfied. The atmosphere had changed; where once it had been playful, it was now harder, more serious. Men were roaring at the fighters, shouting them orders, standing in front of their seats, punching the air.

Shepherd was soon breathing hard, his ribs discernibly pumping and his shoulders low. Sweat shone on his face and sprayed around him as he swung his heavy fists. At the end of round four, Fitzsimmons returned to his corner still bouncing on his toes, whilst Shepherd slumped to his stool, seeming close to exhaustion. It was only then that Vita saw Kitty in the Fitzsimmons corner, calling urgently through the ropes to her husband. This was a different Kitty altogether from the fashionable lady of the newspaper photographs. She wore the plainest white shirt with her sleeves rolled, and a dark skirt under a workmanlike brown apron. One arm held the middle rope as she leaned in to bark orders into Jack's ear. He nodded, swigged water and leapt from his corner as the bell rang again.

Both fighters immediately laid into each other with a determined violence unseen in any of the earlier rounds. Vita found herself looking away to avoid seeing the viciousness of the blows. Instead her attention was drawn to Kitty Fitzsimmons who was on her feet at the ringside, darting along the side of the ring with her face at knee level to the fighters. She was shouting instructions and her voice could be heard, a rare female note piercing a chorus of masculine shouting. Vita could not make out her words, but Kitty's face lit by the lights above the ring was distorted with what seemed to be rage as she punched the air and shrieked orders through the ropes to her husband fighting above. The hall rang with the repeated sound of glove on rib, jaw, cheekbone and grunted exhalation as breath was pounded from chests. Neither man stepped back now, neither broke the rhythm of punches, and then it came, the decider: an uppercut from the Cornishman catching Shepherd on the side of the jaw, jerking his head round with force enough to send his shoulder and finally his feet twisting after.

He crashed to the canvas on his side and was counted out before his men ran over, waving towels, slapping his face and lifting his head to give him water.

'I don't like the look of him,' a man sitting behind them said. And many in the audience seemed to agree. A collective gasp at the repetition of the sights they had seen earlier sounded around the stands. The noise died away as the seconds worked with increasing desperation to bring the fallen boxer round.

'Is he waking?' Vita asked.

They peered towards the ring, but so many figures were now crowded there that nothing could be seen.

Soon a stretcher was run in from the side, passed over the ropes empty, and back out again bearing Sam Shepherd, still senseless. He no longer wore boxing gloves, but one hand, still bandaged at the knuckle, hung limply over the side. The sight drew an intake of breath from the audience.

Almost unnoticed, Fitzsimmons was urged through the ropes and led away from the ring in a protective group of seconds.

The ladies waited in their seats for a while, then followed the muttering crowd out of the hall.

19

They hesitated in the street as people pushed past on either side. It was a chilly night, with the dregs of a sharp easterly wind biting through their overcoats. To their relief, Edward soon appeared. His shoulders were hunched and his coat collar pulled up around his ears. He looked pale to Vita and one eye was swollen to the point of being closed.

'Edward! Are you quite recovered? How are you feeling?' Vita asked him.

He smiled and shrugged, 'I am perfectly well, except for having exactly the headache I deserve. And some slight damage to my pride.'

'What possessed you, Edward, to put yourself forward for such a challenge?' his aunt asked.

He laughed, 'I'll tell you on the walk back to Eden Street,' he said, taking both their arms. 'Some of the blame rests with my fellow students, who thought it would be highly entertaining to see me beaten, but most of it rests with me. It was a fit of madness. I have paid the price with a humiliating defeat, so I hope it will soon be forgotten.'

The crowd was dispersing around them. A passing carriage stopped and a friend within called to Louisa to climb in for a ride home. She accepted and was driven away.

'Did you see Tabitha backstage?' Vita asked.

'Yes, with Fitzsimmons' wife and seconds. I told her we would wait here and she could walk home with us. They are a tight-knit company, the Fitzsimmons cornermen and Kitty.'

'I saw her shouting instructions at her husband during the fight,' Vita said.

'She is from a famous dynasty of boxing trainers. Her father trained two world champions. He made a great fortune at it.' Edward thrust his hands into his coat pockets and hunched his shoulders against the cold. 'Kitty is said to rule over her husband's fighting career. A great deal of money is at stake. Not here, this was just a sideshow event for them, a warm-up. The big fight is early next year. Jack Fitzsimmons is tipped to be the next world champion.'

'And you fought him!'

'I fought him and was duly beaten and given the headache and black eye I deserved for my impudence, but he was not seriously fighting me. The seconds told me he would make light of it, and he did. I got what I deserved.' Edward shivered.

'I hope there is no lasting damage, Edward. I did not enjoy the spectacle.'

'I doubt there will be. We examined the skull of a fighter in an Anatomy class only the other day,' Edward said. They both leaned against the wall, tucking their hands under their arms for warmth. 'He was not a boxer, but he was regularly charged with brawling and had once been a prizefighter. The purpose was to examine the damage that blows to the head could inflict on the brain within.'

'And what did you find?' asked Vita.

' We could see bruising and lesions and patches that

appeared to be scarred,' Edward said, 'but the damage was superficial. It was the drink that killed him, his liver was a sieve.'

'I am glad you took up fencing and not boxing,' Vita said.

'Most people make full recoveries after being knocked out, as I have, but on the other hand a tiny knock or small blow to the wrong part of the head can have serious consequences. Boxers often live short lives or suffer a weakening of the brain in old age. It is a hard life. Its only real appeal must be the money.'

The side door opened and Tabitha stepped over to them.

'How is your cousin?' Edward asked her.

'Well enough, thank you sir, but dreadfully down-hearted and worried about Sam Shepherd. His wife is very angry with him.'

'Angry?' asked Vita, 'why should she be angry?'

'She says he should not have issued the challenge to all-comers before the fight. She did not want him to do it. Excuse me saying it, Mr Edward, but Kitty told him it was unprofessional. It made him look like a prizefighter from a fairground. She was angry about that. My cousin was saying he hated fighting and he had half a mind to give the game up. He is most terribly upset. He said he had near-on killed two men in one night and it was not the life he wanted. Not any more.'

'I certainly bear no ill will of any sort against him. He was doing his job, nothing more,' Edward told her. 'I will tell him in person, if it would help.'

'No, Sir, I do not think that would help.'

The crowds had dispersed. A cold drizzle was beginning to fall. 'Ladies, unless there is anything else we can do here, I think it is time to return to Eden Street. I must admit, I am keen to get back to college and my own bed, too. I have a headache that would kill an ox.'

Edward did not return to his college that night, however. Just as they turned the corner into Eden Street, he stopped, seemed to mutter a few words and fell to the pavement where his body began violently to spasm, his heels kicking the paving stones and his head jerking backwards.

If Vita had ever doubted the usefulness of First Aid training before this, she never did again.

'Tabitha, knock at Doctor Goodman's house. Quickly please,' she said, 'ask him to come at once. Edward is having a seizure.' She was already taking off her coat and lifting her brother's head onto it.

Tabitha sprang up to run, but her foot slipped on the wet kerb and she fell, measuring her length on the flagstones and winding herself badly.

Vita rushed to her, saw that she was not badly harmed, then hurried on to the doctor's house herself, leaving the maid with her brother.

20

Once the fit was over, they helped Edward into his aunt's house. He was already protesting, telling anyone who would listen that he was perfectly well, and needed to get back to his college, but Goodman was firm. 'You will stay where you are, so that I can keep an eye on you,' the doctor told him. 'You'll worry the ladies if you go back. I recommend bed rest and a light diet. Sleep upright and keep your head cold. You must avoid inflammation. I shall prescribe salts of Bromium – Sandow's are the best.'

Out of earshot the doctor told Vita to watch her brother overnight and report any signs of mental disturbance or fever. There were none. Edward slept well and began his protests against being kept away from college as soon as he woke the next morning. His first visitor was Aloysius Derbyshire, who surprised the household by arriving at 7am, the normal time, he said, for Edward's training.

'They told me at college that he had not returned last night. I was alarmed. I came immediately,' he said, standing on the doorstep in a cap and a strange sporting suit of a kind unfamiliar to Vita. His gingery hair was sticking out wildly and he was gasping as though he had run full tilt from Trinity to the door. She let him in. He spent twenty minutes with the patient and left looking unhappy, promising to return soon.

In the course of the day, Dr Philpott, Edward's tutor from college, and two friends also visited. Edward seemed cheerful and well, but Doctor Goodman advised at least a week's rest, preferably with drawn curtains, and far fewer visitors.

'Recovery from an injury to the brain is never predictable, Miss Carew,' the doctor told her on his way out. 'Your brother may feel well, but we must keep him calm. He must have no stimulation. Rest is what that boy's brain needs. Send his friends away. Feed him a light diet. Don't let him read. He must lie still and listen to the birds in the garden. Nothing more!'

THE THIRD SCREAM WAS LOUD AND LONG, SEVERAL TIMES repeated, and first heard at 4.25 am. The other guests of the Red Lion Hotel, when they were questioned later that day, reported being roused from their sleep by a woman's shrieks of alarm followed by running steps on the stairs, men's voices, apparently giving orders, more running footsteps and more again. At breakfast there was discernible dismay among the staff, but no information was given. Uniformed police officers kept passing the dining room and climbing the stairs. Mrs Emilia Foster, whose room at the back overlooked the service entrance, reported seeing a covered stretcher carried out by four men. There appeared to be some uncertainty about the driver's instructions and they spent a long time in heated discussion before the carriage drew away.

At about nine o'clock the same reporters who had crowded the station to meet the boxer the day before began to arrive at the hotel and ask questions. The staff were startled and wary, but several guests spoke to the press. Word soon spread that the disturbance in the night had been Mrs Fitzsimmons' discovery of her husband dead in bed beside her.

This news, whispered from ear to ear, moved round the hotel like a swift invisible gas, penetrating from attic to guest rooms to kitchen and lobby and out into the street. Pedestrians learned what had happened apparently just by walking by, but within the hour the headlines of early editions of the papers were being bellowed from the corners of the street: '*Famous Boxer Dead in City Hotel*'

❦

IT FELL TO AUNT LOUISA TO INFORM TABITHA OF THIS terrible news. She had read it in the paper and hurried home to make sure her new maid did not chance across the death of her cousin without warning, but Tabitha had already heard.

'I can hardly believe it, Madam,' she said, sitting at the kitchen table with sweet tea before her for the shock, 'I was only talking to him last night. I can't believe that Jack could have died so sudden.'

'Did he seem well when you saw him?' Louisa asked, gently.

'He was upset because he had beaten two men into unconsciousness. He kept saying he was sorry I had to see it, or anyone else had to see it. He kept saying it was the game, it was just the way boxing was. He didn't mean Master Edward or Sam Shepherd any harm. He was unhappy, but he was not ill. He spoke clearly and he seemed strong. He was tired, I daresay, and bruised, but he seemed his normal self otherwise.' Tabitha dabbed her eyes on her apron. 'I shall need to write to my poor Aunt and Uncle,' she added, 'I should not like them to get the news of his passing from a newspaper, poor things.'

'And do you think you should go and see your cousin's wife?' asked Louisa. 'She must feel terribly alone at this time. I know what it is to lose a husband suddenly, and she may be in need of a friendly face.'

'I should like to, Madam, yes. Though she was not very welcoming last night.'

'I expect she was in a hurry to get her husband back to the hotel, it was a difficult evening,' suggested Louisa.

'Yes, Madam, I expect so.'

21

At the Red Lion Hotel Tabitha could do no more than send a note of condolence upstairs with one of Fitzsimmons' men. She waited uncertainly as all sorts of people queued at the desk to send similar messages and newspapermen lounged in chairs in the foyer, watching for the widow to appear. Tabitha was about to leave when the same black suited man returned. He spoke confidentially, turning his back to the press reporters and leading her through the hotel lobby to the restaurant beyond.

'Mrs Fitzsimmons will see you. We must use the back stairs. Come with me.'

He led her through the kitchen to a rear staircase and up to the second floor. A broad carpeted corridor spread ahead. Outside one of the doors a policeman stood guard and Tabitha was led there and shown in. Kitty Fitzsimmons, in mourning black, sat at a circular table by the window. Two of her men were with her, but she waved them outside. Tabitha approached, but the widow made no sign of noticing her. When Kitty finally spoke she did so without looking up, addressing the paisley cloth on the table.

'Sit down, you cannot stand there forever.'

'I came only to offer my condolences. Jack was a good man. It is a great loss to us all. And it must have been a terrible shock.'

The widow shuddered. 'Did he say anything to you last night?'

Tabitha was taken aback by the question. 'Only that he was sorry about the men he had injured, Madam, that he did not mean to do them serious harm.'

The widow still did not look up. 'Did you talk about me? Either last night or the day before?'

Tabitha did not, at first, know how to reply.

'He told me you were from a famous boxing family and knew a great deal about boxing.'

'Anything else?'

'No, Madam.'

'You were seen taking money from his jacket pocket.'

'What? No, Madam, no.'

'I should report you to the police. It would mean jail.
'

Tabitha swayed on her feet, reaching for the edge of the table to steady herself. 'But he gave it to me,' she said, eventually.

'Why? Why should he give you money?'

'He wanted to help me. He told me to take the money from his jacket on the chair because his hands still had the tapes on them. He wanted me to have it.'

'Why should anyone believe you?'

Tabitha hung her head. 'I am telling you the truth, Mrs Fitzsimmons. I have had some troubles and my cousin wanted me to...'

'What sort of troubles?'

'I lost my job...'

'Ah, yes, there's always a tragic story,' Mrs Fitzsimmons

suddenly twisted round and stared at the girl. 'Give me your bag.'

Before Tabitha could respond, Kitty Fitzsimmons had grabbed the small handbag she was carrying and opened it. She pulled out a large folded banknote and held it up.

'Ten pounds! How generous! I wonder why? Why was my husband paying you? Was it to keep quiet? Was it to keep a little secret? Something he did before? Something his wife shouldn't know?'

The youngest of the Fitzsimmons men appeared at the door. He looked wary.

'Go away, Liam,' Kitty said, without looking at him.

'It's just that you may be overheard, Ma'am,' he said, 'we are under police guard, if you remember.'

'They treat me like a criminal,' Kitty leaned conspiratorially towards Tabitha, who could smell the unmistakable sourness of whisky on her breath. 'Anyone would think it was I who...'

'Kitty!' Liam stopped her. 'I will take you downstairs, Miss. Mrs Fitzsimmons is not herself, as you see.' He went to take Tabitha's arm, but Kitty sprang up and stood between them.

'Out, Liam. Out! I need a moment more.'

He turned angrily and walked out, closing the door behind him.

'Here's what I will do, Cousin Tabitha,' said Kitty. She pushed the £10 note back into the bag. 'You can keep the money. I will not tell the police you stole it, though I believe you did. In return, you will not tell the police or the newspapers anything Jack said about me. Nothing. If you do, I will report you as the dirty thief you truly are.' She leaned over and tucked the bag under Tabitha's elbow, patting it. 'There,' she said, 'we are family, after all.'

Tabitha, bewildered, looked down at the bag, instinctively clasping it to her side.

The widow's face had changed again. 'I must rest now,' she said and called her man back into the room. Tabitha was led away.

On Monday morning Aunt Louisa paid her own visit to Mrs Fitzsimmons, but was unusually reticent when Vita mentioned it at dinner.

'How did you find her, Aunt?' she asked.

'It was rather distressing, I'm afraid. But perhaps I am making much of little. Manners are different in New York, I dare say.'

It was most unlike Aunt Louisa to keep the details to herself, but Vita did not feel able to question her further, so changed the subject and asked about her most recent portrait commission.

'Oh, something rather interesting,' her Aunt replied, brightening, 'I am to paint Mr Aloysius Derbyshire, Edward's fencing master!'

'Good heavens!' Vita said. 'How did this come about?'

'He has seen my work, and feels it is time he was immortalised in oils! Those were his exact words. He will pose for me with his sword – but it is not called a sword, it has a special name which I forget – and he will wear the white suit that fencers adopt. I was quite taken aback by his request. He is a young man, and generally it is a college or an institution that commissions my work, rarely an individual, but he was at pains to assure me he is perfectly able to pay the price. He was most direct about the monetary arrangements. It will make a pleasant change from painting august members of the University. I suspect my greatest challenge with Mr Derbyshire will be to persuade him to talk a little less and keep still. He was neither still nor silent for a moment of the time he was here; he is quite the raconteur. I found him very entertaining.'

The atmosphere was lifted so thoroughly by this exchange that neither of them thought about Mrs Fitzsimmons or her husband again for the rest of the meal. It was only when Tabitha failed to appear in her usual prompt way to collect the dishes that the issue re-entered their consciousness.

22

'Tabitha seems slow this evening,' Vita remarked.

'She is writing to her aunt and uncle. We are to leave everything on the table for her to collect later,' Aunt Louisa said.

'You called at the Red Lion earlier?'

'That is the strange thing. I presented my card with a note explaining that I was Tabitha's new employer and wished to present my condolences. I waited an inordinate length of time in the lobby while a constant stream of people came and went, but was not given the courtesy of any reply for at least forty minutes. Then a young man who said he was a messenger from Mrs Fitzsimmons came and told me that she was feeling unwell and could not see visitors, but that he would express my condolences to her himself. I accepted this, feeling quite concerned for the plight of the poor young woman, and prepared to leave, but as I did I saw something strange. I do not wish you to speak of this to anyone else, Vita, I trust you to be discreet.'

'Of course!'

'Well, I was sitting in an armchair against a pillar in the

lobby of the hotel, and I had a view through to the dining room from where I sat. The doors were constantly opened and shut as hotel servants passed in and out. I was beguiling the time by making small sketches in my notebook, as I always do. I was particularly trying to capture a waiter in movement, with his tray held aloft, so I was concentrating on that, and not taking any interest in the customers in the dining room, until I suddenly noticed that the lady I was looking at, sitting with a gentleman at a table over in a far corner, was Mrs Fitzsimmons herself.'

'She was not indisposed, then?'

'Well apparently not. I told myself that there could be many reasons a young widow might want to avoid a visit from someone she hardly knew. She has a perfect right to privacy, after all, and grief takes many forms, but she was not alone. She was...I hardly know how to express it...she was speaking privately to a gentleman. They were leaning together. Her manner was, well, I can only call it *coquettish* and she was laughing and tapping his arm and shoulder with her fan.'

Vita considered this information. 'Are you certain it was Mrs Fitzsimmons?' she asked, 'you only saw her at a distance at the Assault at Arms.'

'I wondered that myself, it seemed so improbable. But look,' Louisa took a newspaper from the sideboard and pointed to a photograph, 'this is the woman I saw, I cannot doubt it. In my profession one remembers a face.'

They had all but forgotten Tabitha's absence, but were reminded when they heard the back kitchen door open and close. A few moments passed before she appeared with a tray and began to clear the table.

'Is there anything more I can bring?'

'No thank you, Tabitha. You are quite well, I hope?' Aunt Louisa asked.

Tabitha's face was pale and she hesitated, her hands

nervously smoothing her apron, then began suddenly to weep, hiding her face by lifting the apron to cover it. '...I'm so sorry, Madam, I always liked Jack, he was like another brother. Mrs Fitzsimmons, she only spoke about how she didn't want me to go talking to the newspapers. As if I would. As if I needed telling!'

'Vita,' said Aunt Louisa, 'bring a nip of sherry for Tabitha, she is upset. And perhaps one for me, too. It has been a long day, all in all.'

23

Early the next day the police sent an officer to interview Tabitha on the grounds that she was one of the last people outside Fitzsimmons' immediate team to see the boxer alive. A serious sergeant with a wide moustache and large pale hands removed his helmet inside the door and stood with it under his arm. Aunt Louisa was at a talk, so Vita, who had let him in, called for Tabitha to leave the breakfast dishes and come upstairs. She accompanied them into the sitting room. Vita and Tabitha sat on either side of the fireplace. The police officer stood before them until Vita suggested he take a dining chair and sit down. This he did, leaving his helmet on the table and drawing a notebook and short pencil from his uniform pocket.

'You are Miss ...'

'Tabitha Hindcote' she put in.

'And you are related to Mr Jack Fitzsimmons, I believe?'

'I am his cousin.'

'And you know him well?'

'I know...knew him well when we were children together, but I have seen less of him since he left Cornwall.'

'But you saw him last Friday night?'

'Yes, sir.'

'At the fight would that be?'

'I saw him before, during and after the fight, sir.'

'Would you say that you and Mr Fitzsimmons were on good terms?'

'Yes sir. I always got on well with Jack.'

'And Mrs Fitzsimmons? Were you friends?'

'Not friends, sir, I can't say that. I met her only when they came here to Cambridge and there was hardly time to talk.'

'But she seemed friendly?'

'Friendly enough, sir.'

'And you say you saw the fight. Did you see anything unusual?'

'I saw Jack knocking the other men down. It did not seem unusual for that to happen at a boxing match. It was unusual for the man not to wake up at the end, though. It was terrible. I went afterwards to see Jack and he was very upset. He told me he never meant to harm Sam Shepherd, or Mr Edward. He regretted hurting them both very much. 'I think I shall give up this game' he told me. He said that several times. He was nearly breaking his heart, sir.'

The policeman wrote slowly in his notebook, bending over and frowning in concentration.

'And how was Mrs Fitzsimmons at this time? Was she present?'

'After the fight? Yes, sir. She was trying to take his mind off it, telling him not to upset himself. Sam would soon wake up and he shouldn't worry. She was busy while I was there, packing up his things and getting ready to go back to the hotel.'

'Did she appear worried about her husband's health?'

'His health? No sir. She wanted him to get changed and go back to the hotel to eat his supper and rest.'

'She was anxious about her husband?'

'No sir, she seemed more impatient than worried, but I was not there more than ten minutes. She wanted to get back to the hotel.'

'And Mr Fitzsimmons did not seem unwell to you, other than in the way of bruises and being tired after the fight?'

'No sir, he was upset, as I said, but he seemed well enough.'

The officer cleared his throat and squared his shoulders slightly before asking the next question. 'Were you alone with Mr Fitzsimmons at any time?'

'Kitty was coming and going from the room, it was a small room and she was giving instructions to the other men who worked with Jack.'

'So there was a point when you were alone in the room?'

'Yes, sir, for one or two minutes.'

'On more than one occasion?'

'Yes. As I said, Kitty and the other men were coming in and out, but there were a few times when we were alone together.'

'A few times?'

'Perhaps two or three, but only for a moment.'

'Thank you, Miss Hindcote.' The officer closed his notebook. 'There will in all likelihood be further questions at a later date.' He stood abruptly and took his helmet from the table. Vita showed him out. When she returned Tabitha had gone back to her work in the kitchen.

'You are to turn them away at the door next time,' Aunt Louisa said when she heard about the visit. 'No policeman should enter a house with only two young women present – much less interview one of them without a senior member of the household to observe. Disgraceful! I've a good mind to speak to the Chief Constable.'

Tabitha was offered time off to recover from the shock of

her cousin's death and do whatever duties she owed in notifying the rest of the family, but she preferred to keep working. Louisa and Vita both noticed the strained and crestfallen air of their new maid-of-all-work. Even so, she continued her habit of rising before anyone else and Vita still heard her on the stairs at night.

On Tuesday morning Dr Goodman arrived early to call on Edward and found him increasingly impatient with both his confinement to bed and the light diet. He and Vita both noted a slight rise in his temperature, so the patient was firmly told to stay where he was.

The doctor joined Vita and Louisa at the breakfast table on his way out. He waited until Tabitha had left the room before saying, 'I hear the Fitzsimmons post mortem examination is to be carried out by Professor Rusbridge.'

'Will you attend?' Aunt Louisa asked.

'There will not be room for mere General Practitioners,' he said, 'besides, I have patients to see.'

24

They broke off as Tabitha returned with hot water for the teapot and attempted small talk until she was safely outside the room again.

'The poor girl is most distressed about the circumstances of her cousin's death,' Aunt Louisa said, 'it may be a matter of academic fascination for medics, but this is someone she has known all her life, we must show consideration.'

'Why is a post mortem examination necessary?' Vita asked. 'Is there any doubt about the cause of his death? Surely he died as a result of his injuries during the fight?'

'Very probably he did,' Goodman told her, 'but that is only an assumption. He did not show any signs of injury when he was examined after the fight. The post-mortem examination is likely to confirm that what you say is true, but it is unusual for someone to walk away apparently well, and then die in their sleep without warning or other symptoms.'

'What sort of symptoms might be expected?' asked Vita.

'Well, if the brain were damaged there might be slurring of the speech, perhaps, or co-ordination problems – a staggering, uneven walking gait, for example.'

'Or a seizure, like Edward's?' Vita added.

'Yes, that would be another indicator, though in your brother's case there seems to be no lasting damage.'

'I saw none of those things, sir.'

Tabitha had returned to the room unnoticed. The others started uneasily and looked toward her.

'This must be very difficult for you, Tabitha,' Aunt Louisa said.

'It is, Madam. But ... may I speak?'

'Of course.'

'I saw him that night, and he was walking about, he was talking just as he normally would. He had bruises, but he didn't even have a swollen eye or a cut on him. It was always his proud boast that he was so good at dodging punches that he kept his looks. He said he was the best-looking boxer in the country. It was a boast and a joke, I know that, but there was some truth in it. His nose was not broken and his ears were not like cauliflowers like some boxers. He was a handsome man and proud of it. He had not taken many hard punches to the head that night. Mrs Brocklehurst and Miss Vita are witness to that themselves. When I saw him he was in good health, the only thing wrong was that his heart was heavy with anxiety for the man he had sent to hospital, and with the harm he had done to Mr Edward.'

'Please, Tabitha, do not upset yourself. Forgive us for talking about your cousin without including you,' Vita said. She pulled out a chair, and Tabitha, now in tears, sat suddenly on it, burying her face in her apron.

In pained silence the others watched her a moment, but then she wiped her eyes and sat up straight. Addressing Dr Goodman she said, 'If you could see the examination of his poor body, sir, I would be glad of it. I have a feeling in the back of my mind. I should not say it, and I hope you will forgive me for telling you, but I have an idea that my poor cousin did not die in a natural way, sir. Something was wrong.'

'Did you mention this to the police officer?' Aunt Louisa asked.

'He did not give me the chance to, Madam. He did not ask my opinion, why should he? I am only Jack's distant cousin and only a maid-of-all-work from Cornwall...' she paused here and wiped her tears away again, 'but if he had asked, I would have said that I don't like the way Kitty Fitzsimmons has acted.'

'You must be very careful what you say about this in public,' Goodman told her.

'I know that,' Tabitha said, 'she is a grand American lady who has lost her husband and everybody must pity her and feel charitable, but I do not.'

Tabitha sat up straight and took her apron from her eyes. Speaking clearly and without a tremble in her voice, she looked round at them. 'To speak plain, I don't like Mrs Kitty Fitzsimmons. I think that lady behaved badly towards my cousin. She did not want me there and she did nothing to make him feel better. She only chided him for weakness when he was sorrowful after harming his opponents.'

'You surely do not think that his new wife could have meant him any harm?' Aunt Louisa said.

'I cannot say, Madam. All I know is that she was not a kind lady and she seemed only to care for the fighting, for the fighting game and the money, and not to care for my cousin in a wifely way. And she is always with that group of men, his 'seconds' she calls them. They are a secretive lot and they act more like her guards. And when she spoke to me she was only thinking about what the papers might say. That's what I saw with my own eyes. So, if anyone could find out any more information about my poor cousin's death, then I should be most grateful to them.'

Tabitha stood, briskly gathered plates and cups onto her tray with trembling hands, and left the room. A brief silence followed her departure.

'You said Professor Rusbridge would supervise the post-mortem?' Louisa asked.

'Indeed. He has been invited to do so. He is eminent in the field of Anatomy. There will be a police pathologist present as well.' Goodman told her.

'Dr Goodman, would you be willing to attend on Tabitha's behalf, as it were, if you were invited?'

'Of course, though I cannot claim any great expertise.'

'I shall send him a note requesting an invitation,' Louisa said.

Goodman laughed. 'Your portrait of him must have been particularly fine, if it gives you such powers!'

Already at her bureau, Aunt Louisa picked up her pen and began to write.

'It was,' she said quietly.

Goodman's invitation to the post mortem was delivered by teatime.

25

In her room, Vita found *The Undergraduette*, the little newsletter Clara Benn had given her in the cafe, tucked into her notebook. In search of distraction, she took it out. Printed on a single sheet, so that it could be folded small, it was already soft and frayed as though many readers had handled it. There were items of news, opinion pieces and short essays, all apparently written by women students or would-be students at the university. Its tone was playful and ironic, but there were also practical tips for women whose studies were thwarted by the regulations. *Gaining Entry to the Three Ls* was one headline, and below it were listed a number of imaginative methods women students had successfully used to gain access to libraries, lectures, and even laboratories.

Vita read the list with amazement and stared out of her study window across the peaceful back gardens of Eden Street. Minmou, the little cat from next door, sauntered along a wall and the wind tilted the trees, blowing leaves in twisting shoals from one garden to the next. The feeling of being one of a group engaged upon the same endeavour was entirely new to Vita. She knew such women existed, she had met Clara, but *The Undergraduette*, printed on rough paper and handed round secretly, was her first indication that there was a grouping of people - women mostly, but there were men writing in support too - all sharing the same goal. That sensation was new, delightful, but also unsettling. It meant that something she had imagined as distant, vague, and probably unachievable might now, in reality, be possible. It would, however, call for great determination and a rule-breaking audacity that Vita was not sure she possessed. Would she have the courage to dress as a man in order to enter a library, or as a cleaner to gain access to a laboratory, both methods described in *The Undergraduette*?

Vita stood and walking to the window, looked down into the garden. As she watched, Tabitha let herself in through the back gate and walked quickly up the path by the garden wall towards the scullery door. The cat came over and rubbed against her skirts. Tabitha paused and seemed to be talking quietly to the animal, leaning over to stroke its ears for a moment before she moved away. Even from a distance her whole bearing was stooped with the burden of sorrow.

This brief scene was enough to remind Vita of the shadow that the death of Jack Fitzsimmons was casting upon the household. The pugilist's death, a matter of newspaper headlines and scientific curiosity, brought not only fascinated public and medical speculation, but private grief and questions that needed to be answered.

Was Tabitha right to doubt Kitty Fitzsimmons? And why did she come and go at such strange hours?

VITA CARRIED THE NEATLY FOLDED COPY OF THE Undergraduette into her brother's sick room, when it was her turn to sit with him later. He was dozing, so she free to read it discreetly. One of the ideas struck Vita particularly. '*Women,*' the article said, '*being generally ignored and considered insignificant are, if plain in appearance, and therefore invisible to the male eye, often able to move about in the world with peculiar ease. Which gentleman of significance would think to question, for example, the comings and goings of cooks, maids, cleaners, bedders, serving women, launderesses and all the other members of the below-stairs classes?*'

It was in this manner that several young women gained regular access to libraries and even laboratories outside the usual hours in order to pursue their studies. One lady, who signed herself 'Annabella Architect', revealed that: '*I have been able to work every night for three months at a time in the Architecture Library by entering the building at six o'clock dressed as a cleaner and pretending to dust books until all the readers in the library went back to their colleges for dinner. From seven until midnight the place is mine to read in as I will, in perfect peace. My studies are advancing well. I am at pains to replace the books exactly where I find them, and I must say the library is exceedingly well cleaned, for if ever anyone enters, I spring up and dust another bookcase.*'

At five o'clock Vita noticed her brother's temperature was almost 100 degrees. He was quiet and made no remarks about the smallness of his dinner. She went for Dr Goodman immediately.

'I am concerned about this change,' he told her. 'Have you noticed anything else?'

'His ear bothers him still, and he complains of the headache he had before.'

'Come and observe as I examine this ear. I'm not sure what is causing the discomfort.'

A small unexplained wound behind Edward's ear was reddened and raised. A clear central mark made it look like a puncture or a particularly severe insect bite, but the pain it caused was so severe now that Edward could hardly bear it to be touched. Dr Goodman applied Magnesium Sulphate on a dressing to help draw any infection out. 'We must do everything we can to avoid inflammation,' he told Vita. 'Raise his head on pillows and cool it by applying damp towels. I know it is cold, but keep the window open. Warm his limbs with blankets, but keep his head as cool as possible. Take his temperature every quarter of an hour. Fetch me if it rises again. Is all that clear? He is to take water and nothing else for the next twenty-four hours. If he begins to ramble or become incoherent or delirious, or suddenly becomes irritable, let me know. Likewise if he suffers spasms or another seizure. I will come at any time if needed, just knock.'

As he left, the doctor stopped on the landing and put a hand on Vita's arm. 'Miss Carew, I realise I speak to you unthinkingly as if you were a medical professional. This care of your brother is a heavy responsibility. I have no doubt of your abilities, but I should not make assumptions. Perhaps you would prefer me to recommend a professional nurse for your brother? I can easily...'

'No. I want to do as much as I can,' Vita said.

'You are skilled in the sickroom.'

'Alas, I have had a great deal of practice.'

26

The newspapers, naturally enough – the local newspapers in particular – were making much of the sensational outcome of the biggest boxing fixture the town had ever seen. New editions seemed to be printed hourly, with street sellers shouting new headlines and holding up front pages bearing the same large photographs of the boxers every time anyone speculated or mentioned a new detail. Cockney Sam's sister was on her way to her brother's bedside from London. Doctors confirmed the boxer was still alive and breathing, though senseless and unresponsive. They feared a lengthy paralysis. 'Needles pressed into his arms and legs produce no movement,' one medical man was quoted as saying. Photographs of Mrs Fitzsimmons, now always dressed in black gowns, her face usually veiled, being ushered into or out of a building in a press of supporters, were also popular. '*Pugilist's Widow Attends St Barnabas Church*'.

'I spoke to the lady at length and was able, I think, to offer her some words of comfort,' Reverend L.B. Sumersfield told the Cambridge News, as part of a lengthy statement.

'It was the largest hat I have ever seen in St Barnabas,'

was what he later told his mother, 'from the pulpit it looked like the roof of a small circular building. And I must say the lady was brief to the point of rudeness when we spoke at the door, but then she is American, mother, we must make allowances, I suppose.'

'The unfortunate woman is alone in a foreign country and recently bereaved, Lawrence,' his mother reminded him, cutting her son a smaller slice of fruit cake than usual.

EDWARD'S SICK ROOM WAS KEPT SO COLD THAT VITA DID not want her aunt to risk her own health by spending too long there, but Louisa insisted on sitting with her nephew until about eleven that night. Vita then took her place, recording the patient's temperature at a hundred degrees at ten past eleven. She bathed Edward's hands with ice water and soaked the towels that were wrapping his head to keep them cold. Edward was half asleep, only shivering as the cold towels were applied and moaning a little. Just after midnight he complained of a headache, said his neck was hurting and took a little water. Vita recorded his temperature as a hundred and one degrees.

A little later she heard a knock at the door and Tabitha put her head into the room. 'I cannot sleep, Miss, may I fetch you a cup of tea? There's a terrible chill in here.'

'Yes, tea would be welcome,' Vita told her, 'and I may need to ask you to knock for Doctor Goodman. I'm afraid Edward's temperature is still increasing.'

By one in the morning Goodman was back at Edward's bedside. He re-applied the dressing to Edward's neck and noted the continued rise in temperature. Edward was not fully conscious any more. He groaned and thrashed from side to side, muttering and tearing at the bedding and his bandages. Several times the doctor and Vita re-settled him with his head raised and wrapped, but now he shrugged them aside, squirming. It was harder to get a temperature reading, but it seemed to be over a hundred and two degrees.

'What is the cause of this fever?' Vita asked, 'is it the original blow to his head?'

'It could be that, but I am inclined to suspect the wound in the neck. It feels hot to the touch and there is a discharge. It may by deeper and more serious than I thought. Is your maid still awake?'

'She said she would be in the kitchen.'

'I want her to go for my colleague, Dr McCardle. He's a head and neck man at the hospital. He will come immediately. I warned him he might be needed.'

McCardle lived three streets away and was in the room within the half hour. The doctors sent Vita to rest while they considered the case. She was reluctant to leave, but had to allow them their professional discussion. Tabitha brought her tea.

'The doctors will know what to do for the best, Miss,' she tried to reassure her. 'Your brother is young and strong, and they are very clever gentlemen.'

Vita took the tea, hoping she was right. Several times that night she listened outside the door. Once she knocked, but Goodman came to the doorway and told her they needed only hot water and clean towels to wash their hands. When she and Tabitha brought them, they were received at the door. There was a sharp chemical smell, the lamps had been lit and both doctors were in their shirts with their sleeves rolled to the elbow. Dr McCardle seemed to be wearing a brown apron.

'Wait downstairs,' Goodman said. 'We have work to do here and must not be interrupted.'

The door was then closed. For the rest of the night they

could hear low voices and purposeful movement within, more water was asked for and Goodman went across the road to collect something from his own medical stores, but there was nothing the women could do but wait. Vita and her aunt, who had been roused by the all the movement, dozed a little in their chairs. Tabitha did the same in the kitchen.

Around five a.m. there was activity above and Dr Goodman escorted his colleague to the front door. Aunt Louisa slept on and they whispered to avoid disturbing her. 'Come, Vita, and see the change,' he said.

She found Edward peaceful on his pillows. His head was hugely bandaged.

'Why is he bandaged?'

'We have operated. He was endangered by pressure on his skull from the inside. We made a small opening and drained it. He is in less pain now, and the fever is diminished. McCardle has performed the procedure successfully many times.'

'I don't understand. Did you drain the wound on his neck?' asked Vita. She touched her brother's forehead with the back of her hand and found it cool.

'The infection was in the skull,' Goodman said.

'You opened his skull?'

'Yes. At the side, behind the ear. There was no alternative. We are lucky that McCardle was here and had the skills.'

Vita looked at him in alarm.

'How? How did you do it?'

'He used a drill. A special one, and sterile, obviously. Only a small hole was needed, but it enabled McCardle to drain the skull of infection. The procedure undoubtedly saved your brother's life.'

Vita felt the room sway around her at the thought of her brother's skull being drilled opened. She held the bed post tightly. They both looked at the patient, now breathing easily.

His colouring was normal. There was little sign of the feverish flush his face had shown earlier.

'We are lucky McCardle was on hand,' Goodman repeated.

'Yes, we are,' Vita said, but left the room quickly to hide her horrified reaction. Tears were running down her cheeks and she could no longer trust herself to speak.

27

Nobody had slept that night except the patient, but Vita persisted with her quarter-hourly recording of Edward's temperature. By midday it was close to normal. As she entered the figure on her list, Dr Goodman returned to the room. She showed him her temperature chart and he nodded in approval, throwing himself wearily into the other chair in the room.

'Dr Goodman, do we know what caused Edward's fever?' Vita asked, 'It seemed so sudden.'

'McCardle and I both have some doubt about the cause, Miss Carew,' he said. 'I will speak to you as someone with a scientific interest. Frankly, the sudden fever was unexpected. In the case of a severe concussion, such as one caused by a head injury in a boxing match, a stroke or seizure might occur – even those are rare enough – but a fever is more likely connected to a wound or infection. There seemed little evidence of such a wound.'

'Except for the tiny scratch behind his ear,' Vita said.

'Indeed. We speculated that it might have been incurred earlier – some accident. Do you know of anything that happened? A fall, or accidental encounter with something sharp?'

'He mentioned nothing of that sort,' Vita said, 'but we had watched him fight with a sword before the boxing match.'

'A thin-bladed sword?'

'Yes. An epée.'

Goodman shrugged. 'Perhaps he will remember something when he wakes. McCardle speculated that a fairly minor wound was aggravated to the point of infection by the concussion. He may be right. We may never be able to explain it.'

'I wish I knew more!'

Goodman smiled at her.

'Your brother is studying Medicine, is he?'

'At Trinity, yes.'

'And you, Miss Carew, you are outshining all the eager young police officers in your First Aid classes. How are your other studies progressing?

Vita waved a hand towards the pile of notebooks she had been working on while her brother slept. Dr Goodman pulled his spectacles from his top pocket and surprised her by opening a notebook and inspecting it thoroughly, leaning over the table with his hands on either side. It seemed to Vita a long and piercing scrutiny, considering the notes had been made in her own way, entirely for her own use.

'There is promising work here, Miss Carew,' he finally declared. 'If you are serious about pursuing your studies, I would recommend Miss Emily Shorto on the Hunstanton Road. Her rates are reasonable. She is an excellent instructor who has saved many undergraduates from humiliation in their examinations.' He left a card which said 'E. Shorto, Instructor in Anatomy and Biological Sciences, Albert Cottage, Hunstanton Road, Cambridge. Laboratory facilities available.'

'She must be the daughter of Mrs Evelyn Shorto,' Aunt Louisa remarked, when she saw the card, 'I met her mother at an exhibition of plant drawings. Her own were very fine, as I recall. I believe she is a distinguished botanist. She and her daughter work together since her husband died.'

AT FOUR THAT AFTERNOON, AS THE LIGHT BEHIND HIS curtains was fading to darkness, Edward opened his eyes and said quietly, 'Cheese. That is what I would like most of all. A good strong cheddar and perhaps some pickle.'

'You are permitted water or a little broth,' his sister replied, smiling, and stepped out of the room to hide tears for the second time that day.

Aunt Louisa wrote to her brother giving the news of Edward's fever and recovery. The danger had come and gone so swiftly that it was a difficult letter to compose. Nobody had told her of the operation, either. By silent mutual decision Goodman and Vita kept those details to themselves. Vita added a few notes of her own and posted the letter to catch the 5.15pm collection. After that she set out to find Miss Shorto.

28

Miss Shorto and her mother lived in a plain terraced house with steps up to the front door. The front of the house was dark, but a light shone distantly inside. A note pinned beside the bell pull read, '*Please ring hard several times and be patient. We are in the laboratory at the back and may take some time to answer.*'

There was, indeed, a considerable delay before the door was thrown open by a woman in her thirties with her sleeves rolled to the elbow and a skullerymaid's brown apron over her skirt. Behind her Vita glimpsed an Aladdin's cave of books. They lined the hall and all sides of the room beyond.

'Did you want Miss Emily or Mrs Elizabeth Shorto?' asked the woman, wiping her hands on her apron. Her hair was tied up in a scarf, as if for cleaning.

'I was hoping to speak to Miss Emily about a course of study. I was sent by Dr Goodman in Eden Street,' Vita said, uttering lines she had rehearsed on the way.

The woman in the apron looked Vita up and down as if she were a piece of furniture in an auction room. 'This way,' she said, leading her into a tiny parlour, where there was just room for a table and chairs among the bookcases. 'I am Emily Shorto. I may not be able to teach you immediately, my mother and I are finishing an important publication, but I'm sure we can manage something.'

Until that moment Vita had thought she might be speaking to the maid. They sat at a small table crowded with books and papers. After rummaging for a moment, Miss Shorto retrieved a large diary and opened it. 'What is it that interests you, Miss...'

'Carew, Vita Carew.'

'What is it that you wish to study, and why?'

Vita was speechless, her head suddenly as empty as a balloon. A clock on the mantelpiece ticked loudly and passing carriage wheels rumbled in the street outside. Specks of dust floated in the milky lamplight between them. She looked down at her hands and to her surprise and shame found them trembling in her lap.

Miss Shorto sighed, 'Perhaps you are reconsidering. Scientific study is often more pleasant in the imagination than it is in practice.' She laid her pencil to one side and was about to close the diary.

'It is not that, Miss Shorto. It is the opposite. I wish to study everything! I know so very little.'

'I see.' Miss Shorto looked out of the window and flipped the pencil in her fingers. 'But if we had to start somewhere...?'

'Anatomy!'

'You are interested in Anatomy?'

'The structures of the brain, in particular.'

'Good heavens,' said Miss Shorto. 'The brain? That *would* be an unusual starting point.'

'I nursed my mother through her final illness, a brain sickness. My brother recently suffered a head injury and a seizure. So much remains mysterious about the brain. I should like to learn as much as possible about it.'

Miss Shorto now looked back at her visitor and raised her eyebrows. 'And your education so far...?'

'In Science? I have read my brother's books and attended a few lectures.'

'But no schooling?'

'No. I was needed at home.'

'And your aims? Your purpose in studying?'

Vita winced and squirmed in her chair, it was difficult to tell this brisk lady her secret thoughts. 'I should like to study, even if I am not able to join a university,' she said, finally.

'Yes. To what end?' asked Miss Shorto, looking at Vita sharply over the top of her small spectacles. 'So that you can sound clever at dinner parties? So that you can give lectures to the Ladies' Guild? So that you can beat your brother at quizzes?'

'No! I want to become a doctor.'

'Of Medicine?'

'Yes!'

Miss Shorto smiled for the first time. 'Well, Miss Carew, you have a long and difficult path ahead, but others have trodden it before you. Some of them women I have taught in this room.' She picked up her pencil, licked the tip and leafed through her diary. 'Come on Wednesdays at nine o'clock and Fridays at ten. Let yourself in at the back door, down the side of the house. You need an apron for laboratory work. Bring the fee with you each week and post it through the front door as you pass. Science is an honourable pursuit, Miss Carew, but I always warn new students that if it is pecuniary advancement they seek, it would be better to look elsewhere. You will have to get used to a satisfying, but humble existence, if my parents' and my own experience is anything to go by.'

'Can I read anything to prepare?' Vita asked.

'I will lend you Carrington,' said Miss Shorto, and without

needing to rise from her chair, she reached and took a large brown volume from the shelf at her elbow. 'If it is the brain that interests you, we might as well begin with that. Look at Chapter 5, Osteology of the Skull. Learn as much as you can. Return on Wednesday and I will give you a list of lectures. And please be punctual.'

Vita lost her way twice on the walk back to Eden Street. She was filled with a strange energy that made her walk fast but removed all sense of direction.

29

There was, of course, no question of Vita attending the boxer's post-mortem examination, even if she drew, labelled and memorized all the parts of the skull. She did speculate aloud as to whether she might disguise herself as a man or a cleaner in order to slip into the laboratory. 'Wherever did such a preposterous idea as that come from?' Aunt Louisa cried, pressing her gloved hands to her bosom in dismay.

'I have been reading about young ladies who are so desirous of the study of Science that they find ingenious ways to enter into libraries and even Anatomy rooms,' Vita told her.

Dr Goodman had sent both of them out for some fresh air. They were walking down the avenue of chestnut trees along the fields known as the Backs. A large playful dog was jumping in piles of leaves ahead of them.

'Vita, dear, I know you are enthusiastic about your studies, but a post-mortem is not a fairground entertainment. To see a human body...' Louisa struggled for a word, '...*dismantled* before you must surely be the stuff of nightmares to all but the most hardened and experienced observer. And furthermore there is something disrespectful about the eagerness you exhibit, it is unseemly to wish to take part in so tragic an event, whatever you might learn from it.'

'I apologise, Aunt, if it seems disrespectful,' Vita said, 'I did not intend it. It is just that the workings of human anatomy are so mysterious and fascinating.'

'I know you mean no harm,' her aunt told her. 'If your dear mother were still with us, I feel sure she would be delighted at your thirst for knowledge. And your father encourages it. I only wonder whether the direction you have chosen – Science - is one that is so fraught with pitfalls and limitations that you lay yourself a series of terrible traps to fall into and miseries to endure. It seems almost unnatural for a young woman to set herself so overwhelming a challenge. Life is quite hard enough without it. I do not agree that women are unsuited to intense study, Vita, but I should hate to see your energy sapped and your spirit dampened by rejection. It is really very hard for me to know how to advise you.'

Vita put her arm through her aunt's and squeezed it a little. 'You need really not concern yourself about my future, Aunt, there is something about learning facts, scientific facts, that makes me feel I am built of rubber and will bounce up again if I am thrown down.'

'I hope that is true, even if it is rather a strange idea,' Louisa said as they strolled under the dappled archway of the trees, 'particularly as I have decided to review my opinion on one of the topics we have discussed.'

They stopped and watched in amusement as the bounding dog found a friend and the pair ran in wild circles scattering small typhoons of russet coloured leaves. Behind them King's College Chapel caught the sun and an artist at an easel close by attempted to capture its famous profile in watercolours.

'You said you had reviewed your opinion on something,' Vita prompted, as they turned for home.

'Bicycles,' Louisa said, 'I read an article in the Ladies Journal and I have concluded that they may not be quite as dangerous as I had thought.'

'Oh Aunt!' Vita cried, 'Do you mean I may be permitted to ride one myself?'

'I do,' her aunt replied, 'and your father agrees. And for reasons of safety, you may also adopt the divided skirt, but Vita ...'

'Yes, Aunt?'

'...absolutely no pantaloons. We are not in *France*.'

30

A bicycle, however, was not as easy to come by as all that. They were expensive machines and, although Vita spent several pleasant hours the following afternoon visiting cycle shops in town, she could do no more than pretend to ride one, stroke the shining metal of the handlebars and choose which basket she would attach to carry her books. Second-hand cycles were available of course, but Vita had no way of knowing which would be a wise choice. Besides, even the cheapest of these, weather-beaten and a little rusty, was beyond the price her small allowance could stretch to. 'So near and yet so far,' she thought, irritably, kicking at leaves down Silver Street on her way home.

The next day Dr Goodman visited Edward and stayed to dinner. After a polite delay so that everyone could savour Monsieur's *confit de canard*, he reported on the post-mortem.

'It was very formal and unsensational,' Goodman told them. They were in the drawing room and Tabitha had been invited to join them. 'Barnes, the police pathologist, had already made all the preparations, opening the chest and so on, and samples were taken. We looked at the heart and lungs, which appeared entirely healthy and normal in all details, as did all the other organs. After that we attended mostly to the head and neck. There was little to see externally; slight bruising to the nose and jaw, but nothing very noticeable. It was, I confess, even to a professional eye, quite difficult to see him there. It is rare to see an apparently healthy young man, in the prime of his life, on the slab, at least in my experience.' The doctor looked at his listeners, particularly at Tabitha, but all were perfectly calm.

'Did Professor Rusbridge take the lead?' Vita asked.

'He did, it being his laboratory, as a matter of medical etiquette. He made a long examination of the head externally, assessing the skull and its integrity, feeling for anything misshapen or misaligned in the head and neck. He wanted to eliminate any pre-existing weakness or injury that could unexpectedly be aggravated by a blow, in case the blow itself were not fatal, but the combination of some underlying weakness and the blow together might be so. He and the other doctors - there were five examining in all, McCardle was one - all took it in turns to examine the head and neck in great detail.'

'And *was* there any pre-existing condition?'

'They found no external evidence of one. The skull was sound and the jaw and vertebrae of the neck all intact and correct. They found evidence of a previous injury to the nose, which had been broken some time ago, but that was expected, given his profession.'

'So it was not a skeletal injury that killed him, then?'

'There was no evidence of one, no.'

Goodman looked into the fire, seeming to admire the flames.

'When the skull was opened there was a small amount of surface scarring,' he went on, 'but very little. There were no contusions or irregularities and when it was cut into sections, none of the pathology of external damage. Interest was focused on whether he had suffered a clot or a bleed to the brain. That would usually be clearly visible. Of this there was little sign except in one small area.'

'So what was the cause of his death?'

Goodman did not answer but continued his quiet description of events. 'We were invited to come and examine the brain ourselves once it was laid bare. I confess I do in general find the brain a disappointing organ to look at. It is the extraordinary engine of control for our whole being, immensely subtle and mysterious to Science, but, as you know, its appearance is of little more than a well-ordered mound of putty. I could see little of note. There were no marks other than one or two patches of very slight discolouration which were perfectly in keeping with the injuries a pugilist might sustain. We were quite a crowd, circling round the table. The undergraduates were eager to impress the Professor with their expertise. They all appeared extremely well-informed, and I felt I had nothing to add to their erudite observations. But on one side, the left, I observed a minute circular...I hardly know what to call it... an indentation of the subtlest kind. It was the size of a glass pinhead.'

'Did you call attention to it?'

'I explained what I had seen and Professor Rusbridge and two of the senior doctors said they had remarked on this odd shaping but concluded that it did not amount to anything significant. They all looked again and declared it to be part of the natural contour of the brain.' Goodman shrugged and his face clouded for a moment. 'Further into the skull,' he went on, 'there was an area of damage, as I said. It was small, but it appeared to be the only unusual feature. It was the kind of staining one might associate with a spontaneous bleed. A stroke.'

'He died of a stroke?' Vita asked.

'As I said, there was an obvious patch of discolouration. At the conclusion of the post-mortem they deferred a decision and arranged to reconvene for further examination of the brain itself, but their provisional conclusion was that he had suffered a stroke in the ring and died later in his sleep of its effects.'

'Do you agree?'

'My knowledge is far too limited to disagree. It is an unusual sequence of events, but perfectly plausible.'

'Would he not have shown signs of a stroke earlier?'

'Not necessarily,' Goodman said, 'as we know to your brother's cost, symptoms can take many hours to develop. It is perfectly possible that Fitzsimmons and his supporters mistook the symptoms for the usual after-effects of a fight. They might be very similar.'

'None of this is very reassuring for you, Tabitha,' Vita said. The maid had sat stiff and silent as she listened to Dr Goodman's report.

'I am glad to know that so many great doctors are trying to find out what happened,' Tabitha replied. She smiled ruefully. 'Poor Jack would be surprised if he knew how much trouble everyone was going to.'

As he left, Goodman looked in on Edward, who was sleeping peacefully and whose temperature was now normal.

'He has a little difficulty remembering things,' Vita said, as they crept out of the room without disturbing the patient.

'In what way?'

'He has no recollection of what caused his illness. He did before the fever, but now he no longer has.'

'Amnesia is not uncommon after a concussion or a seizure,' Goodman told her. 'Normally the memory returns over a few days. You need not worry. But there is one further thing I wanted to mention to you alone, Miss Carew.' They were standing now at the foot of the stairs. Goodman, his coat already on, was holding his hat with his gloves inside it. 'I noticed that Fitzsimmons had a small wound near his ear very similar to the one your brother had. I would probably not have noticed it, but for attending your brother. I had it included in the report.'

'Do you think it contributed to his death?'

'I cannot say. The brain sections have not had their detailed examination yet. That will take place on Monday. Perhaps there will be new observations then. Now goodnight. And do not worry about Edward's memory. Prompt him with a few questions to help him remember.'

31

Vita's first lesson at Miss Shorto's was due the next morning. She did not want to leave her brother, but both he and her aunt urged Vita to continue as normal. Louisa promised to take temperature readings and keep the patient to his meagre diet while her niece was away.

It was a cold grey morning, and just as chilly inside the Shorto household as in the windy street. Emily Shorto seemed immune to this, except for wearing a muffler and gloves. No fire burned in the grate and a draft seemed to blow upwards through the floorboards from an icy basement. Vita lost all feeling in her feet within the first quarter hour. Despite this the lesson on the osteology of the skull went well. Miss Shorto produced a real skull, which they passed between them. She admired Vita's notes, particularly her sketched reproductions of the illustrations in the textbook.

'Are these your own work ?' she asked, peering over.

'Yes. I copied them out to help me remember the names.'

'And you do remember them. To an impressive degree, as a matter of fact.'

'I've always found remembering things quite easy. It annoys my poor brother.'

'And these are notes from lectures you have attended?' Miss Shorto was openly leafing through the notebook now.

'Yes.'

'You have been busy.'

'I have a lot to learn.'

Miss Shorto smiled. 'I believe you met Clara Benn.'

'I did,' Vita said, 'how did you know?'

'Cambridge is a small world. She is very gifted. She was top of the list in the Tripos exam in the summer, did she tell you? It is only the third time a woman student has achieved such a thing. It caused quite a sensation.'

'She said nothing about that.'

'No, she wouldn't. Clara is the most promising student I have ever instructed, and I have worked with some very clever people indeed. You would do well to stick by her, Vita . Now, in our next lesson we return to the cranium, so I refer you to Carrington pages 69 to 75.'

Still feeling chilled to the bone, Vita found Clara in their usual spot on the stairs outside the lecture theatre at eleven.

'Did you attend the boxer's post-mortem, Clara? It must surely have been of great interest to you,' Vita said, as they settled their papers before the lecture began. Young men in twos and threes were sweeping past them into the lecture hall.

'There was no possibility of that,' Clara replied, 'Professor Rusbridge only allowed a small group of invited guests to observe. Most were professors and police officers, I imagine, although he probably filled the operating theatre with his favourite undergraduates. No ladies were invited. They have a terrible fear of ladies fainting or running mad in the presence of a cadaver, despite the fact that nurses lay out bodies every day. I have seen a forensic post-mortem examination on one occasion. It was extremely interesting.'

'Do you not find it frustrating to be kept away from interesting occasions?' Vita asked, taking a pencil and notebook from her bag.

Clara smiled, 'I decided long ago that I would not entertain thoughts of frustration or anger,' she told her, 'it does no good. I know some young women in our situation – aiming to study Science or Medicine - who have become so enraged and ill-tempered that their very sanity has been ground down by it. Such powerful resentment can be quite harmful.'

The lecturer, in his black academic gown, passed with his books under his arm, closing the doors behind him. He did not seem to notice them.

Clara lowered her voice, 'I believe our best method is to be silent and stealthy, to avoid drawing attention to ourselves, and to concentrate instead on using every method our wits can devise to find and learn the subject matter we are intent upon. We are intelligent enough to find ways, if we put our minds to it - that is my programme. Public show and protestation are necessary at various times, I can see that, but it is not something that appeals to me. My health is limited. I do not want to exhaust myself in battle when I could avoid it and still achieve my aims.'

After the lecture, whilst they were walking along King's Parade towards the café, Vita was aware that Clara's pace was slowing. 'I hope you are not unwell, Clara,' she said, 'I am sorry to hear that your health is not strong.'

Clara shrugged. 'I have a weak heart. It is a condition I have had all my life. It means I have no great stamina and must rest sometimes, but I am not affected in any other way. I sometimes think that my fascination with Anatomy stems from the condition. There is no cure, but I should very much like to know exactly what is wrong in here.' She tapped her chest lightly as she walked. 'If only nature had provided us with a means of seeing inside our bodies. I imagine I would see a heart with a single valve that is misconnected, a few fibres in the wrong place, that is all, and yet it has altered my destiny entirely.'

They reached the café and found a table.

'But you appear so...'

'Serene? Resigned?' Clara laughed, 'I am now, perhaps, but it has taken a long while to reach that stage. There have been times when the limitations I live by have chafed me most painfully. But now I feel there is so much to study and so little time that the work itself is all I care about. And, Vita, on the subject of the post-mortem, I may have an idea.'

Their poached eggs on toast arrived and they set about them with the good appetite of students who have been hard at work all morning.

32

There was no doubting Kitty Fitzsimmons' beauty. Vita sat near her and found herself cataloguing the elements which combined to such effect: delicate features, pale, almost pearly skin, chestnut hair swept up and pinned, but softly enough to curl gently at the temples and along her neck. Kitty's eyes were a dark blue and wide beneath thick lashes. She wore, as she always did now, black from hat to boots, but there was the sheen of silk and the rustle of delicate petticoats as she sat and a light perfume seemed to shake from her skirts. She removed long gloves with great concentration and folded them in her lap. She did not smile, seeming ill-at-ease and the tension spread with her perfume through the room, so that Vita and Louisa felt unrelaxed as well. The visit was a surprise. A note had arrived that morning while Vita was at Miss Shorto's. There had been little time to prepare.

As hostess, Louisa did her best to overcome this.

'Please do come in, Mrs Fitzsimmons and Mr...?' Their guest had arrived in the company of a tall dark-suited gentleman. He was not introduced.

'He will wait in the hall,' said Mrs Fitzsimmons, following her hostess into the drawing room.

'May I offer a little tea, Mrs Fitzsimmons? Or perhaps you would prefer coffee?' Aunt Louisa had prepared herself for American tastes.

'I do not care for either,' the guest replied, 'but I could take a seltzer or a root beer, if you had one.'

Neither of these was ever drunk in the house, but Louisa took the request calmly, rang her little hand bell and relayed it to Tabitha.

Kitty Fitzsimmons looked only at her gloves while Tabitha was in the room and did not acknowledge her.

'I do hope you have everything you need at the Red Lion, Mrs Fitzsimmons,' Aunt Louisa began again.

'It is satisfactory, I guess,' the lady replied, 'I shall not be there much longer.'

'Will you change hotels?' asked Louisa.

'Heavens no. I shall return to London. I am not...comfortable in this city. It is an unhappy reminder to me of the...of the dreadful events. I am obliged to stay for a time to attend to the funeral proceedings etcetera. It is most trying.'

Mrs Fitzsimmons made a languid gesture of dismissal with one of her delicate hands. It then slumped back into the black silk of her lap.

Vita had never heard anyone pronounce the word 'etcetera' before.

'I can imagine something of your situation,' Aunt Louisa remarked, 'I myself lost a husband in very sudden and difficult circumstances.'

Mrs Fitzsimmons looked directly at Louisa for perhaps the first time. 'Is that so? Why then you must understand the tender nature of my feelings at this time - and the difficulty of being alone and far from home.'

'Certainly I do.'

'The newspapers...' Mrs Fitzsimmons said vaguely, waving her lovely hand close to her face, '...it is unimaginable! The things they write! They follow me day and night. They have attempted to photograph the room where my husband...' here she broke off and struggled with the catch on her tiny jewelled purse before pulling out a lace handkerchief and holding it briefly to each eye.

'It must be dreadful for you.'

'I cannot move or speak to anyone without a flash going off in my very face. I have asked the police commissioner - Superintendent Collins, I find him very obliging - to restrain them, and he has stationed his men in the hotel, but he does not seem to have the power to prevent the reporters' constant invasions. They are without mercy.'

Vita and Louisa could do little other than nod in silent sympathy.

'I have no alternative but to stay because of the - oh! I have forgotten the name - the medical inspection...'

'...the post mortem?' Vita suggested. Her aunt frowned at her.

'They will not allow a funeral until that is satisfactorily concluded. It seems to take an endless time. They say it is a technicality. I try...I try not to think about it.' Mrs Fitzsimmons pressed her tiny handkerchief into service again.

Tabitha arrived and set out the tea things. They were all glad of the little diversion this provided.

'Will I take some tea to the gentleman, Madam?' she asked.

'No. He will take nothing,' replied Mrs Fitzsimmons, dismissing the maid with a gesture.

'Your family is long associated with the sport of boxing, I am told,' Aunt Louisa remarked, pouring a pale cordial from the jug Tabitha had brought into her guest's glass.

'We are well-known in boxing, certainly. My father's

training establishment in New York City is famous for the high quality of its fighting men. We have won a great many titles, All American Titles, *World* Titles. Why, last year my father trained more champions than anyone else in the world, the world that boxes to the Queensbury Rules, that is. I have been brought up in the sport, as was my father. English ladies are not always able to understand my liking for the sport of boxing. Some American ladies, also, find themselves looking askance at my livelihood, but it is my home, my realm, my whole life.'

This manifesto seemed to have exhausted Kitty. She broke off and took a sip of cordial. 'I do not know how the sporting life is conducted in England, Mrs Brocklehurst, but I do know that horse racing is the sport of kings, as you would say. You must imagine that I am a trainer of horses - and champion horses, winning horses of the finest kind - and then, perhaps you can understand how I see things. Why, pugilism is the finest sport of them all, to my eyes. There are few ladies who truly know the business as I do, having been raised in it from my earliest childhood, but there are one or two in England, I believe.'

This sudden speech was delivered with an energy that brought a flush of pink to the young widow's delicate cheeks and a new light to her eyes.

Neither Vita nor her aunt had any ready reply. Their glance met briefly and both registered only bewilderment. The widow was in full flood now and continued her monologue.

'I have found the police to be most gentleman-like in England, at least. They have been polite and considerate at every turn. But the press are not so polite. They will not leave me alone and I really cannot stay in my room all day and every day. A walk, a short stroll, a little lunch - even the smallest of activities brings them out in a pack, like wolves. It is perhaps because I am a foreigner to them and seem... exotic. The rash impertinence of their questions, too. They ask where I am going, who with, for how long. *Kitty! they call out. Kitty! Over here, Kitty!*'

'I am sorry that you are so distressed...' Aunt Louisa began, but Kitty cut across her.

'...they look at me, Miss Brocklehurst, they look at me as if I had a hand in it. As if I were responsible.'

'Oh! Surely that is not the case!'

'But it is! They question the hotel staff, the police question the men who work with me, they take fingerprints, they take photographs. It seems endless, endless!'

33

Aunt Louisa stood and put a hand lightly on Kitty's shoulder. 'My dear,' she said, 'I sympathise deeply with your situation. If there is anything I or my niece can do to help you...'

Kitty started at Louisa's touch and pulled away. She dabbed her eyes, then laid a hand flutteringly at her own throat before sighing and straightening her back against the chair.

'Please excuse me, my main intention was to enquire after the health of your nephew, Mr Edward Carew. I heard he was not well.'

'He is much recovered, thank you,' Aunt Louisa told her.

Kitty straightened the silken fingers of the gloves in her lap. 'Has he spoken to you about the fight?' she asked.

'He has no clear recollection of events, as a matter of fact. The doctor says he will only slowly regain his memory.'

'But otherwise he is well?' Kitty asked.

'Much better than he was, thank you,' Aunt Louisa told her.

'Does your maid attend him?'

'I beg your pardon.'

'Does she take him food and drink to his room? Is she alone with him?'

'Why do you ask this?'

'I am speaking to you in confidence, ladies. I do not believe that young woman is trustworthy. She tells lies. I have good reason to say this. I believe she may also present a danger, a physical danger.'

Louisa and Vita, bemused, watched the widow sip her drink, wince slightly, and return her glass to the table.

'What makes you say this?' Vita asked.

'Tell me this. Was she ever alone with your brother?'

'Well, yes. Occasionally.'

'Was she alone with him after the fight on Saturday?'

'He walked us both home, then he was taken ill and I ran for the doctor. She was alone briefly, very briefly with him then.'

Kitty looked up and tucked a curl of hair absent-mindedly back behind her ear. 'She was alone with my husband, also.'

'But why is this significant? You surely don't think she is implicated in what happened to them?'

'Why should I not think it? Why? I believe she has done something to them. It has killed my Jack and injured your Edward. You may think this is far-fetched, ladies, but I have grown up in a harder world. Something is wrong. The only connection I can make is that young woman, and you have her living under your roof. I want you to send her away. For your own safety and for my peace of mind. I should feel happier by far if she were to return to...' she seemed to forget the name of the place.

'...Cornwall, do you mean?'

'Cornwall, yes. Send her there. And soon.'

This silenced Vita and her aunt and the silence deepened as Tabitha came in and re-filled the tea pot, before curtseying and retiring, puzzled by the lack of conversation, to the kitchen.

'But why do you ask this?' Louisa enquired.

'I beg you. Do not to ask me to go into further details,' the widow said, waving her hand as if to fend off a blow, 'but she has added to my misery and continues to do so. I would like her gone and I ask it of you as a favour to a widow who is alone in your city. I throw myself on your mercy. Please!' Kitty cried, 'please do not ask me to re-live the worst moments of my life! I beg of you to take me at my word. I would not ask it without very good reason. This young woman is spreading terrible rumours about me. What she has said, I do not know, nor do I want to know, but it has turned the eye of suspicion onto me. Onto *me*! His bereaved widow, who woke...' her voice was rising to the pitch of hysteria, 'who woke and found her dear husband lying cold and dead beside her! What further tortures could possibly be dealt to me than this? I beg of you, as a widow yourself, as a woman of sympathetic feelings, *send this girl away*! She is not honest. I truly believe that she may even be dangerous.'

Perhaps she heard the outburst from the garden, or sensed the tension in the house, for whatever reason the cat, Minmou, began at this moment to howl outside, uttering a series of long, eerie calls from beneath the window. The sound, echoing around the brickwork of the walled garden, distracted the widow for long enough to interrupt her outburst. She regained control with a noticeable shudder.

'I shall leave now,' she said, springing to her feet. 'Would someone else kindly bring my coat? I do not think I can bear to set eyes on that young woman. I am obliged to you for your hospitality. You see that I am not fit for company. Good day.'

Vita fetched Mrs Fitzsimmons' coat and the widow and

her man left without another word. Vita watched their departure from the front window.

'Whatever was all that about?' her aunt asked, falling into an armchair and pouring herself a much-needed cup of tea with a slightly trembling hand.

'She has certainly taken against Tabitha very strongly,' Vita said, 'what could she have meant? Do you think it could be true that she is dangerous or spreading rumours?'

'Do you?'

'I am not inclined to. Did you hear her man moving about in the hall? I thought I heard him on the stairs while Mrs Fitzsimmons was talking.'

'Tabitha has not been here more than two weeks. You do read of such cases. A new maid comes and dreadful things occur. References can be forged. There was a case in Bury St Edmunds where the maid put poison in the teapot because the mistress would not allow her to have the afternoon off.'

Both momentarily looked at the teapot, which sat plump and silver on its tray.

'We checked Tabitha's reference, did we not?' Aunt Louisa continued.

Vita looked alarmed. 'I may not have reminded you. I meant to.'

'I shall write tonight,' said her aunt.

'I have noticed that Tabitha comes and goes at odd hours,' Vita said, 'I hear her on the stairs.'

'Yes. Monsieur mentioned it to me too. He was not concerned.'

'Will you send her away?' Vita asked.

Her aunt sipped her tea. 'I am not inclined to do so,' said her aunt. 'Mrs Fitzsimmons is a very unfortunate young woman and I truly pity her, but I fear grief has made her susceptible to strange ideas. Besides, Tabitha's work pleases Monsieur. You know that is rare.'

Vita sighed, wondering what crimes a maid could get away with as long as Monsieur approved of her. 'Shall we tell Tabitha what Mrs Fitzsimmons alleges against her?'

'What good could come of that?' Aunt Louisa said, 'It is bad enough losing her cousin without being suspected of all sorts of vague rumour-mongering and worse. Let me sleep on it.'

34

The ladies were preparing to retire for the night when a loud knock at the door announced a pair of police officers. The sergeant who had interviewed Tabitha before had brought a senior man, a detective, with him.

'We would like to search your maid's room,' the sergeant announced. 'Would there be any objection?'

'Are we allowed to enquire why you wish to do this?' Aunt Louisa asked him.

The senior officer turned to her. 'Do you object?'

'Shall I send for someone to be with you? Your relatives at Meeks, for example?' Aunt Louisa asked Tabitha.

Tabitha said nothing, looking fearfully between Aunt Louisa and the police officer. 'No, I...'

The policemen began to move towards the stairs. Louisa, Vita and the maid followed urgently. They followed Tabitha to her room in the attic. Standing at the door, Vita was struck by the tidiness of the maid's few possessions. A spare apron and a coat hung on one peg on the wall with a pair of boots, clean and polished, under them. Her Sunday hat, black straw with a pale blue ribbon, hung nearby. Besides that a few books, a threadbare woollen bedspread and a single dog-eared church magazine seemed to be all the girl owned. The detective stood aside and motioned his sergeant to open a small wardrobe. He did so, rifling through, pushing dull-coloured dresses aside and opening the single drawer beneath, impatiently feeling between piles of pale undergarments and dark stockings. The sergeant's face remained sternly inscrutable. Standing up, he then ran his hands over the bed, and looked under the mattress and pillow. The three women watched in mute dismay, feeling the invasion acutely. The officer reached up and ran his hands over the top of the wardrobe, finding nothing, and then reached beside it, to the gap between it and the wall. There his hand found something and he pulled out a leather handbag and handed it to the senior officer.

'What's this?' the detective asked, showing it to Tabitha.

'My bag, sir.'

'Why is it concealed in this way?'

'I only tuck it in there to be safe, sir. I keep my letters and money in it.'

The man struggled with the catch on the bag before wrenching it open. He peered inside and then walking over, emptied the contents onto the bed. A small blue purse, a few letters and a pair of gloves fell first. He shook the bag harder, reaching into it. After a struggle a narrow black box like an elongated spectacle case and a bunched handkerchief tumbled onto the bedspread. The officer picked the box up and opened it, removing a long metal spike with a wooden handle. He held it, shining, to the light and twisted it.

'I don't know what that is! I never saw that before,' said the maid, 'Oh, Madam, please tell the policemen. I don't know those things. They are not mine. They were not in my bag this morning. Please, Miss, please Madam, tell them. They are not my things.'

Unsmiling, the policeman replaced the spike in its box and took up the handkerchief. This was bunched and thoroughly stained, clouded with overlapping reddish brown blots, each paler inside a dark outline. The officer pulled it apart, and held it aloft by one corner.

'Is this your handkerchief, Miss Hindcote?'

'No sir. I do not know it.'

'What is on it? It looks like blood to me.'

'I don't know, sir. I never saw it before.'

The officer laid the crumpled handkerchief on the bed and turned to the small purse, which he opened and shook. A few coins fell out, followed by a large white £10 note, several times folded.

'And this?' he asked. 'Is this money yours?'

'Yes. It is mine.'

'£10 is a great deal of money.'

'It is mine. Jack - Mr Fitzsimmons - gave it to me before he died.'

'Miss Hindcote,' the senior officer said, 'you will need your coat.'

'Sir, the money is mine. I must have it. It is needed!'

The sergeant put the contents back into the handbag and carried it under his arm out of the room and down the stairs. The detective waited for Tabitha to pick up her coat and followed her.

'Where will you take her? On whose authority do you do this?' Aunt Louisa called, hurrying down behind. In the hall the sergeant waited for Tabitha to button her coat. She was pale and bewildered.

'We will question her further at the police station, Madam,' said his colleague. There is evidence enough to do so. She may pose a risk to the public.'

'A risk? Why? What sort of risk?' Aunt Louisa asked,

indignantly. The men simply opened the front door and walked away into the night, leading Tabitha between them.

After the tall figures of the police officers and the smaller one of the maid had disappeared round the corner of the dark and wind-blown street in the direction of the police station, Vita wrote a careful note of everything that had happened, finding comfort in the meticulous recording of a long and dramatic day. Aunt Louisa wrote a letter to a solicitor whose twin sons' portraits she had painted the year before last.

35

'Was there a disturbance downstairs? I heard something,' Edward asked, as Vita looked in on him. His temperature was normal and he had even been allowed a little chicken broth and toast for supper.

'The police have arrested Tabitha.'

'Tabitha?' Edward appeared not to know the name.

'The maid.'

'Of course. I was forgetting her name. Why ever did they arrest her?'

'They found things in her room. She was one of the last people to see Jack Fitzsimmons alive. It has made her a suspect of some sort.'

'Who is Jack Fitzsimmons?' Edward asked.

'You know, Edward, the boxer. The one who knocked you out.'

'I've never heard of him.'

'You fought him, Edward, at the Assault at Arms. The Hero's Challenge. Don't you remember?'

'I have no idea what you're talking about, Vita,' he said.

As they retired Vita decided to say nothing of this to her

aunt until the morning, feeling the strain on her was quite enough for one day. But as they climbed the staircase, her aunt suddenly grasped Vita's arm. 'I knew I'd seen that wretched man before!' she said.

'Which man?'

'That rude and unpleasant detective. The one who took Tabitha away. That is the same man I saw at the Red Lion talking to Kitty Fitzsimmons.'

'There is nothing strange about her talking to a police officer,' Vita said. 'Surely interviewing the widow would be routine in such an enquiry.'

'She was not just being interviewed, Vita, she was fluttering her eyelashes and using all her feminine wiles to manipulate him, by the look of it.'

'But why? Why should she need to do so? She is an innocent widow!'

'I regret to tell you this, Vita, but there are some women who can only converse with gentlemen on such terms. You meet them in every circle of society. But no, I do not think that is the explanation. I think Mrs Fitzsimmons is convinced that Tabitha knows something about her that she would rather keep secret.'

'I believe I heard her man go quietly up the stairs while we were talking in the drawing room, Aunt,' Vita said, remembering. 'You don't think he could have taken something up to Tabitha's room? He could easily see that she was occupied in the kitchen and slip up while we were talking.'

'You suggest that Mrs Fitzsimmons' role was to distract us while he ran up and left something suspicious in Tabitha's room?'

'Her outburst was certainly dramatic enough to do so,' said Vita, 'but why should they need to? No crime has so far been committed.'

'Except a possible theft of £10 by our maid.'

'Do you believe she took it?'

'I don't know what to think. Casting suspicion on Tabitha might be useful if they were hiding something. It is one possible explanation for what was found in her handbag. The other explanation is that we have been harbouring a criminal and are lucky to have escaped harm ourselves.'

'Perhaps she really did attack Edward.'

'We are too tired, Vita, our ideas are running away with us. Good night,' said her aunt, and quietly closed the bedroom door.

36

By seven the next morning newspaper sellers had a fresh headline to call to passers-by in Regent Street, '*Suspect arrested in Fitzsimmons case. Maid held for questioning*'. The familiar portrait of the boxer now paired with a blurred and grainy image of a young woman being escorted up the front steps of the police station with her hands in chains. Readers were provided with Tabitha's name and the fact that she was '*newly arrived from the West Country*'.

It was Aloysius Derbyshire who delivered the first edition to the household when he arrived for his portrait sitting at nine. He clutched the newspaper to his chest and burst into the hall in full cry when Vita opened the door.

'Oh Mrs Brocklehurst, Miss Carew! Have you seen? How dreadful for you!' he cried, waving the paper.

'Seen what, Mr Derbyshire?'

'This!' He unfolded the paper and held it up. Louisa and Vita peered at the headline and then both reeled back.

'Well, they certainly wasted no time,' Louisa said.

'What shall we do?' Vita asked. Her aunt read the newspaper story carefully.

'There is nothing to be done. I propose that we continue with our sitting, Mr Derbyshire. Work first is always my motto.'

'Admirable!' cried her sitter.

'But what of Tabitha, Aunt?'

'What indeed!' Derbyshire said, peering at the newspaper himself. 'You may have been sharing your home with a murderess!'

'She may need our help,' Vita said, 'I hate to think of her alone and friendless at the police station.'

'She has exploited your kind hearts, ladies. She has hidden weapons and *a blood soaked handkerchief!*'

Aunt Louisa ignored Derbyshire's dramatic outburst. 'We shall call at the police station this afternoon. We may have legal advice to help us by that time.'

'May I write her a note immediately?'

Derbyshire was rustling the newspaper, 'Oh my word! A thief and a murderer, in this very house!'

'Yes, but only tell her we will call later and do what we can. Now I shall begin my work, and you, since we are without domestic help until Monsieur arrives, will take up your brother's breakfast. After that I suggest you continue with whatever you had planned. In a time of crisis it is important to maintain one's routines.'

With that she led the fencing instructor briskly down the stairs to her studio.

'Such courage! Such *sang-froid!*' he murmured, dancing behind her.

'DID I HEAR DERBYSHIRE'S VOICE?' EDWARD ASKED.

'Oh, you are dressed! I was bringing your breakfast.'

'There is no need to wait on me, no need at all. I will go

mad if anyone makes me stay in this room any longer. Besides it's time I returned to Trinity.'

'You remember Derbyshire and Trinity, then?'

'Remember them? Of course! Why?'

'Last night you seemed to have forgotten how you were injured. I mentioned Fitzsimmons and you had no recollection.'

Edward looked blank for a moment but then said, 'I remember Derbyshire, of course I do. Did you say Aunt Louisa is painting his portrait?'

'His first sitting is today.'

'Derbyshire having a portrait made? I must see this!' Edward said, and went down to the studio.

37

It was Vita who opened the door in answer to the next knock. She found a broad, angry woman in a faded coat standing belligerently with a sack in one hand. Her other fist was grasping the coat collar of a small pale child.

'I can't keep her. I won't keep her. Not without the money. She said she'd bring it yesterday, but she never came. I can't live on thin air. It isn't reasonable,' the woman said, loudly.

Vita could only stare at her in confusion.

'I said I'm not keeping her. Small she may be, but she still eats! She takes up space where another one who pays could be. I told her more than once...'

'I don't understand,' Vita said.

The child hung her head. Vita could see she was wearing unmatched boots.

'They sent me here from Meeks. She didn't even give me the right address, the little madam! Anyway this one's no trouble. She doesn't fuss much or make noise. She's a bit of a sniveller, but most of them do that. I'm leaving her with you. Tell Miss Hindcote, or whatever Miss Pay-You-Soon calls herself, she still owes me three shillings.'

With that the woman dropped the sack on the doorstep, pulled her woollen shawl around her shoulders and stomped away up the street.

The child's shoulders were shuddering. Vita had not yet seen her face. A keen wind was turning people's umbrellas inside out and rocking the trees. Vita picked up the sack and put her hand to the child's shoulder to urge her into the house. Her shoulder was bony and trembled through the thin coat.

At first all four of the adults present, that is to say Vita, Louisa, Aloysius Derbyshire and Edward took turns to ask the child questions, but this had no result. She sat wordlessly shivering, even when they put her directly in front of the fire.

'I expect it is an orphan,' Derbyshire announced. 'It is thin, certainly, and not very clean.'

'She is a little girl,' Vita reminded him.

'But whose?'

'Was that lady your mother?' Edward asked the child.

'She did not behave like a mother,' remarked Louisa.

'She seemed to be talking about Tabitha,' Vita told them. 'She said something about Miss Hindcote owing her three shillings.'

All four looked again at the child.

'I am developing a theory,' said Louisa, finally. She began taking off her painting apron. 'Mr Derbyshire I shall have to postpone today's sitting. As you see, we have an...unexpected event to deal with.'

With no experience of younger children, Louisa and Vita called on Mrs Goodman, mother of five and employer of a new and capable nursery maid called Ginnie.

The child knew an expert when she saw one and stopped weeping and shivering as soon as Ginnie swept her up into her warm and starchily aproned lap.

'What's your name, my darling?' Ginnie asked her,

stroking the straggly hair back from her grimy face. The larger of the child's odd boots fell off, revealing a small and very dirty foot.

'Hetty,' she whimpered.

Very soon they carried her off across the road for Ginnie's prescribed treatment: 'A good scrub and something hot to fill her insides '.

'WELL, THAT IS SOMETHING ELSE TO ASK TABITHA ABOUT,' Louisa said. 'I begin to wonder which tempest will hit my household next.'

'Should I take anything to the police station?' Vita wondered. 'A little food, perhaps, or some clean clothing?'

'You can send some later, if she needs such things,' Aunt Louisa said, 'for now, just see how she is. I admit I am confused now as to our responsibilities.'

'She is a solitary young woman in an unfortunate situation,' Vita said, 'we need not look further than that, surely?'

'Indeed,' her aunt agreed, 'but Vita, this young woman has been less than truthful, at the very least. We may not be in a position to help. I hope you will not mind visiting on your own. I feel exhausted by the day's events already.'

38

Approaching the police station, Vita could see a crowd of men with cameras huddled near the doors. They stood up and watched her curiously as she approached, but she hurried past ignoring their questions. The police officer at the counter was one of her classmates from the First Aid course. 'Miss Carew,' he asked, surprised, 'what brings you to the police station?'

'I hope to see a young woman you have here, Tabitha Hindcote,' she told him.

'I shall enquire whether visiting is permitted. Please wait a moment,' he said.

It was a long wait, but eventually the same officer returned and led Vita through the building and downstairs to a row of cells. Tabitha was in the first one, sitting at a table.

'You have ten minutes,' the officer said, 'I must lock you in, but if you need to be let out earlier, you can ring this bell.' He handed Vita a small handbell. 'A guard is within earshot.'

Vita sat opposite the maid, appalled at the stark grimness of the surroundings as well as by Tabitha's evident distress.

'I'm so sorry for this trouble, Miss,' Tabitha said. There were dark shadows under her eyes, as if she had not slept.

'Are they treating you well?' Vita asked. It felt a foolish question, but she did not know, otherwise, how to begin.

'They keep asking me questions,' Tabitha told her, 'I don't know how those things came to be in my bag, Miss. I truly have never seen that horrible sharp bodkin or the nasty handkerchief before. They are not mine, Miss. I have told the policemen that, but they don't believe me. Mrs Fitzsimmons has taken against me and they believe her. She is a grand lady and I am nobody - a maid from the country.'

'Why should she take against you, though?'

'I don't know. She thinks Jack told me something about her. Something she is worried about. I don't know what. He didn't say anything except that she was from a fighting family and knew a lot about boxing.'

'She said something similar to my aunt. She wanted us to send you away.'

'She wants me hung, Miss, if you want my opinion. And she winds policemen round her little finger.'

The implications of her own words seemed to drain Tabitha's strength. Her shoulders slumped. She could not look at Vita directly, but drew a ragged breath and turned her face away.

Vita took a deep breath of her own, aware of the tang of damp and dirt in the air of the cell. 'Tabitha, a woman brought a child to our house this morning.'

Tabitha looked round in shock and covered her mouth with her hands. 'Oh no. No.'

'Who is the woman? She said she was owed money.'

Tabitha hid her face in her hands. For several minutes she seemed unable to speak, but then she sat up and squared her shoulders.

'I asked this woman to take care of the child. I paid her to give the child board and lodgings. This child is my responsibility.'

'But you could not pay?'

'No. I had some money for her, but then the policeman took it in my bag. He won't give it back to me because they say I stole it. I didn't steal it, Miss. I didn't. Jack gave it to me. He wanted me to have it for the child.'

'Why Tabitha? Whose is this child?'

'It is my sister's child, Miss. My sister died and the little girl was in an orphanage. I took her away and brought her here to Cambridge. The woman was paid to look after her. I should most probably have left her in the orphanage, but it was a horrible place. I couldn't do it. Now I have made everything worse.'

Vita looked at the whitewashed wall of the cell, trying to collect her thoughts. 'Is that why you kept coming and going at odd hours?'

'I tried to be quiet. Yes, the girl is only a few streets away. I walk past the house whenever I can. Sometimes I leave her a bit of food. Your French cook, Miss, he gives me a few little things. I do not steal anything.'

'I did not imagine you did,' Vita said. She was struggling to absorb the information.

'The cook found out about her because he saw me going out. I just walk past the house and wave to her some days, or try to catch sight of her when the lights are on in the evening.'

'You are fond of the child,' Vita said.

'I am, Miss. I got to know her on the journey up here from home. She has not had a good start to her life. I have made it worse now. They will take her to the workhouse or another orphanage. It breaks my heart.'

The maid wept in a helpless and defeated way, sobbing stiffly, tears washing her cheeks.

'Why did you not tell us?'

'When I told Mrs Meeks she said I was lying to cover up that the girl was my own child. Your aunt might think the same. I needed the money badly by then. I was truly desperate to have the job.'

The maid was overcome with weeping, leaning forward, her shoulders convulsing. Vita could only watch in pity. A smell of damp and disinfectant crept out of the walls which seemed to press in on them. The loud clang of the cell door being opened made both women jump.

'You must leave now, Miss Carew. Only a short visit is allowed,' said the police officer.

'Can I bring her anything? A change of clothes? Some food?'

'That is allowed, but you will only be able to talk to her once a day for a short time. I believe she will not be here for long.' The officer locked a second door behind them and shook the keys on their ring.

'They will release her soon?'

'No. I am told they will charge her soon.'

'With what will they charge her?'

'With murder and theft, I believe. The evidence is strong.'

Vita was so shocked that she walked past the waiting pressmen outside without noticing them.

39

By the time Vita returned to Eden Street, a small revolution had occurred. Her aunt opened the door with the sound of childish laughter behind her. It was coming from the kitchen together with a song in a rich French baritone.

'Monsieur is making Hetty supper,' Aunt Louisa said with a shrug, 'he seems to have taken to her. And Mr Derbyshire has appointed himself our bodyguard. He has a sword and refuses to leave the house.'

'I have a great deal to tell you about Tabitha.'

'Then please wait until I have poured a little sherry, dear. I need something to sustain me.'

AUNT LOUISA'S RULE OF CONTINUING AS NORMAL IN A TIME of crisis extended to another early portrait sitting for Mr Derbyshire the next day. Little Hetty was easily absorbed into the playful scrum of Goodman children across the road for the morning, and Edward was packing to return to college, so there was nothing to prevent Vita accepting Clara's impromptu offer of a first bicycling lesson.

They chose a quiet corner of the wide chestnut walk along Jesus Green and first adjusted the saddle and handlebars to Vita's height. Even this small preparatory activity filled Vita with excitement. She was delighted by the toolkit which was hidden in the tiny leather bag behind the saddle and even more impressed that Clara knew the purpose of each little instrument inside it. Clara demonstrated loosening the nuts and how to move the saddle and handlebars up or down. They needed to apply a little oil from a tiny bottle before they could move them, but even doing this gave Vita the heady feeling of conquering a new type of skill.

'I shall become an engineer!' she cried, 'a bicycle engineer!'

'You're only adjusting the thing, Vita, there is a fair way to go before you could claim the status of engineer, but still, it is a start,' Clara laughed.

Before long it was time for Vita's first attempt at cycling. With no divided skirt yet in her wardrobe, she could only fasten her skirts to one side with a kilt pin and hope for the best. Clara pushed the bicycle from behind and Vita attempted to press down on the pedals, steer with the handlebars and stay upright all at the same time. The first hour of this was not a success. The furthest she rode was about ten feet of freewheeling before veering off and into the trunk of an ancient horse chestnut tree. Passers-by, particularly those of the younger male variety, chuckled at the spectacle of Vita, helplessly wobbling, as she plunged off the path before her front wheel hit a root and she was thrown into a pile of leaves. Several bruises resulted. Both friends were panting, picking dried greenery out of their hair and brushing mud off their skirts, when they decided that was enough for the first lesson.

'You'll get it,' Clara told Vita, 'it just all comes together if you keep practising. You should take the bicycle home with you. My doctors forbid me to use it, so it is yours.'

Vita could only gaze back at her friend. 'But this is too generous.'

'I want you to take it, Vita . Please accept.'

'I will look after it as well as I would care for a beautiful pony,' Vita said, 'It is the finest machine in the whole of Cambridge and I already love it! Shall we have a cup of tea at the park cafe? I could die of thirst. Anyway, I want to pick your Anatomy brain, if you will allow me yet another favour.'

'My Anatomy brain is at your service, for what it's worth.'

'Excellent!' Vita said, reaching into her pocket and counting the coins she found there, 'I might even be able to run to a scone. '

IT WAS ON THE WAY HOME, PUSHING HER NEW CYCLE BESIDE her, that Vita first heard the news about Sam Shepherd. The newspaper sellers at the corner of St Andrew's Street could hardly hand out papers fast enough. The usual man had brought along a small boy for assistance and the lad folded and handed out the papers as his father took the money and yelled, '*Cambridge News! Boxer Recovers! Exclusive!*'

With no money left in her purse, Vita could only hurry home to read the copy Aunt Louisa had delivered. It was on the mat and she rushed to it, and was standing in the hall reading when Aunt Louisa came up from her studio.

'Something important?' Aunt Louisa asked.

'It is the other boxer, Aunt, Sam Shepherd. He has recovered his senses and is able to sit up and speak.'

'I am glad to hear that, his family must be very relieved indeed.'

'They are. He was very sad to hear that his opponent had

died, apparently. It says here that the first thing he did was to send his condolences immediately to Mrs Fitzsimmons.'

'Well, that is only proper.'

'And the next thing he did was to make a large donation to the hospital so that others who have accidents can receive such good treatment.'

'He sounds a very thoughtful gentleman.'

'And Aunt, I have stored my new bicycle - it is on loan from a friend - in the toolshed in the back garden.'

'Have you ridden it?'

'I have tried. It is more complicated an activity than one might imagine. I was thrown from the saddle several times.'

'Oh dear! No injuries, I trust.'

'None whatsoever, and it is a very pleasant sensation when one succeeds in balancing, even for a moment.'

'Ride slowly and stay far wide of horses - I have read of unfortunate mishaps when cycles and horses come into contact.'

'Do you think I might visit the boxer? He might know something that could help Tabitha.'

'Is it our business to help Tabitha?' Aunt Louisa asked.

'Clara says there might be some connection between Edward's illness and Jack Fitzsimmons' death.'

'Clara? Do I know Clara?'

'The friend who has given me her bicycle and is teaching me to ride it. She is at Newton College and knows about Anatomy.'

Aunt Louisa looked weary. 'Is it complicated? My head is full of Hetty and what to do with her, and the change in Monsieur has left me a little dizzy.'

'I'll tell you when I know more,' Vita said and went to her room to write a note to the boxer.

40

The boxer's reply was rapid and positive. On Monday morning Vita arrived at the hospital and found him sitting in his bed surrounded by vases of flowers and a surprising number of books. The boxer seemed pleased to meet her. Vita explained her connection to Tabitha without mentioning that her maid was being detained.

'I am most sincerely sorry for her loss, Miss, I knew her cousin well. He was a fine sportsman and a fair one, an excellent boxer and a very decent and generous man outside of the ring, too. I was shocked when they told me the news. A terrible thing it is, upon my word, truly terrible.'

Bruises coloured the boxer's jaw purple and yellow and a cut was healing over one eyebrow. One ear was bandaged. 'I am not half the boxer he is - *was*,' he told her, 'he had a natural gift for the ring. I am just an old slogger.' He looked away sadly. 'He was by far the better fighter, and he deserved the win. I sent to tell his wife that, too. I wanted her to hear it from me, although she would know it well enough for herself. '

'Do you know Mrs Fitzsimmons well?' Vita asked.

The boxer seemed to consider for a moment. 'Not well, exactly, but I trained at one time with her father,' he said, 'that was years ago, she was a youngster then. I saw her at the ringside during the match on Saturday, but not to speak to. When I have the opportunity, I should like to tell her in person what a gentleman I thought Jack was, and how respected he was among fighters and in the boxing game in general, but I suppose she knows it already, for she comes from that world. His reputation was well known.'

The boxer's bruised face fell as he remembered his opponent. 'I dread to think how he was feeling after he saw me carried out of the ring senseless. It is a terrible way for a boxing match to end. People imagine we hold feelings of hostility toward each other, but we rarely do, Miss. We are both in the same game and nobody wants to cause that sort of an injury. I am truly sorry if anything I did contributed to Jack's death. It truly fills my heart with sorrow to think of it.'

'He was greatly troubled by your condition,' Vita said, 'I'm told he was anxious that night and asked again and again when you would recover.'

'Did you see him after the fight?'

'No, but his cousin said he spoke normally and his health did not seem damaged. His face was much less marked than yours is now.'

Sam laughed a little.

'Aye, he was known for his unmarked face, it was a kind of joke among the boxers he fought,' he said with a wry smile at the memory. 'We used to say he wanted to keep his freckles just as they were.'

Here the boxer broke off, frowned and looked aside, troubled by the thought. 'It grieves me very much to think that I shall not see Jack again. I sent two letters to Mrs Fitzsimmons, but she has not replied. Perhaps she blames me. For all the dangers of her husband's occupation must have been well known to her, she may still hold me responsible.'

'Is it a commonplace thing for a boxer to fall sick and die so suddenly, just after he has fought in the ring? I am sorry to ask if it upsets you.'

The boxer looked gently at Vita. 'Do not apologise to me, Miss, I am pleased to do you any little service I can. In answer to your question, no, I have not personally known another fighter to...to pass away soon after a fight in this manner, but I have heard stories. It damages the head, you see, all the buffeting and pounding of the ring. I have known older men begin to limp and slur their speech and they say that is the damage caused by fighting. We are not made of stone, the hurts we do and which are done to us all leave their scars inside or out.'

'I have seen this for myself. It was my brother that Jack Fitzsimmons knocked out in the Hero's Challenge.'

Sam Shepherd took this in for a brief moment, looking steadily at Vita. 'I am very sorry to hear that. I have never held with that sort of play-fighting, but the promoters insist sometimes. The crowds love it. Is he recovered, your brother?'

'He had a narrow escape. Even now his memory is not restored completely.'

'I am deeply sorry to hear that, Miss Carew.'

'How can you bear to do it, Mr Shepherd?' Vita asked him.

The boxer looked down at his huge hands on the neat white sheet. The knuckles were calloused. 'I am not sure I *can* bear to do it any more, Miss. To speak plainly, the reason I have done it until now, and the reason poor Jack did it, is for the money. It does not sound brave or honourable to say it, but the fighting game gives men like us a chance to earn a good living. And it sucks you in. You think you will just fight a few times and then buy a little farm or a pub or some such and retire, but the money and the crowds, the fame, they get their claws into your soul and it is very hard to say no to the next fight. Jack had a big family of brothers and sisters back home, as you know, and a new wife to support. He had some big successes and the world title was next. The next fight is always going to be the best one yet. And then there's the gambling...' he was about to say more, but looking up at Vita he seemed all at once to notice her youth. 'But I must not trouble you with that. I am very grateful for your visit.'

'And what about your own recovery, Mr Shepherd,' asked Vita, 'are you quite well again now yourself?'

'Aye, they only want me to rest. I shall be right as rain by Friday, thank you for asking. I shall travel home to London and take it easy for a short while. I like reading, as you can see. I shall settle to my books and take a little holiday, I daresay.'

Vita left, having wished the boxer well, and walked home through an autumnal mist which drifted in ribbons across the college playing fields.

'Is gambling important in boxing?' Aunt Louisa asked, after she had heard Vita's account of the visit.

'I don't know,' Vita said, 'I imagine there is gambling over who will win a boxing match, but I cannot say how it works, or how much money is involved. I will ask Edward. There are young men in his college who gamble, I believe, even though it is very strictly forbidden.'

'Imagine that!' Louisa said, 'I may visit Mr Shepherd myself. I should like very much to paint him. Now that I have begun with Mr Derbyshire I find sportsmen hold a great interest for my work. I wonder whether he could be persuaded to sit for me? Would it be improper to ask, do you think?'

'It might be improper at this moment, Aunt, given the tragic death of Mr Fitzsimmons.'

'Well, perhaps you are right,' her aunt agreed, 'I would not want to appear insensitive,' but her attitude suggested only a temporary postponement of the plan.

41

The second bicycling lesson was planned for that afternoon. The weather obliged with a cloudless sky and sunshine warm enough to make young men remove their hats, and even sometimes their jackets, as they strolled over Jesus Green. Vita found even wheeling the bicycle delightful. The ticking of its turning wheels seemed full of promise - she could go anywhere, do anything! At least she could once the small matter of being able to ride without falling off was overcome. Autumn smells of damp leaves and woodsmoke were about and a soft mist was rising from the river where racing eights were being lifted in and out of the boat sheds by muscular crews.

Clara was waiting by the oak tree, as they had agreed. Their plan had been to practice on the towpath, where it was level and where there should be fewer spectators to laugh and offer sarcastic advice. Usually this would have worked, but the unseasonal warmth of the afternoon seemed to have brought half the population of Cambridge to the river bank, so that part of their plan was not a success. They decided to proceed anyway, walking further away from town until there were slightly fewer strolling families to get in their way.

Cycling, like swimming, is one of those activities that looks easy, but actually demands a high level of co-ordination. Some find it easy, some can learn, and others find the physical skills impossible. Telling one of these unfortunates that it is a simple matter of kicking their legs or holding their breath, or pushing off and lifting their other foot to the pedal, is like telling a table to dance - it simply will not work.

Clara had not found cycling easy. She was of the group who learn by considering intellectually what is required and then using reason to school their limbs to perform the task. Vita, on the other hand, was all for launching herself as fast as possible and hoping that her natural sense of balance and the momentum of the machine would somehow take over and save her from too many disasters. The combination of the two women's natural inclinations meant that Clara spent a lot of time calling sensible instructions which Vita ignored, and Vita spent a lot of time picking herself and the bicycle out of the grass. By now though, she could travel about twenty feet before the handlebars began to wobble and all steering was lost, though on one occasion she managed about thirty-five feet, before the path took a slight right-hand bend and the bicycle did not. There were cows in the fields around them, gentle beasts accustomed to passing humans and normally more interested in chewing the cud, but on this occasion several stopped eating and stared.

'Well, I declare the end of the lesson for today,' Clara announced after the sun had began to hide itself behind clouds and the crowds had dispersed home to their firesides. 'Miss Benn's academy for lady bicyclists is in need of a rest!' She threw herself onto a riverside bench and set about tidying her hair, which had fallen out of its fastenings left and right.

Vita propped the bicycle against the seat and sat beside her, but instead of relaxing, she grasped Clara's arm and said in an urgent whisper, 'Clara! Over there in the distance, that couple. I passed them earlier. I've just realised that the woman is Mrs Fitzsimmons. Look, if you can, but be subtle about it.'

'Why should I be subtle?' asked Clara.

'Because she is not alone.'

Clara stood up and made as if to shift the bicycle and check its basket, glancing, as she did so, up the towpath. There was indeed a couple walking there, far beyond the paved towpath on a track across the field. They were - it was easily discernible even from a distance - arguing angrily. The woman wore a veiled hat and both were in black. They stopped and turned to one another, the woman gesticulating, the shrill tone of her voice clear, although the words could not be heard.

'Is it her?' Vita asked.

'I have only seen her in the newspaper photographs,' Clara said. 'I cannot be completely certain, but it looks like her.'

'Do you recognise the gentleman?'

'No, why should I?' Clara looked rather sternly at her friend. 'Vita, there is nothing unusual about a lady taking a walk with a gentleman on a pleasant afternoon, even if she is recently widowed. She may have a relative with her, or be discussing legal matters with an advisor. It is quite wrong to suggest anything scandalous. It is this sort of loose talk that...'

But as she spoke, to their great astonishment, the distant couple turned to one another and the woman slapped the man's face with the full force of a blow from the shoulder. The sound of her gloved hand on his cheek reached them across the field, faded, but clearly audible. The man reacted by snatching the hat from his head and striding furiously away. The woman looked after him, but then turned back. She dusted her hands together, smoothed her skirts, and looking perfectly untroubled began to walk towards the towpath alone.

42

'You will perhaps think it very improper, Clara,' Vita said, as they walked back toward the centre of the city, 'but I have developed some suspicions about Kitty Fitzsimmons' honesty. She has made serious accusations against our maid, Tabitha. They have led to her arrest.'

The path was almost empty now, and peaceful, apart from a few walkers exercising their dogs. A family of swans dipped their long necks into the water near the bank, searching for food among the reeds.

Clara walked on, saying nothing.

'And then there was the post mortem.'

'What about it?' Clara asked, sharply.

'My brother's doctor was there and he said there were some details that could not be explained.'

'The people carrying out the examination, if my reading of the newspapers is correct, were some of the most distinguished experts in the field,' Clara remarked, looking towards the river.

'I know,' Vita said, 'it's just that...'

'It seems to me, Vita, that the implications of what you say are very shocking indeed. You suggest that these very expert observers have made an error and perhaps even that the boxer's widow is in some way implicated in his death. These are dangerous and slanderous accusations to make against people who are powerful in their different ways, and you make them as a raw beginner in Science and - I am sorry to say this - in life too.'

Vita looked away from her friend and down at her boots for a few moments. The grass was long and the boots were muddy and wet. Two of the buttons had been torn off the left boot at the ankle, probably in a fall from the bicycle.

'What are the grounds of your suspicions?' Clara went on, 'could you let me into your confidence far enough to share them?'

So, as they took the path towards Jesus College, Vita explained about Edward's fever, the odd little puncture mark on Jack Fitzsimmons' brain and the damage deep inside it. Clara listened in silence.

At the corner of Jesus Lane they stopped, one to go left and the other right from this point. Vita looked at her friend unable to tell how the information had been received and was surprised when Clara said, 'If you are free tomorrow, I believe I might know someone who can help.'

'Who?' Vita asked, 'how?'

'Meet me tomorrow in Burleigh Street at ten. I shall be outside Arthur Booker and Sons, the photographer's shop. And, Vita,' Clara laid a hand on Vita's arm, 'if your suspicions have any justification, you must be very careful. You may put yourself and even your family in danger.'

A NOTE, WRITTEN IN A LARGE BUT ELEGANT COPPERPLATE hand, was waiting for Vita when she came home. It was from

Sam Shepherd asking her to return to the hospital. Puzzled, she did so immediately, though it was almost dark.

'It occurred to me, Miss Carew, that I have more to tell you,' the boxer said.

'Oh?'

'I read about your maid being at the police station - it was in the newspaper - and it reminded me of something. I couldn't fathom what it was at first, but then it came to me.'

'What is it, Mr Shepherd?'

The boxer looked uncomfortable. 'Please, Miss Carew, sit down before I say it. I hate to pass rumours. I try to avoid gossip and scandal.'

She sat in the chair beside his bed.

'Only, when I read about the maid, it brought something to mind. I had to struggle to remember the details. I suppose my poor head's had a fair few knocks, it isn't good for the memory. What I remembered in the end was this, Miss Carew: it was a maid that got the blame before.'

'Before?'

The boxer rubbed his chin with his hand, frowning. 'I've been thinking about this all night long. It was so long ago. Miss, people here don't know Kitty very well. I've known her for years. I trained, like Jack, with her father. Anyone who wants to win in the boxing game goes to Loftus's place in New York, if they can. He's still the best there is.'

Vita waited. Whatever he wanted to tell her was clearly causing the big boxer a struggle.

'There was a scandal while I was there. Just after I arrived, it was.'

'What sort of scandal?'

'That's the problem. I hate that sort of thing. I tried not to know. I was only interested in my training.'

'But you did hear something?'

'They said she'd run off and married.'

'Why was that such a scandal?'

'We only heard the edges of it, you know. The nasty rumours. They said her father didn't like the man. He was a boxer, a lad called Radway, if memory serves.'

'And that caused outrage?'

'No not that. What caused the scandal was that he died on their honeymoon.'

43

Vita took a moment to consider this.

'So Jack was not her first husband? She had one before, in New York?'

'I believe so.' Sam Shepherd spoke quietly, looking down at the book he was holding.

'It is not so unusual to be widowed and then to remarry, I suppose,' Vita said.

'No. But when you asked me if I had heard of any other fighter dying without warning, it reminded me. Her first husband was a boxer too and he died suddenly.'

'After a fight?'

'He died on their honeymoon. She found him in bed.'

Vita looked steadily at Sam's battered face.

'This has happened to her before?'

'It has. Kitty was not so grand in those days. Her husband - his name was Joseph Radway - was only a middle-ranking fighter. There was all sorts of gossip about it at the time, but Kitty's father is a big man in New York. The fight world and the police are close, they always have been in that city. The general feeling was that her father had it quieted down, if you know what I mean.'

'No, I'm not sure I do,' Vita said.

'He had powerful friends; police chiefs, lawyers, some of them not too honest. He greased a few palms – gave away a lot of free tickets – asked a few favours. He kept it out of the papers, it was only known about in the boxing world and even there people hardly dared to whisper about it. You couldn't risk getting on the wrong side of old man Loftus. There were ugly rumours at first, but they soon died down.'

'Rumours? But what were they about?'

The boxer stopped. He turned a volume of poetry over in his hands. 'I hate that sort of thing, Miss Carew. There's a lot of it in boxing. People pitted one against the other, they have to rely on favours. It leads to behind-the-hands talk. I try to keep out of it. Least said, soonest mended, that's my motto.'

Then, as if a decision had been made, he sighed and placed the book back on the bedside table. 'They said she killed him. They said she took against him as soon as they were married, and did away with him.'

Vita sat back in her hard hospital chair. A nurse passed down the ward behind her.

'But you didn't believe any of these rumours, Mr Shepherd? How could anyone believe Kitty capable of such a terrible crime?'

The boxer looked at her calmly. 'I knew her, Miss. I knew her when she was just a girl. She had a fierce reputation, even then. You couldn't cross her. Her nickname was Vicious Kitty. I never saw such a temper. But her father would never see it. He would never hear a word against her.'

'And you say a maid was blamed? How?'

'I don't know the details, Miss. I put them out of my memory. But I know there was a court case and a maid at the hotel was found guilty. They said she was trying to steal something from the room and attacked Radway when he woke and saw her.'

'Did Jack even know Kitty had been married before?' Vita asked.

'I don't know. This was seven or eight years before Jack would have met her. I heard Kitty and Jack married quickly and came over here to get him a few wins before going for the big titles.'

It was only then that Vita noticed that the boxer's head was no longer bandaged.

'You're feeling better, Mr Shepherd, I hope. I see your bandage has been removed.'

'I am stronger every day. It was just a small cut behind my ear. I probably did it when I fell.'

'Mr Shepherd, did someone examine Kitty's first husband after he died?'

'A doctor, you mean? They must have, if there was a court case, I suppose.'

'Who would it have been?'

'It happened in New York. A police surgeon there, I imagine.'

'And what happened to the maid?'

The boxer, looked down.

'I believe they found her guilty of murder and sent her to a madhouse.'

44

The hospital visit had almost driven the meeting in Burleigh Street with Clara the next day out of Vita's head, but she remembered at breakfast and left hurriedly, pushing her bicycle. There was a thin drizzle falling.

'You cycled?' Clara asked, as they met.

'No, I only pushed. Where can I leave it? I do not want it left in the street in the rain,' Vita told her.

'It's not a baby, Vita, a little rain won't hurt it in the least! Few bicycles would be sold in England if they melted in wet weather.'

Vita leaned the cycle against a wall, hoping the overhang of the roof would offer a little protection. Soon they both stood under umbrellas with rain dripping in overlapping circles about them.

'Why are we here?' Vita asked.

'I want you to meet someone very clever and interesting,' Clara explained, 'but, be warned, she is also a little...unusual.'

'How fascinating!' Vita said, looking around. There were very few pedestrians about.

'In here,' motioned Clara, and she stepped into the nearest shop. A bell sounded somewhere far inside. It was a photographer's studio. There was a desk before them and a curtain to one side. Around the walls dozens of images of families, smartly dressed men and women, children in their Sunday best, banks of students in serious rows, school classes with children in pinafores and teachers with stern expressions, professional shots of churchmen, shopkeepers, solicitors, councillors and even a butcher holding a large cleaver, all looked down.

They waited, examining the photographs for several minutes, but eventually they heard a door open somewhere beyond the curtain and an uneven step approached. The curtain flicked aside and a very small woman with steel rimmed glasses and a short haircut stood before them.

'Ah,' she said, 'Clara. And this must be your friend...'

'Vita Carew,' Clara said, by way of introduction. Vita had hardly ever seen a woman with short hair. It was difficult not to stare.

'Vita Carew,' the lady said, as if considering the name, 'welcome. Follow me, ladies.'

The studio beyond was like the backstage area of a theatre. Down one side of the long space were all manner of props and artefacts for photographs. There were large columns made of plaster of Paris and a waist height model Acropolis for those who preferred a classical Greek background. There were potted palms and climbing ivies for subjects who wanted greenery. Over to one side was a backdrop painted to look like an Indian raja's palace and another which might have been the Scottish highlands. Draperies and rich coloured silks hung over screens painted in the Japanese style and numerous ornately framed mirrors reflected the gorgeous jumble from several different angles at once. The far corner was the magnificent library backdrop, painted mahogany bookshelves filled with trompe l'oeil books disappearing into the distance. Here, at a table, the lady proprietor sat them down, first moving a stuffed bird of paradise and a small harp to one side.

'So what can I help you with?'

'Do you recall that I spoke to you once about the work you do in the laboratories?' Clara asked.

'Yes, of course.'

'I was wondering whether you could explain your work to Miss Carew. She is interested in Science and needs assistance with the practical side. Laboratory work and so on.'

'And why, Clara, could you not explain my work to your friend yourself?' the lady asked, mildly. Her tiny, silvery spectacles glittered as she angled her head to scrutinise her visitors.

'Well, what I am in fact asking,' Clara said, moving the tip of her gloved finger in a small circle on the table, 'what I am in point of fact asking is...'

'...is?'

'Is whether you would consider extending to Vita the same great favour that you have allowed to me once or twice.'

The photographer studied Vita for a moment, as if assessing her. 'Is your friend qualified, and suitable?'

'I believe that she is.'

'Does she understand how necessary discretion is? Have you explained that?'

'I have not yet done so, but I shall, and I am sure she is trustworthy.'

It was an odd sensation being spoken about as if she were not there. Vita pretended to be as deaf as the stuffed bear silently roaring nearby.

'Well then. What would you like to see? I expect it is the pugilist last week.'

'It is.'

'I will fetch them,' she said, and left them through a door Vita had not even noticed.

45

'What is happening, Clara?' Vita asked. 'Who is this lady and what has she to do with Jack Fitzsimmons?'

'She will tell you herself,' Clara replied.

The lady returned with a ribboned portfolio under her arm and set it on the table before them.

'Vita,' she began, smoothing the flat surface of the tablecloth carefully, before beginning to untie the ribbons, 'this is what you need to know.'

Miss Booker laid her hands over the folder as if pressing it into the table. 'Eight years ago my father was approached by the Board of Studies for Natural Sciences. They wanted to experiment with photographs as a means of recording dissections and other procedures carried out in their laboratories. It was, at the time, an advanced and experimental idea.

Since that time photographs have been taken regularly in the laboratories after the students have completed their work. They have not, however, been taken by my father, who was struck down by ill-health almost immediately after taking on the commission. They have been taken by myself. We here at Booker and Sons - there are no sons, incidentally, only a daughter, myself, we use the name for business reasons - hold a complete record, therefore, of the activities in the laboratories. If a post mortem examination takes place, we photograph that too.

The photographs form part of the University's archive, but we lodge the plates here, having the facilities to keep them in the best condition. The images are as accurate a record as can be made. They may be used in a court of law as evidence, so it is a heavy responsibility. If the Board could have found a gentleman to take these photographs, after my dear father's illness, they would have done so. However, I can fairly claim to be the most experienced and skilful scientific photographer available in this city, so the responsibility has fallen to me.'

'Soon after I took on this work, I was approached by some women students who wished to study, but whose ambitions to attend dissections were thwarted by the regulations. They asked whether they might be allowed to inspect my laboratory photographs. I agreed on the understanding that there must be absolute discretion.

The University authorities need my work. They appointed me to the task quite unwillingly, believing it to be unsuitable for a woman, especially since I am required to enter the laboratories outside the normal hours. I am frequently alone at night with a corpse, which for academic purposes has been cut up and taken apart. Not surprisingly, perhaps, the University authorities were concerned that this would be unsettling for any photographer, and particularly so for a woman.

It took me many months to persuade them that not only was I able to do this work, but that I could be efficient, and produce photographs of the highest quality. I pride myself that this is still the case. And if I choose to share the images with a group of students, there is nothing unusual in that.

Any student has the perfect right to examine them. All I do is to make my photographs available to them here.'

Vita stared at the cover of the portfolio on the table before them. 'You make a photographic record of all dissections?' she asked.

'Yes. As I said.'

'Goodness!' was all Vita could say.

'Now, if you wouldn't mind being reasonably swift, I have a sitting at noon,' the photographer said, consulting her small wrist watch. With that she left, and as she did Vita noticed for the first time that she walked with a limp.

46

Clara lifted open the portfolio and there inside was a pile of photographs. The corpse was seen close up in most of them, but one or two more distant shots showed the whole body, draped on a metal table in a room bare except for a table of tools. The tools looked to Vita, for the most part, like the sort of thing you might find in a carpenter's workshop.

The two women spread the photographs out on the wide surface of the table, having first set aside a pile of silk shawls. Displayed before them, the images were, to Vita's eye at least, solemn and strangely beautiful. The body had the look of a marble statue. The face, at least in the early images, appeared serene, with only a slight, indefinable vacancy to confirm the permanence of its resting state. In a laboratory, Vita thought, there would be smells and living people moving around in contrast to this utter stillness, but in a photograph it seemed possible that life might yet return to the face, still freckled and uninjured, lying on the slab so calmly.

The later photographs, tracing the post-mortem, were not so reassuring. The skin lifted from the skull, the skull itself opened at the top, much as you might open a boiled egg, Vita could not help thinking. The brain inside, looking exactly like a fat walnut in its shell, was shown removed, then sliced through. A separate image recorded each section. They were about the thickness you might use for toasting, if it were a loaf.

The darkening, or bruising that Dr Goodman had mentioned was easily discernible, occurring from the third to the fifth slice and located low in the centre of the brain's wrinkled bulb. They peered at this photograph for some time.

'Can you see slight lines, or...' Clara leaned close in to the image, peering at it, '...some sort of trail or...I don't know what to call them...*striations*, lines of some sort criss-crossing the darker area? They are not very clear. Perhaps your eyes are sharper than mine. I think I shall ask Miss Booker for a magnifying glass.'

Clara left, picking her way through the scenery to search for Miss Booker at the back of the studio.

Vita examined the photographs minutely, moving them round to catch the light from different angles. When Clara returned, they both peered again, raising and lowering the magnifying glass.

'I can see lines,' Vita said, 'and look, on this one there is a single line that runs right to the edge. It is faint. Do you see, Clara?'

'Yes. There.' Clara traced the line, hovering her fingertip above the photograph. It ran from the blot that represented the damaged part of the brain, in the centre, at a slight downward angle - perhaps ten or fifteen degrees - to the edge, where the grey mass of the brain would meet the skull.

'What could that be?' Vita asked.

'It is difficult to be certain,' Clara said, 'but it looks like a very thin line of damage. As if something very long and sharp had been driven into the brain. But there is no suggestion of any such thing in the post mortem report. Is there a puncture wound anywhere on the outside of the skull?' She straightened up and began re-arranging the photographs on the table.

'Dr Goodman did mention a very minor nick, or cut,' Vita said, moving round the table to examine the images of the outside of the boxer's head and neck before the brain had been opened. 'Yes, look, Clara, look there.'

Almost hidden by the shadow of the boxer's left ear, and by the mass of freckles, there seemed to be a tiny dot. It was surrounded by a very slight discolouration, a fractionally darker patch of grey on the photograph, about the size of the fingernail on Vita's little finger.

'Well,' Clara said, taking the magnifying glass from her eye and turning toVita, 'if it matches with the line we have traced across the brain, I suppose it *could* be an entry wound. But I can make no connection between that mark and the lines in the brain. If that were an entry wound, made, for example, by a needle or something similar, it would have left a line or trail at right angles to the one we have observed here. The trajectory of the line we saw here would take us approximately to the front of the skull. That entry wound is on the side, under the ear.'

Vita's attention was on another image. 'I think I can see something here,' she said. She had lined up images of three of the cross-section slices of the brain. 'Can you see it, Clara? There is a very small dot, or what looks like the shadow of a dot on this section, and if you look on the two sections beyond it, you can see a similar dot, but at a slightly higher point.'

Clara seized the magnifying glass and looked for herself. 'You're right, I think. It could be a similar long narrow line of damage, but at right angles, so in these images we see only a series of dots.'

'And, if you drew a line between them, where would it lead?' asked Vita .

'Exactly to the puncture wound,' Clara said.

'And the other line? Where does that begin? Can you work that out?'

'At the eye, I should say.'

47

The women looked at each other, as the thought took hold, then back at the rows of photographs on the table.

'So, just to clarify,' Vita said, 'it looks as if one line of injury runs from behind one ear into the brain and another runs from the eye?'

'I believe so,' Clara agreed.

They were still silently contemplating the implications of this, when Miss Booker returned.

'I hope what you saw was worth the visit,' she said, looking at the frozen women curiously.

'Miss Booker,' Vita asked, 'when you were taking these photographs, was there anything that struck you? Any little detail about the body? Did you change or clean it in any way? Did you move or re-position it?'

Miss Booker drew herself up and clasped her hands before her. 'Certainly not,' she replied, 'I would never alter a cadaver in any way. It is my responsibility to record things precisely as I find them at every stage. That is an unbreakable rule of my work.'

'Forgive Vita, Miss Booker, it's just that we found something, an anomaly, and we wondered whether the post-mortem had overlooked...'

'It is very presumptuous of you indeed to imagine that you could see something, anything, that a group of the most distinguished professors had overlooked, if you do not mind my saying so,' said Miss Booker. She surveyed the photographs herself for a moment, which seemed to calm her. 'Perhaps there was one thing. You can barely see it.'

She leafed through the photographs that had been set aside, the ones of the boxer before the examination of had begun. 'You can see it here,' she pointed to a very minor discolouration, little more than a minute darkening, around the outside corner of the left eye. 'I am called upon to photograph the body at various stages, but the eyes almost always remain closed and I am not usually required to re-position the eyelids or photograph the eyes themselves. What I saw was a bruise, a small bruise right at the corner of the eye, here, such that if I were to open the eye there might be a slight pooling of blood. It is very small, as you see.'

'Was it recorded in the post-mortem examination?' Clara asked Vita .

'I don't know. I will have to ask Dr Goodman,' Vita replied, 'but surely such a bruise would be the result of the boxing match?'

'It might be so, but in scientific investigation we make no assumptions,' Clara said.

'I have one more evening to complete the photographic record before the body is released to the undertaker,' said Miss Booker. 'I am due to return tonight for the final few shots. And now, ladies,' she continued, beginning to collect her photographs and place them carefully back into their portfolio, 'I must prepare for the arrival of the Bursar of Jesus College and his six children for a portrait. I suggest you make your escape before they arrive. They are not a quiet or well-behaved brood and he insists on them dressing as wood nymphs for the photograph, which is bound to over-excite them.'

THE RAIN HAD STOPPED, AND A MILKY SUN WAS BEGINNING to show between steel grey clouds, but there were still very few people around.

'Is she right, Clara? Are we outrageously presumptuous to imagine we could see something on the photographs that the professor and his team have missed?'

'She may be right,' Clara said, 'but a fresh pair of eyes occasionally sees things that even experts overlook.' She walked a little further, frowning at the pavement in front of her feet, then suddenly stopped. 'Vita, I cannot rest until I have an answer to this. I must know more about the bruise on the eye that Miss Booker observed. Was it caused by the fight, or has it some connection with the marks we saw in the poor man's brain?'

'Perhaps you could ask Miss Booker to photograph that area specifically?' Vita suggested.

'That will not be enough. I truly think I must see it for myself.'

'How?'

'I am going back to ask Miss Booker whether she will allow me into the post-mortem room with her. In fact, I should like another witness to be present. If I can persuade her to take both of us, will you come too? Have you the stomach for it, Vita ? It will not be easy.'

'I believe I can withstand the sight of a dead body, Clara, but I doubt whether Miss Booker will even consider any such request. She seems very rigorous in adhering to the rules of the University.'

'I shall have to do my best to persuade her,' Clara said, 'wait here, and we will soon see whether I am successful.'

48

Clara turned abruptly and hurried back to the photographer's shop. At the far end of the street Vita noticed a large family turn the corner and begin to make their way towards her. Their progress was slow because two older boys had hoops which they were attempting to roll along the street, and three smaller children kept stopping to play or splash through puddles. The lady and gentleman who appeared to be their parents were deep in conversation.

The lady, pushing a perambulator, was pointing into shop windows on either side, and the gentleman paused, studying first an extraordinary cake in the bakery window and next some particularly fine gloves in the haberdasher's next door. All in all, progress was irregular and unhurried, but even at that rate their arrival would not give Clara very long.

Glancing to the other end of the street as she retrieved her bicycle, Vita could see only one other pedestrian, a gentleman in black. He was slightly familiar to her, but she was not sure where she had seen him before.

He walked briskly her way and surprised her by stopping

abruptly as he came close. Looking around as if ensuring that nobody could hear, he leant forward and said in a menacing tone, 'You want to watch out. We know that maid's got you running her errands.'

He had an odd way of speaking, turning his head from one side to the other without looking towards Vita, so that the words came out of the corner of his mouth. She was too startled to move.

'What do you mean by talking to old Sam Shepherd? What did he tell you? We know what you're up to. We keep a pretty close eye on your comings and goings. You're not so very clever, you and your lady friend. You think you are, but you're not.'

By way of farewell he reached out and, seizing the handlebars of the bicycle, wrenched it from Vita's grasp and hurled it to the ground, where it landed with a loud crash and lay with its rear wheel spinning.

The noise alerted the children, and the two oldest boys ran over and helped Vita lift up the bicycle and set it to rights.

'He pushed it over,' said the eldest, 'I saw him do it!'

'Are you hurt, Miss?' asked a younger boy. 'Shall I send for my Mama to help you?'

Vita thanked them, but assured them she was unharmed, and the bicycle seemed to be the same, but it was never going to be an easy matter to escape the attentions of such a large and kindly family, and it was a full ten minutes before the last of the wood nymphs was gathered into the photographer's studio and Clara was beside her again.

'Thank you, Vita, whatever diversion you created gave me all the time I needed.'

'I would gladly take the credit for such quick thinking, but it was a passing brute muttering threats and throwing the bicycle onto the pavement who created the diversion, I'm afraid,' Vita told her. 'I think he was one of Mrs Fitzsimmons' men. He knew I had seen the other boxer, Sam Shepherd. He said they were watching us.'

Clara led the way towards Jesus Green, hurrying Vita along with the bicycle between them. 'They must have something to be anxious about,' she said. 'They are bullies and we've clearly irritated them. Anyway, Miss Booker has agreed that we can go with her, but there are strict conditions. I will explain them as we walk.'

49

Mr Vernon Todd, the solicitor Aunt Louisa found to represent Tabitha, was an angular, anxious man. In some lights he looked thirty and in others twice that age. He spoke very slowly, considering every word, and wore spectacles that had been repaired using a drop of lead solder right at the bridge of his nose. Something about the angle of his neck and his natural slowness reminded Vita of a tortoise. When she asked if she might go with him to visit Tabitha he paused so long that she thought at first he had not heard.

'I shall have to offer her a confidential meeting,' he finally told her in a dry whispery voice, 'but if she is willing to have you present, then that would be acceptable.'

It was difficult for Vita to believe that the young woman they saw in the cells that afternoon was the same person as the busy maid who had hefted sofas and scrubbed ranges so energetically in Eden Street before her troubles had begun. This Tabitha was grey-skinned, her eyes reddened and ringed with deep shadows. Her fingers twitched and picked ceaselessly at the hem of her shawl as they spoke. They struggled to hear her muttered answers. It was difficult to make her understand what was happening.

'You have been charged with theft, Miss Hindcote,' the solicitor told her. 'And there is likely also to be an allegation of murder. Do you understand?'

'Theft,' she repeated, 'murder.' The tone of her voice gave no indication of emotion, but changed when she asked, 'Will they send the child to the workhouse? Has she gone?'

There was a long pause as Tabitha sobbed and Mr Todd formulated his reply.

'We will come to the child later. Miss Carew has told me about the child.'

'Who are you, sir?'

'I am Mr Vernon Todd, your solicitor.'

'I cannot pay you, sir. I am sorry, but I have no money.'

Another long silence before Mr Todd began again.

'You have been charged with theft, at present, as I said, Miss Hindcote. Is that clear?'

Tabitha turned to Vita in desperation. 'I cannot speak to this gentleman, Miss, I have no money for a solicitor.'

'Tabitha, my aunt has sent Mr Todd. She will see to his fees. He is here to help you.'

'Have they taken the child, Miss?'

'No. She is at home with Monsieur and my aunt. She is quite well.'

Tabitha looked at Vita and at last a glimmer of understanding appeared in her eyes.

'She is at your house?'

'She will not be sent anywhere without your knowing. I promise you.'

Tabitha, speechless with relief, could only clasp Vita's hands, weeping again. 'Thank you, Miss. Thank you. I am so ashamed. I have caused you so much trouble. And the child. The poor, poor child.'

'The prisoner must not touch her visitor,' the duty police officer reminded them.

Vita removed herself gently from Tabitha's grasp. 'I am going to leave you now with Mr Todd. You are to tell him everything. He is going to help you. Tell the truth, Tabitha, and do not worry about the child. She is well and will be cared for.'

The dreadful scene in the cell so preoccupied Vita that she hardly noticed an escort waiting for her outside the police station in the stylishly dressed person of Mr Derbyshire.

'Why Mr Derbyshire, what brings you here?' she asked with a start, when he came out of the shadows and fell into step beside her.

'I was passing and thought I should like to accompany you home,' he replied. He carried a cane and walked with a dancer's spring.

'My aunt sent you, didn't she?' Vita said, walking a little faster.

'Well, yes, she did, as a matter of fact, but I hope I am not intolerable as a companion.'

'Is she afraid for my safety?'

'She believes there are people watching the house,' Derbyshire said, sounding perfectly cheerful.

'Why should anyone...?'

'Because you are going about asking questions, Miss Carew. Some people do not like that.'

'Which people?'

'People like the gentleman who is following us now. Do not turn your head. He has just stepped into a doorway.'

'Are you sure?'

'Sure enough to wish to stay by your side.'

'You have no weapon. Without a sword, how could you protect me anyway?'

Mr Derbyshire looked momentarily offended. 'Miss

Carew, I know many ways of rendering an attacker powerless with only my hands. I am quite the expert in the Eastern arts of fighting.'

'Goodness, what foolish nonsense!' Vita said, as Derbyshire bounced along beside her. They continued for some distance across Parker's Piece, but then a sudden thought struck Vita. 'Mr Derbyshire, are there any Americans among your pupils?'

'Why should you care? You have just told me I speak only foolish nonsense!'

'I take it back, Mr Derbyshire, I hope you will forgive me.'

'Of course,' he replied, 'and yes, I do have a number of American pupils.'

'Would any of them happen to be New Yorkers?'

'I believe Roland Hathaway is from there. He's at Pembroke. Why do you ask?'

'I need to speak to someone who knows how the police work in that city.'

'Well, I believe Roland's father is a lawyer. That might help.'

'Excellent!' Vita said, 'My aunt can invite him to dinner.'

Mr Derbyshire cleared his throat.

'Oh, and the invitation will include you, Mr Derbyshire, of course.'

50

Short notice invitations were a Cambridge tradition. Aunt Louisa sprang into action and Vita had only a day to wait before the American was enjoying one of Monsieur's special Wednesday dinners. They were introduced over drinks, but even Vita's determination could not divert Roland Hathaway III from mixing amiably with the rest of the company before they filed into the dining room. Her aunt had paired Vita with the American, so he walked her in and sat opposite. There were many courses to be eaten and any amount of dutiful conversation to be made with guests on either side, so it was well into the dinner before Vita managed to direct a question over the table. Roland was a dry-witted young man in a snugly tailored suit. He had a pale moustache and a coloured bow tie which caused at least one elderly guest to start and glare in disapproval.

'Mr Hathaway, if I wanted to put a question to someone in New York, what would be the quickest method to do so?' Vita asked at the earliest opportunity.

The young American smiled across the table, 'If it were a short question, then I guess a cable would be best.'

'A telegram?'

'Exactly. One merely fills in a form at the Post Office, Miss Carew. It could scarcely be easier.'

'And would the response be rapid?'

'That would depend on the person at the other end, I suppose.' Roland was smiling at Vita now, it was a look more suited to a child or a dog, she thought, and did not feel like saying more. Roland, however, was now languidly intrigued. 'May I ask the nature of these international inquiries?' he asked.

Vita was inclined to evade his question, but the need to make use of him overcame this. 'I would like to put a question to the New York police.'

'I see,' he said. He looked at her, expecting more, but she added nothing. A brief lull in their conversation occurred during which the fruit course was served. Artfully piled pyramids of fruit were passed around. Vita watched distractedly as Mrs Welney-Granger peeled grapes and removed their seeds with a pair of ornate fruit scissors, while the Bishop of Norwich, seated next to her, proceeded to eat a banana with a small knife and fork.

'I never could get the hang of eating fruit with silverware,' Roland told her confidingly, 'I guess I am just a Barbarian.' He picked up an apple and bit into it, attracting looks of astonishment from several diners. 'To return to your question, Miss Carew, I think you would greatly improve the chances of a swift reply if you took pains to direct your inquiry to exactly the correct recipient. That is to say you need to address it to a named official. A generally directed question would almost certainly take more time.'

'And how might I find the name of the correct official?' Vita asked.

'Now there I believe I can be of assistance,' Roland said, 'my parents are residents of the Upper West Side of

Manhattan and can, in all likelihood, provide you with the name you require. My father is a lawyer - not of the criminal kind, he specialises in land - but the information you need would be easy to come by, I imagine. There are directories. If you like, I can wire him first thing tomorrow. Just tell me what you need to know.'

'I need the name of the police medical examiner who investigated the unexpected death of a boxer called Joseph Radway. It was seven or eight years ago.'

Roland did not look at her. He bit thoughtfully into his apple and then asked, 'Is this something to do with...'

'I would rather not say, Mr Hathaway, if you will forgive me. But the matter is most urgent.'

'I will cable my father tonight and send word as soon as I hear.'

IT WAS ONLY EIGHT THE NEXT MORNING WHEN DERBYSHIRE and his American pupil both appeared in running clothes on the doorstep. Hathaway was out of breath, 'The man concerned was not so easy to locate,' he said. 'He has retired from the police force. My father recommended that you direct your enquiry to the Chief Examining Medical Officer. His name is J. Mulhearn M.D. and he can be found here.' He handed Vita a slip of paper.

'Why should he answer me?' Vita suddenly asked.

'He is a public servant in the realm of justice,' Roland replied, still running the spot. 'In my country we are particular about such things. Of course he will answer you.'

'But the story was kept quiet at the time.'

'There are still people honest enough to resist improper pressure,' Roland said, 'let us hope that Dr Mulhearn is one of them.'

Vita telegraphed Mulhearn as soon as the Post Office opened.

51

The first condition imposed by the photographer was utter discretion. This made it difficult for Vita to be completely honest with her aunt, which she regretted. An absence late at night would, however, need some sort of explanation. She settled uneasily on half-truth, asking her aunt whether she might be permitted to go to the library out of hours because that was the only time women students could gain access.

As it happened Aunt Louisa was committed to a late night in her studio, forging ahead with her portrait of Mr Derbyshire, having promised it to him by the end of the month.

'How impertinent of him to impose such a demand upon you, Aunt,' Vita remarked. 'I never knew you to submit to such pressure from your sitters before.'

'Yes, it is unusual, but then everything about Mr Derbyshire is unusual,' Aunt Louisa said vaguely, 'and he has paid a premium for me to complete the picture in time for a special occasion, although he will not divulge what the occasion is. All in all it is very irregular and I have half a mind to be put out about it, except that he is a most entertaining sitter. We laugh so, and you would hardly believe some of his stories. The time flies by, so it is no hardship. Anyway, what were you saying dear?'

'The library, Aunt, I should like to go this evening. It will be quite late before I come home.'

'But how will you get in, if it is closed?' Aunt Louisa asked.

'There is...a special *arrangement*,' Vita told her.

Her aunt looked at her scrutinisingly over her pince-nez. 'And how will you get home? It will be very late by then, I presume.'

'I could take my bicycle with me, Aunt.'

'A bicycle will not prevent ne'er-do-wells intent on criminal activity, whatever young women cyclists believe!' her aunt told her sternly. 'Besides, you have not yet conquered the riding of it. I'm afraid you may only go on this studious late-night jaunt if you can persuade an appropriate chaperone to meet you and accompany you back here afterwards. What would your father say, if he heard of you wandering the dark streets alone? He would never forgive me!'

'I understand, Aunt,' Vita said, and left immediately to write an imploring note to Edward at his college.

Clara had some elaborate arrangements of her own to make, for she had a college Mistress, rather than an aunt in loco parentis. There was no question of a request to stay out after ten pm being granted, college rules completely forbade it. This left no alternative but to climb out of a ground floor window and leave the gardens by crossing the lawn and slipping between laurel hedges. It was a well-known route - so well-known that the path between the hedges was well-trodden and the ground floor bathroom window left permanently unfastened - but it still risked terrible penalties from the college authorities. Careers, and even whole lives had been ruined for less.

Nor was it easy to recruit Edward to the cause. He was now well enough to be attending a college dinner and had no intention of leaving before the port had circulated several times. He would not guarantee to be outside the laboratories before eleven pm.

It was a windy night. When Vita left home the trees along the river were thrashing and their last leaves flew along the quiet streets at speed, wrapping themselves around street lamps and gathering in flurries at the foot of high college walls. There were still people about. Whole families, warmly dressed and in high spirits, making their way to bonfire parties, for it was November 5th and effigies of Guy Fawkes were being burnt in gardens all round the city. The smell of woodsmoke permeated the streets and there was the occasional bang or flash of a distant firework. In one large garden Vita could see children gathered round a huge fire as she passed, the light flickering on their upturned faces as they bit into toffee apples.

The plan was to enter the back door of the laboratories as inconspicuously as possible. Miss Booker would let them in and had assured them that she was rarely disturbed in her late night work. How she had been persuaded to allow them to join her, Vita had no idea. Clara's sudden determination and the authority of her scholarly nature had somehow been enough. Until this moment; until she stood here, in a dim doorway across the street from the tradesmen's entrance to the laboratories, Vita had not really considered the scale of what they were doing. They were trespassing into a private laboratory in order to examine the corpse of a man whose death they considered suspicious. On nobody's authority but their own, they were seeking to establish the true cause of the boxer's death.

A firework exploded loudly nearby, and Vita jumped.

. . .

SHE FELT UNTRAINED, INEXPERIENCED, IGNORANT; generally ill-equipped to carry out this examination, and quite suddenly she feared being in the presence of the dead body lying so pale and still in the photographs. A quick pressure on her arm made her turn, and she saw with relief that it was Clara.

'Are you afraid, Vita ?' her friend asked, joining her in the doorway and looking across to the small laboratory gate.

'A little,' Vita admitted.

'You must not feel obliged to come with me,' Clara said, 'I am experienced in post-mortem work, but I know it will not be easy for you.'

'I want to be there. You said you would need a witness.'

'Nobody will accept my word alone. Even with photographs as evidence it will not be easy to present findings if they differ from those of the professors. And we may be wrong in our suspicions. I rather hope we are.'

'Forgive me if I seem anxious. I am braver than I appear.'

'If you are concerned at any point, give a sign and I will find a way for us to leave immediately.'

'What sign should I give?'

'Just hold up your hand.'

52

As Clara spoke, a dim figure appeared behind the gate they were watching, unlocked it from within and waited in the shadows. The two women crossed the street and passed through, following Miss Booker into the back door of the laboratories and up a long flight of winding stone stairs.

To either side corridors stretched into darkness, unlit except for a single dim lamp. They continued upward, their footsteps echoing, Miss Booker's lantern throwing a watery pool of light ahead as long shadows flicked around the curved walls behind. At the attic level they left the stairwell and moved into the laboratory corridor. Here the smell of chloroform and an underlying hint of formaldehyde and disinfectant reminded them of the activities carried out in these rooms. A brighter light shone from under the door Miss Booker now opened. She led them in, setting the lantern aside and closing the door silently. The laboratory was bright, lit by a series of lamps on stout wooden stands. They surrounded a large table upon which the unmistakable form of a body was lying, covered in crisp linen drapes.

Miss Booker began to roll back her sleeves. She unfolded a long apron, put it over her dress and slipped her arms into sleeve protectors which reached to her elbows.

Dread squirmed in the pit of Vita's stomach. Her mind filled with the photograph of the man's skull opened at the top. She tried to set it aside, but it persisted and her eyes were drawn to the draped top of the head, her thoughts fastening on the unnatural shape that must lie there beneath the stiffly starched covers.

'There is a chair over there by the wall,' Miss Booker told them. 'You will sit on that if you feel faint. If you need to vomit, you will withdraw to the sluice room there,' - she pointed to a door in the far corner - 'and you will clean up after yourself. I will proceed with my work exactly as usual. You are welcome to observe, but not to get in my way. Be careful not to cast shadows across my shot. Above all you must not touch the body, not in any way. You must not even consider repositioning so much as a single hair. Am I making my instructions clear?'

'Yes, perfectly clear,' the women agreed. Clara's voice far stronger than Vita's.

'I will explain what I am doing at every step. There will be no shocks, but I must work quickly. I have only this one evening in which to complete the autopsy record, so there is a great deal to do. I will start now by uncovering the cadaver.'

Vita took a deep breath as Miss Booker deftly rolled the canvas back from head to toe of the body. She lifted the roll of fabric and placed it over a table to one side. To Vita's surprise the body, as it lay before them, held little to terrify. A short towel was draped across the hips and a soft flannel hat, something like a nightcap, concealed the damage done to the skull by earlier examinations.

Clara left Vita's side and stepped forward to examine the chest. Huge incisions had been made and then repaired, so the boxer's freckled chest now bore a very long raised seam, a truly horrible disfigurement to the body which otherwise, as it appeared before them now, had no visible injuries apart from a few bruises. Clara peered closely at these discolourations, leaning forward and moving her head this way and that as if scanning the surface. On the other side of the body Miss Booker adjusted the height of one of the large lanterns and pulled it closer. She then began tightening the brass keys on the legs of the wooden tripod upon which her large box-shaped camera was positioned. Many times she put her head under the black fabric behind it and emerged again to re-position the camera or alter the height of the tripod, but at last it was satisfactory and she called, 'Stand clear!' to the ladies, before the shutter was operated and the first plate was exposed.

This pattern continued as Miss Booker moved further up the boxer's right hand side and began to aim her camera at his neck and right ear. Seeing her struggle with one of the heavy lamps, Vita moved round and helped her. Being taller and stronger, Vita soon had the knack of moving it. This left the photographer with only the camera to adjust. 'A little left, a little more...' she instructed Vita over her shoulder, and the next shot was taken in half the time. Miss Booker, whilst still businesslike, appeared to relax a little and they proceeded together to take low-angle photographs as close to the boxer's head and neck as the lens of the camera would allow.

Meanwhile Clara, careful to step back and retreat from the shot every time the 'Stand clear!' was called, had continued her minute visual examination. She had begun to take notes in a small book, and was using a tiny ruler, carefully held well above the skin, to take measurements which she added to her sketches and notes.

After half-a-dozen photographs had been taken, Miss Booker paused and stood up to stretch her back. 'I have completed the usual set of photographs now, ladies. I believe they are all satisfactory. I have also been asked to re-take one or two images of the brain itself for purposes of clarification. It is in the dish on the side-table over there, covered by a blue cloth. I propose removing the cloth and photographing the sections of the brain again, under brighter illumination.'

'May I help by moving this lantern?' Vita asked.

'Yes, I would be most grateful. It needs to go there, to the right of the small table and the height should be lowered so that it is at about 45 degrees, if you can manage it.'

53

Vita busied herself with shifting the weighty lantern on its stand, and was so absorbed in this that she was not prepared for the sudden uncovering of the sliced brain contained in fluid in a small tank. The quick flick of the blue cloth to one side caught her eye and she gasped. Both the other women froze and looked anxiously her way, but she steadied her breathing and went back to twisting the brass fitting on the lamp stand.

'I am requested to photograph each section separately in bright light,' Miss Booker told them. 'In the case of a brain and internal organs I am permitted to touch for purposes of re-positioning only, and I must record each of my contacts. I am required to take a contemporaneous note, that is to pause each time I touch something and write down what I have just done.'

'Might I help with that?' Vita asked. 'I could write to your dictation.'

Miss Booker seemed taken aback by this suggestion, but then said, 'I type my report, so the handwritten notes might as well be made by you as by me, and it would certainly be very much more convenient, if you think you can write quickly enough.'

Vita took her own notebook and pencil from her skirt pocket. 'I take fast notes, I can assure you,' she said.

Miss Booker stepped forward and plunged her hands without hesitation in to the tank holding the brain. She lifted the grey mass out and placed it carefully onto a shallow tin tray before separating the sections and then placing them in a row on a black marble slab. While she washed her hands and returned to operate the camera, Clara stepped over and began her own examination of the brain slices, sketching and measuring as before.

'Write this down please,' said Miss Booker, 'I have removed the brain from its container, drained it and laid the eight sections horizontally on a dark background for contrast. The order is left to right. The leftmost section of the brain seen from the front is laid on its left side on the far left and the other seven sections, also on their left sides are laid out in succession. I will now place the numeral cards beside each section for the purposes of identifying each one in the photographs.'

Miss Booker took eight small labels from her pocket and placed them next to a brain section, numbering them left to right.

Clara and Vita looked closely at the putty-coloured slices neatly lined up in order as Miss Booker adjusted her camera. There was evident damage - a darkened and more open-textured area about half an inch across - in the two largest central sections. The traces of this darkening extended to the sections on either side, but only as a scattering of tiny dot-like blemishes. What was clearer under the lights was the faint line, discernible only at certain angles, that ran from the dark area, cut across the blank inner mass of the brain tissue and ended at the exterior surface.

'That, I believe, is what we saw on the other photographs,' Clara said quietly.

Miss Booker frowned and peered at the line Clara was tracing above the brain matter with her finger.

'It will be difficult to capture so faint a line, but I will certainly try,' she told them, and began moving the camera to a better angle, bringing it in as close to the marble topped slab as she could.

With no warning the door of the laboratory was thrown open and a bearded gentleman with wild grey hair burst in, closely followed by two other men in black suits and bowler hats.

'What are you doing here?' he demanded, 'Who are you? Who gave you permission...?'

Although both Clara and Vita started and reared back, Miss Booker stood her ground with complete composure.

'Good evening gentlemen,' she replied in the mildest of tones. Then, smiling and calm, she walked over. Taking a card from her pocket as she crossed the laboratory, she handed it to the bearded leader of the intruders. He bristled with indignation and took the card with a bad grace, glaring as if it might explode in his hand.

'As you will see, I am from Booker and Sons, the official laboratory photographer, and these are my two assistants.'

'By whose permission do you take photographs here?' demanded the gentleman, but his tone already showed signs of doubt, concealed under irritation and bluster.

'My company works on behalf of the University. We are here tonight specifically at the request of Professor Rusbridge,' said Miss Booker. 'This work is something we do routinely.'

'I was not informed of this!' was all the gentleman could say. At the mention of Professor Rusbridge's name he felt forced to read the card he had been given, squinting at it at arm's length. 'I shall be speaking to the Professor about this arrangement. I consider it highly irregular for anyone, let alone three unaccompanied ladies, to be permitted to enter the laboratories at night. Highly irregular! It breaches every scientific code. Who knows what tampering, what damage might be done to evidence needed in court!'

'Professor Rusbridge has trained my company to the highest standards of forensic evidence,' Miss Booker told him. 'I recommend that you do take the matter up with him to put your mind at rest. Meanwhile time is passing and we have several more photographs to take. Professor Rusbridge is extremely desirous of this work being completed tonight. That was his specific instruction.'

The grey-haired gentlemen wavered for a moment, then turned on his heel and addressed the two porters he had brought with him. 'I want you to ensure that everything is left as it should be. And kindly escort these people off the premises when they have finished!' And with that he marched out of the room and his footsteps could be heard in fading echoes as he stamped down the stairs.

The two porters, one tall and young, the other short, round and considerably older, looked nervously beyond the women to the body on the slab behind. They shrank away and backed toward the door.

'If you would like to wait downstairs, gentlemen, I will let you know when we are leaving in the usual way,' Miss Booker said mildly.

'Yes Miss, thank you Miss,' they said and withdrew as quickly as their boots could take them.

The ladies listened as footsteps hurried into the distance.

'Have you been interrupted in your work before?' Clara asked, once they had all caught their breath.

'Never,' said Miss Booker, 'and I fear this will not end well. Ladies, I can hardly emphasise enough to you how much this special commission means to my family. My father can only help a little in the business now, I do most things, and the business supports nine of us. The loss of this university commission, and the consequent loss of business any rumours or scandal would bring - you know what a small town this is - would quite simply be the ruin of us.'

Vita and Clara could only look at her anxiously.

'Ah well. On with the job at hand,' Miss Booker said, 'I shall not rush towards possible bad news. Honest work is the best solution. You would do well to learn that, as young women.' And with that she walked back toward her camera and ducked her head under the black cloth.

54

After they had finished and left, they found Edward leaning against the wall under a streetlight. His black academic gown was slightly askew.

'Ladies!' he cried, 'your escort awaits!' He swept his mortar board off in a bow so low that he almost lost his balance.

'Edward, this is my friend Clara Benn,' Vita told him, 'Clara, may I present my brother, Edward, who I believe has been at a college dinner and enjoyed his fair share of port this evening.'

'Delighted. You need only accompany me as far as the cab rank,' Clara said.

Edward set off unsteadily down the street. They followed him. The ladies' heads were full of serious thoughts about the frailty of the human form and the transience of life, while Edward's was full of the delights of a convivial evening and the surprising difficulty of walking in a straight line.

Glancing back as they turned into King's Parade, Vita thought she saw someone following, but the dim figure slid into an alley, so she could not be sure.

❧

IN BED TRYING TO SLEEP, VITA FELT A SURGE OF RELIEF, and even a certain pride at having kept her composure in the presence of a dead body, without the need to run for the sluice room or hold up her hand. Then to her surprise she found that tears she could not reasonably explain were dampening her pillow. Somehow the smell of the mortuary was still around her and later her dreams were full of pale corpses crying out for help.

AS THEY PARTED, CLARA HAD JOTTED DOWN A LIST OF books they needed to consult in order to complete their research. Several of these were in her brother's collection, so Vita set off for his college very early the next morning. They hoped to complete their report that day. The sooner the better, if it were to prove Tabitha's innocence.

The porters at Trinity were friendly, but notoriously vigilant. They knew Vita because she often visited, but they knew also that few scholarly brothers welcomed unexpected early morning visits, even from their sisters; *particularly* from their sisters. The senior man on duty, Mr Briggs, accepted Vita's note and despatched a smartly dressed apprentice boy to deliver it to Edward's room, but firmly insisted Vita should wait in the Porters' Lodge, and not on any account go up to Edward's room herself. The very idea! The porters were former military men; one did not argue with them. So Vita sat on the well-worn visitors' chair in a corner, read the notices pinned on the students' noticeboard, and watched the bustle of the college's early morning routine.

Letters were being sorted into pigeon holes; a deliveryman with a tray of apples on his head was waved through to the kitchens and bedders, the cleaning women who looked after the scholars' rooms and lit their fires for them, passed in groups of two or three, all greeted with a cheery 'Good Morning!' from the porters. These women, a talkative and purposeful lot, passed through a doorway Vita could see on the other side of the ancient stone archway that formed the college entrance. A few moments later each group emerged in aprons, carrying brooms and buckets, which they took over the flagstones and out towards the open square of Great Court. There they dispersed and disappeared from sight, presumably to climb the ancient stone stairways that led to the gentlemens' rooms.

After more than ten minutes' wait there was no reply.

Vita approached the desk again and told the porter she must, she really must go to Edward's room, it was an important matter.

'Sorry, Miss, if the young gentleman will not come down himself, there is nothing I can do,' he said.

'But this is a matter of great urgency,' she told him.

'That is the rule, Miss. I can send a note, but I am not at liberty to permit you to go any further,' Mr Briggs insisted, ending her protests by picking up a pile of letters, and turning away with an air of supreme concentration to sort them into pigeonholes behind.

Vita, taut with rage, left the porters' lodge and stood against the outer wall of the college, partly to gather her thoughts and partly to shelter from the rain. Bedders were arriving in raincoats and umbrellas. A smartly liveried cart drew up beside her, and two men jumped down and threw open its tailgate. Shouldering sacks of potatoes and string bags of onions, they began to deliver the day's vegetable order to the kitchens, which also seemed, as Vita peered after them, to be down the passageway opposite the porters' lodge. The porters could see everything, but they were now also busy. One or two students and professors began arriving from the opposite direction to collect their post or ask about keys; there were delivery sheets to sign and parcels to be stored for collecting.

At the moment when three big sacks of potatoes and another of carrots were lifted from the cart, Vita pulled up her hood and fell in beside the men. The kitchen porters turned left towards the kitchens and Vita slipped alongside them past the porters' window and darted into the passageway after a pair of bedders. They walked to a large storeroom where buckets, mops and dustpans were ranged beneath rows of coathooks, each with a long brown apron hanging from it. Vita followed, but hesitated at the doorway.

'You looking for someone, Miss?' asked one of the women.

'Yes,' Vita replied, 'I am to see Mrs Lightwell'. The head housekeeper's memorable name had been on several of the notices Vita had been reading in the porters' lodge and sprang easily to mind. The two women looked mildly curious, but were obviously pressed for time, they were busily removing raincoats and changing into their aprons.

'She's at the bottom of Q staircase,' the woman told her. She pointed down a passageway.

55

Edward's room was on R staircase, which must be in the same direction. She could see both staircase entrances directly across the courtyard when she reached the doorway. It was tempting to run straight across, but Vita knew college rules well enough not to do so. She walked instead right round the paved perimeter, trying to look as inconspicuously servant-like as possible. The grassy expanse of the court, looking vividly green in the falling rain, was crossed by diagonal paths, but bedders never used them. Only scholars could do so, and only fellows of the college were permitted to walk across the grass itself. The cobbles shone in the downpour and water gushed from ancient downpipes.

It was still only eight o'clock and the spiral stone staircases and passageways were empty. Climbing the staircase marked R, there was a smell of toast and she heard a whistling kettle as she approached the attic rooms her brother shared. The gentlemen were not going about their morning routines particularly quietly. There were shouts from one room to the next, sudden roars of manly laughter and on the corridor below her brother's there seemed to be a rumpled but fully-clothed young man face down on the carpet. 'Come on Biggers, don't be all day!' someone yelled from behind a door.

Vita, still hoping she would pass as college servant, knocked on her brother's door. She dare not call, for fear of attracting attention, but placed her face close to the door and stage whispered as penetratingly as she could manage. The door opened suddenly and a tousled young man in a silk dressing gown stood behind it. She had no idea who he was.

'Alarm call for you, Ted,' he called over his shoulder and turned away saying nothing to Vita .

She followed him into the sitting room where he waved an indolent hand towards the door of Edward's room, saying, 'You'd better knock loudly, he was out late last night. In fact I didn't hear him come in. And make the fire up while you're here, would you? It's perishing cold and I should like to boil a kettle.'

Vita knocked hard on her brother's door and called out in tones she imagined would suit a bedder making a formal wake-up call. There was no reply. The other young man paid little attention, but pulled on a pair of slippers, picked up a kettle and strolled out of the door, presumably to find the nearest tap and fill it.

'Edward!' Vita called and tried the handle of the door, 'Edward. It's V...' but her own name faded on her lips as the door opened easily and revealed Edward's room to be completely empty. The bed was made. The whole room was meticulously tidy. A large pile of books sat on the desk alongside a blotter and an inkstand. Vita stepped over and examined the titles of more books in a bookcase. Pairs of shoes were ranged under the coat hooks by the door.

'Perhaps he did not return,' shrugged the other young man. He was leaning round the door to watch her. 'Though it would not be like Teddy to stay out all night. Not like him at all. That sort of thing's more my style, if you know what I mean.'

'I have been asked to collect some books from his room,' Vita told him, testing the story to see if it would arouse any curiosity.

The young man showed no interest, so Vita gathered the textbooks she recognised from Edward's desk and carried them out.

'Send someone to make up the fire, will you?' he called after her.

At the foot of the staircase she ducked through an entrance on her left and along the perimeter path of a different, smaller courtyard. On the far side there was a wooden gate with a smaller door set in it. By her reckoning this should lead towards the river. Vita heard footsteps coming behind her, but she did not want to stop for long enough to look, so when she reached the door, she stepped through and found herself on Laundress Lane, a little alley leading over a humped bridge. This was close to the path where Clara should be waiting, so Vita, still weighed down by the books, hurried over the bridge towards the Backs. Only when she was over the crest of the little bridge did she dare look back to see whether anyone had followed. She could see no-one.

IN THE DISTANCE AHEAD THE BRISK FIGURE OF CLARA WAS approaching along the beech tree avenue. What happened next was so swift that later Vita found it difficult to put into words. One moment Clara was walking towards her on a wide paved path scattered with dried leaves, dwarfed by the archway of ancient beech trees on either side; the next she was knocked from her feet by a dark figure which ran at her with startling violence from behind a tree. The man, having tackled her and hurled her down, held Clara to the ground and Vita, as she ran towards them, could hear shouts, from both victim and attacker, but could not understand what was being said. The sounds, though loud, were deadened by the trees and the thick carpet of leaves that lay around. There seemed to be nobody else nearby. Vita raced towards them, calculating that with no other weapon to hand she might be able to hit the attacker with the heavy pile of medical textbooks she had in her arms, or, since he was on the ground, stamp over his legs, which might at least distract him. The man, however, saw her coming, stood up with impudent calm and dusted the leaves from his black hat before putting it back on his head and darting off through the trees in the direction of Sidgwick Avenue.

56

Clara lay, her hat askew, gasping among the golds and browns of the fallen leaves. Her lips were slightly blue. Too breathless to speak, she could only put her hand to her chest.

'Are you hurt?' Vita asked, dropping the books to kneel beside her. 'Shall I send for help?'

'No, I…I just need to…to catch my breath.' Her face was grey with the effort of breathing.

Looking round frantically for help, Vita noticed a pair of runners in the distance change direction and make towards them.

'What can I do, Clara?' Vita asked, but Clara could only concentrate on catching her breath.

'May I be of any assistance, Miss Carew?' The voice was familiar. Vita looked up and saw Aloysius Derbyshire, in his white running clothes, leaning over them. Beside him, panting and red-faced, was another young man in white.

'My friend has been terrified and she has a weak heart,' Vita told him. 'We may need a doctor.'

'I can soon run to Trinity and fetch one, but perhaps we could move her to this bench first?' Derbyshire suggested. The two men raised Clara to her feet and helped her to the bench. Once there, her breathing became a little easier. She reached up and pulled out the hatpins securing her now rather battered hat, pulling it into her lap.

'Arnold Foster here is training as a medic,' Derbyshire told them, by way of introduction.

'How do you do,' said Foster with a bow. 'I am not qualified, and I would not presume to offer any advice, but I could, if you would allow it, take your pulse, Miss...'

'...Benn,' she said.

'...Miss Benn, your pulse, you see, will tell me...'

'I am perfectly aware...what it will tell you...thank you,' Clara told him, between breaths, but she held her wrist in his direction all the same.

Derbyshire watched as his running companion looked off into the distance, holding Clara's wrist and counting for a few moments. 'It is strong, but a little irregular. I think it would be wise to...'

'Oh, but... I thought you were *not*... presuming to offer any advice,' Clara said, between gasps.

'Well, this is no more than an opinion, obviously, but I believe you should...'

'...you are going to tell me to rest, are you not? All doctors, and apparently all student doctors too, give me exactly the same advice. Rest. Rest. Rest.' Clara interrupted, irritably.

Foster, who was rather a plump young man, looked like a scolded puppy.

The momentary contretemps was interrupted by Vita who suddenly said, 'Mister Foster, do you have borrowing rights at the Medical Library?'

'Why, yes, naturally.'

The two women caught each other's eye and something was instantaneously agreed.

'Would you consider helping us?' Clara asked.

'Of course...'

'At the library, I mean?'

Derbyshire and Foster now both looked confused. 'Should I not call for a police officer? It was a robbery, I suppose?' Derbyshire asked.

'That is not important. Would you borrow some books on our behalf, Mr Foster?'

'Which books?'

Clara reached for her skirt pocket, finding it with some difficulty among the thick fabric and produced a small folded piece of paper, which she passed to Foster. Puzzled, he opened and read the list.

'You want these?'

'It is a matter of urgent research,' Clara said.

The young man blinked and looked at the list again. He shrugged.

'We will return them to you here in exactly twenty-four hours.'

'I guess the libraries at the women's colleges are less well-equipped than they might be,' he said, cheerfully. 'I suppose I can see no harm in it. The young lady...'

'Clara Benn,' Vita reminded him, 'and I am Vita Carew.'

'How do you do. If you would care to wait here, Miss Benn can rest and you, Miss Carew, can watch over her with Mr Derbyshire, while I go and find your books. Make sure she does not exert herself,' he told Vita, 'and if she feels faint or cannot breathe easily, you must ask Derbyshire to run quickly for a doctor.'

'I will,' Vita assured him.

'We are most grateful,' Clara said. The young man did not move. 'Our request is urgent, Mr Foster, if you please!'

'Ah! Of course!' said Foster. He turned and broke into a run, taking the path that headed for the medical library.

57

'Poor boy,' Derbyshire said, watching the figure bounce away, 'he'll never be an athlete, I'm afraid. Now ladies, the attack, was it a robbery?'

Clara continued to draw deep breaths and began attempting to re-shape the hat in her lap, turning it to pull out the dents.

'I have not introduced Mr Derbyshire, Clara,' Vita said. 'I do apologise. Clara, this is Mr Derbyshire, my brother Edward's fencing coach. Mr Derbyshire, I looked for my brother this morning, but I could not find him. Do you know where he is?'

'No. He should be here running alongside Foster, ' Derbyshire said. 'I believe there was a college dinner last night, but he rarely misses training, even after a late night. Now, Miss Benn, how are you feeling?'

'Much better, thank you.'

'Was it an attempt at theft?'

'No. I believe it was intimidation. The man told me to stop interfering in things I didn't understand. Something about the maid. We weren't as clever as we thought, he said. It was vague but intimidating.'

'Good Heavens!' exclaimed Derbyshire.

'The same thing happened to me,' Vita said, 'he did not touch me, but a man who looked similar threw the bike down while I was outside Miss Booker's shop. He used the same words.'

'I was certainly right to suspect you need protecting. Do you know this man?' Derbyshire asked them.

'He is one of the men in Jack Fitzsimmons' corner at the boxing match,' Vita said.

'Why should they waste their time bothering us?' Clara asked her.

'They must think we know something about the boxer's death...'

Derbyshire gasped in horrified delight.

'...Mr Derbyshire, this is in the strictest confidence,'

'Of course!' he said.

'They believe,' Vita went on, 'that Clara and I have made some sort of discovery and they want to dissuade us from doing anything about it.'

Clara, having straightened the hat, placed it back on her head and secured it by pushing a hatpin through the crown into her hair. 'He may be correct about a discovery,' she said, 'but he is very misguided if he thinks that a few threatening words would be enough to stop us. And why should it concern him? How could any discovery we make harm him?'

'If the boxer did not die from his injuries at the fight, something else must have killed him. Perhaps the Fitzsimmons men themselves are implicated,' Vita suggested.

Derbyshire, standing in front them, turned his head from one woman to the other as if watching championship tennis.

'I need the library books to confirm it, but I have spent the night puzzling over my drawings and I can only conclude that Fitzsimmons' brain shows signs of having been penetrated by a very fine blade of some sort.'

'Oh my word!' said Derbyshire.

'Something like this,' Clara said, and held up her second silver hatpin. It shone for a moment in the morning sunshine before she slid it into the other side of her hat.

'Or like the sharpened bodkin they found in Tabitha's bag,' said Vita.

❧

THE SMALL LIBRARY OF BOOKS THAT WAS ACCUMULATED once Foster returned was too heavy for Vita on her own, and Clara was forbidden exertion, so Derbyshire and Foster insisted on fetching their own bicycles and delivering them to Eden Street. The four walked together as far as the bicycle rack outside Trinity and the ladies were taking their leave when Vita was spotted by the ever-vigilant Mr Briggs in the porter's lodge.

'Miss Carew. I'm glad you have returned,' he said, hurrying out. 'Might I ask you to step inside? It concerns your brother.'

Fully expecting to be reprimanded for her earlier secret visit, Vita followed him, but instead of reading her a lecture on the privacy due to brothers in their rooms, he led her along a corridor to the infirmary.

'I am sorry to tell you that your earlier anxiety was well-founded. Your brother has suffered an injury and been brought here.'

58

In the quiet of the infirmary Vita found Edward sitting in a chair. A swollen and blackened eye showed under his bandaged head.

'What happened, Edward?'

'I don't know. That's the thing. I can't remember. They found me outside in the court.'

'He has suffered a brain injury recently. He needs very careful observation,' Vita told the nurse.

'Doctor McCardle has seen him already. He will be well attended,' the nurse assured her. 'We are not sure what happened, but it seems to have been an assault. He was punched and beaten about the head.'

'Was it one of Fitzsimmons' men who did this?' Vita asked, after the nurse had left.

'Perhaps. I simply have no recollection. I cannot trust myself to remember anything clearly. I know you; I know the college, but I couldn't say where my room is or what the last lecture I attended was about. It's serious, Vita. I can't depend on my memory at all. How can I study?'

It was ten o'clock. They could hear footsteps and voices in the court outside, a bell chimed.

'What did McCardle say?'

'Amnesia. He said my memory will probably return, but it may take a long time. I'm supposed to rest.'

'Then rest you must. I'll send Aunt Louisa with something diverting for you to read. A few copies of the Ladies' Journal, perhaps.'

The patient sighed. 'I'd prefer one of Monsieur's venison pies,' he said.

'At least you remember Monsieur's food. That is a good start.'

She left on that cheerful note, but all the way home Vita was haunted by the gloomy prospect of her brother never recovering his memory. What would become of him?

59

Once the library books were delivered, the two women carried them, with some effort - they were weighty - up to Vita's room, this being the most convenient place to study.

They needed not only to convince themselves, but also to write a paper on their findings which would convince Professor Rusbridge, the police and the Coroner. This was Clara's job, as she knew how such a paper ought to be presented. It needed to be scholarly and convincing; there should be illustrations - both Miss Booker's photographs and Clara's sketches - supported by references to the medical textbooks and similar cases. Finding these was Vita's work. She searched the books diligently, but whilst bullet wounds to the head were surprisingly well-documented in post mortems, very few of the textbooks mentioned injuries of the kind that they had observed.

They were well into their work - a report taking shape and perhaps two-thirds written, when Clara stopped, and said to Vita, 'The implications of these findings of ours, they are very serious indeed. We are claiming that Jack Fitzsimmons was murdered.'

'Yes,' Vita agreed.

'Murdered with an implement such as a hatpin...'

'Yes, that is how it seems from our reading of the evidence.' It was the first time that Vita had dwelt on the terrible act they were investigating.

'We have tracked the trajectories of the lines we found in the brain and they enter via a wound just below the ear in one case and the corner of one eye in another. This is not the sort of injury that could possibly occur by accident, Vita . It would take considerable force and determination to drive a hatpin, say, or some kind of sharpened bodkin into a living man's skull and...'

'Yes, yes,' Vita stopped her. The details were truly horrible. 'Clara, I have not told you before, but the boxer Sam Shepherd told me that Kitty Fitzsimmons was married before and that her first husband's death was also sudden and suspicious. If there were similarities between that death and this...'

'...it would certainly raise difficult questions for Mrs Fitzsimmons.'

'But surely,' Vita said, 'no woman would have the strength to plunge a hatpin deeply into her husband's head? A man as fit and strong as Jack Fitzsimmons? He was in the prime of life and a sportsman, even if he was exhausted after the fight, he was exhausted because he had *won* it.'

'She could have drugged him, or incapacitated him in some other way.'

'But that is an enormous assumption. There is no evidence for this, as far as I know.'

'No. That is true,' Clara was forced to agree.

'Kitty may be innocent. It could be someone else who attacked Jack. Someone with a grudge. Perhaps over a betting matter. Large fortunes are wagered on boxing matches, I'm told.'

'All that might be convincing if not for this earlier marriage. Whoever committed this act, it was ruthless and carefully designed to go unnoticed. It may have been inspired by high emotion, but it was carried out with absolute precision. This is not the kind of killing someone commits simply in a state of rage or on the spur of the moment. It would have taken considerable forethought and detailed research. It is the work of a calculating and intelligent mind.'

'But an evil one,' Vita added.

'Evil or deranged. And this person is still at liberty and may continue to pose a threat.'

'Do you think so?'

'I do. He or she has almost succeeded in persuading everyone that Jack's death was an accident, and then along come an inquisitive pair of young women who start interfering. It must be frustrating, to say the least.'

Vita, sitting on the bed surrounded by open books, looked over at Clara who was at the desk, rolling a new sheet of onion skin paper into the typewriting machine. Her friend's spectacles were slipping down her nose and there was still mud on the hem of her skirt from having been thrown into the leaves that morning. She seemed completely unafraid.

'Are we in danger, Clara, do you think?'

'It certainly seems possible.'

'Should we take precautions?'

Clara turned and looked over her glasses, 'I heartily dislike the idea of being intimidated,' she said.

'I too, but I dislike the idea of either of us being attacked and hurt or rendered useless even more. Somebody has already set upon my poor brother.'

'That is a good point. What suggestions do you have?'

'For one thing, I think it would be better if you stayed here tonight and did not chance the long trip back to Newton alone. It is almost dark already.'

'I would need to provide a very good reason to stay away.'

'My aunt could write and explain that you were unwell earlier today and need to rest. It is no more than the truth.'

This was agreed. The situation explained, Aunt Louisa obliged with a note to the Mistress of Newton College, and the spare bedroom was prepared. It only remained to take the letter to the post box in Fitzroy Street.

'It is a ten minute walk and well lit all the way, Aunt,' Vita said, when Louisa voiced her anxiety, 'You do not usually concern yourself so acutely.'

'You are not usually under threat from desperate criminals, my dear,' her aunt replied. 'Wrap up warm and speak to no-one. And take this whistle.'

'Whistle?'

'The Ladies' Suffrage Group distribute whistles for self-protection. You blow it if you are in danger and it alerts people.'

'Which people?'

'Law-abiding citizens, who will come to your assistance of course,' her aunt said, inspecting Vita in the hallway. 'Perhaps I should accompany you. Not even the vilest criminal would attack a lady my age, I'm sure.'

'No, Aunt, I won't hear of your coming. You and Clara can watch me out of the window as far as the corner, and even when I'm out of sight, you will still be able to hear the whistle.'

'Carry my umbrella too, then,' her aunt said.

Thus armed with a whistle and her aunt's particularly large umbrella, Vita hurried through the dark streets to post the note to Newton College.

From the windows upstairs in the drawing room, Clara and Louisa watched her step energetically from one pool of streetlight into the next. They did not see the dark shadow which resolved itself out of a doorway at the corner and began to follow Vita .

60

Clara continued reviewing her report and Aunt Louisa returned to her studio for a while, but as time went by and no Vita returned, neither could concentrate and they returned to the parlour window.

After half an hour both were beginning to fidget. Clara had re-read the same page of her notes half a dozen times and Louisa's sketch of the dried head of a sunflower was making no progress.

'I think I will go and have a look...' Clara began.

'You will most certainly do no such thing,' Aunt Louisa interrupted her. 'Forgive my insistence, but you have been ill and you have a heart condition. Rest is what you need. No, I will take a little stroll toward the letterbox myself. I expect I shall meet Vita half way. I have another umbrella, luckily. Clara, your role is to stay here and keep a lookout and be ready to welcome us home. I have no doubt we will be back soon.'

Alone in the house, Clara watched Mrs Brocklehurst set briskly off down the street, then settled down to try and finish the report summarising their post mortem observations. Coals shifted in the drawing room fire and a grandfather clock ticked in the hall, but otherwise she was enveloped in the silence of the empty house.

A violently loud knock at the front door suddenly interrupted this calm. Clara jumped and ran towards the door, but hesitated. This was not the knock of the ladies, it sounded far too forceful and insistent.

'Who is it?' she asked.

'Police. Open the door!'

Clara unlocked the door only to be confronted by the man who had attacked her earlier that day.

With one swift movement he pushed her backwards and closed the door behind him. 'Give me the papers,' he said, 'and you will not be injured.'

❧

KITTY FITZSIMMONS SAT BESIDE THE SMALL FIREPLACE IN her room at the Red Lion Hotel. Though there was needlework in her lap, she was not sewing, but staring, immobile, at the flickering coals instead. The room was dim and silent, the firelight picking out a tray of food, untouched, on a table beyond.

When a soft knock came at the door she sat upright and turned towards it without surprise. 'Come in.'

'We have her below,' the black suited gentleman told her.

'Below? Why not bring her upstairs?' Kitty spoke slowly and looked back at the fire.

'No, Kitty. Someone will see her. There is a store room behind the stables, remember?'

'Ah yes,' Kitty said, 'the storeroom, yes.' The coals shifted and hissed a little under her gaze. She made no move.

'Will you come? You wanted to talk to her. She is not a calm young woman, Kitty, she might make trouble.'

'Yes, yes, I will come, of course,' Kitty said. Picking a handbag off the floor by her feet she walked towards him. Instead of leading her away, he stood his ground, his back against the door.

'Kitty,' he said, 'you do not mean this young woman any harm?'

'I must talk to her,' Kitty muttered, but she did not look towards him, 'she has some wrong ideas and I must put her right.'

'But you do not mean to hurt her?'

'Why should I hurt her?'

'I don't know why. It is bad enough that we terrify her this way. That's all very well if it's necessary because she is spreading lies about you...about us, but Kitty if we cause her injury there will be...'

'Of course we will not cause her injury, of course not. I only mean to speak to her.'

'We have terrified her already. She is only young, Kitty, only a girl, really.'

There was sudden rage in Kitty's quiet voice. She looked directly into the man's face and said, 'You are soft, all of you. Do you not see that this vixen is capable of destroying our way of life? Stop blathering, Liam, and take me to her.'

THE STOREROOM HAD BEEN LENT TO THE BOXER'S PARTY AS a storage place for training equipment. It was across the hotel's cobbled livery yard. Being part of an old tack room it still held sacks of feed for the horses and a row of saddles and bridles on pegs. The yard was quiet now, but still lit, and horses could be heard in the stables on either side quietly shifting their hooves and feeding. Some of them snorted at the unaccustomed sound of movement in the storeroom.

Vita had been blindfolded and sat on a bale of straw in

one corner. Her hands were tied at the wrist. She was quiet, her head low as she tried with all her concentration to hear what was happening around her. Two other men were lounging in another corner, with only a dim lamp to light an interrupted game of cards.

Vita started as Kitty and her man, Liam, entered.

'Take off her blindfold,' Kitty told him.

'But - is that wise?' he asked.

'Do it, please.'

Liam signalled and one of the card players untied the blindfold, a long silk scarf. Vita blinked and squinted up. It took her a moment to recognise the people around her.

'Mrs Fitzsimmons is that you? What is it you want with me?'

'Want? What is it I want? Fair treatment. Fair treatment and respect for my pitiful situation as a widow and a stranger alone in...'

'You do not appear to be alone...' Vita interrupted, 'you seem to have a small army of strong men...'

In a startling movement, Kitty stepped forward and struck Vita across the face with a small gloved hand, saying, '...you are an ill-raised and ignorant young woman with too much to say. Your opinions are not important here. You will remain silent and allow me to speak. If you do not, I will encourage my men here to *make* you silent. Is that clear?'

61

'Why should I? What is this about?'

Kitty Fitzsimmons unhooked a short riding whip from a row that hung against the wall. She flexed it once or twice, as if considering its quality, and then touched its tip, a folded flail of leather perhaps an inch long, against Vita's cheek.

'I don't understan...' the word was unfinished. With a hiss as it cut through the air, Kitty had lashed the whip across Vita's cheek.

There was a distinct, though minor ripple of movement among the men in the room, but nobody spoke. A horse nearby shifted iron-shod hooves on the cobblestones and another made a gentle whinnying sound.

Tears of both pain and rage ran hot from Vita's eyes. She raised her bound hands to try to brush them away.

'Now hear me out,' Kitty told her. 'You and your vicious bluestocking friends have cooked up quite enough evil rumours. I do not understand why you should want to do this. Why would you pursue me so? I have suffered a tragic loss. Tragic,' she paused here, a sob causing her voice to break, 'I want only to mourn my husband as any widow should. But I seem to be imprisoned in this dreadful hotel in a city full of people with nothing better to do than turn themselves into scandal mongers and interfering busybodies. Is this how your country treats innocent widows?'

She broke off and glanced around at the men, hoping for confirmation. The men looked away.

'Can you imagine what it is like to wake up, the night after a great triumph, the night after a long but successful fight - to wake up and find a beloved husband dead, cold and dead, beside you in the bed? Can you imagine *that* you stupid, heartless child? This is not some enjoyable little riddle for you and your friends to puzzle your heads over. This is not some little diversion for dull provincial people with stupid lives to entertain themselves with over their endless cups of English tea, this is the *death of my husband*!'

The tone and the volume of Kitty's voice were now such that the three men glanced sidelong at one another, the one in the far corner repeatedly rubbing a rough hand over his mouth and chin.

Liam, the tallest and youngest of them, and the one who had stood beside Kitty so far, stepped slightly further away. 'Kitty, I...'

'...I will not be interrupted!' She was screaming now. 'This young woman is persecuting me! I thought it was the stupid maid at first, but she has neither the wit nor the education, to do such a thing alone. No, this creature here has sown so many seeds of doubt in the minds of the idiot local police and whatever ridiculous professors they found to run the amateur investigation into Jack's death, that they have actually begun to believe that I killed him! *I!*'

Vita tried to say something, but Kitty silenced her by placing the whip against her other cheek.

'You have been spreading lies, you nasty piece of work!

You need to be taught a lesson,' Kitty said, and flicked the whip against Vita's face, raising another red welt. Vita gasped and flinched with the pain. Her eyes filled with tears, but her voice, when she had caught her breath enough to speak, sounded unexpectedly challenging.

'We know you have done this before, Mrs Fitzsimmons. Your first husband, Joseph Radway...'

Kitty screamed as she heard the name. Breathless with rage she threw the riding whip aside and grabbed for the silk bag at her feet. The men looked at one another, uncertain.

She raked violently through the bag, muttering, then looked up with a quick smile, as her hand fastened on something. Her face was white in the light of the lantern, dark shadows exaggerating the glitter of her eyes.

'Get the girl out!' The man she called Liam shouted to the others. 'Quick, move her. Get her outside now!' He stepped between Kitty and Vita, his hands outstretched in a pacifying gesture. This enraged Kitty even more.

'You will not! You will not touch her! I mean to show this young woman the damage she has done me.'

As Kitty turned towards Liam, the object that she had taken from her bag caught the light and they saw for the first time that it was a twelve-inch hatpin.

'Kitty,' Liam was pleading now, 'Kitty, you go too far...'

The blow was swift and subtle. All they saw was a confusion of movement. The slight figure of Kitty reached out with one hand for the much taller figure of Liam, the gesture seeming almost affectionate, as if she were about to admire his pocket watch, or show him a loose button on his waistcoat. The observers, as they described it later, noticed only a brief darting movement by her other hand. For a moment it made no sense, but as this other hand drew back, the shaft of the hatpin followed it; Kitty had plunged it into Liam's waist.

Vita's eyes saw it all, but the information took a moment

or two to reach her brain, which wanted to reject and deny so appalling a sight. Everyone in the room, aghast, looked toward Liam, who in turn looked helplessly back, his gaze moving around them, and then down at the hand which he had instinctively pressed to the wound. He lifted it away. It was perfectly clean.

'Christ almighty! She's never skewered Liam too?' one of the other men said under his breath.

This broke the strange spell that had held them.

62

'Don't interrupt!' Kitty told the man who had spoken. Her tone was calm. 'Liam wouldn't let me explain to this wretched girl.'

'We bloody saw you. You did it! You stuck that thing in Liam. I'm off,' the man said, 'I never liked your ways and now you've really done it. You'll swing for this, but I'm not going to. Come on Con, let's leave the mad witch to it.'

'You will not leave!' Kitty hissed, raising the hatpin, but the two men were already scrambling for the door. There was nothing she could do to prevent them hurling themselves out. She turned back to Liam. 'Liam, you are not hurt, just do as I ask and help me with this girl. We must keep to our plans, Liam.'

But Liam's face was pale and his eyes unfocused. 'Your plans included me once, Kitty,' he gasped, his hands clutching his side.

Kitty ignored him and spoke to Vita confidingly, 'He is weak. They cry like babies when they are afraid.' She passed the blade distractedly across her fingers, then rubbed the fingertips together, as if feeling for damp.

'I am the fourth,' Liam said. He opened his waistcoat showing a darkening smear of red on the shirt beneath, then groaned and leaned heavily back against the whitewashed stable wall, pressing his hands to the wound and bending over.

'And my brother?' asked Vita quietly. 'The young man who fought Jack in the Hero's Challenge?'

'Oh, who cares? Hero's Challenge indeed! Fool's Challenge! Idiot Amateur's Folly! God knows I tried to talk Jack out of it. The boy had it coming to him!' Kitty was suddenly angry again.

'She used him for practice,' Liam said, 'nothing more than that. It wasn't well done or he'd be dead. The same with Shepherd.'

'Is that true, Mrs Fitzsimmons?' Vita asked, but Kitty was distracted by the blade in her hand, turning it to catch the light.

'She used the pin on your brother because he annoyed her. Nothing more. Her mind is overrun with it now. With killing. It's easy for her. She...' Liam broke off and fell heavily forward onto his knees in the straw.

'You are a coward, Liam,' Kitty sneered. 'Where is your courage? Where is your fight, man?'

Vita watched the fallen man begin to tremble. He was groaning now with each breath.

Kitty ignored him and turning to Vita continued, 'At least you are no beauty. Beauty turns them all into babbling fools.' She turned the tip of the pin through the air and pointed it towards Vita's face.

With his last strength, Liam threw himself forward, reaching for Kitty, but fell short.

'Never trust them,' Kitty said, turning back to Vita . The blade was still in her hand. 'When it comes to the important work, always do it yourself. They are like babies. You can never depend on them. I forget your name...'

'Vita,'

'Ah yes. Vita. Remember this, Vita, it is an important lesson. Whenever there is an important or difficult job to be done, the gentlemen you depend on will let you down and you will have to do it yourself.'

'What was the important job you needed to do, Mrs Fitzsimmons?' Vita asked, quietly.

Kitty sighed. 'Jack had to be killed. He had lost his nerve. He was no good to me anymore. Like the other one.'

Kitty, the hatpin still in her hand, now walked over and sat on the bale of straw beside Vita. She seemed to have lost concentration. 'What was I saying? What was I doing, Liam?'

Liam groaned. He pulled himself onto his side. 'You have stabbed me, Kitty, and now I suppose you are planning to murder this young lady. Get out, Miss! Run!'

Kitty ignored him. She placed a hand on Vita's arm. 'Oh my! So melodramatic! I really only mean to stop you both from interfering. I have worked on these plans for a very long time and I cannot allow anyone to upset them. I'm sure you understand that...'

'...Vita,'

'...ah, yes. *Vita* – I find it hard to remember your name, forgive me. I'm sure you wish to keep to your plans as much as I do.' Kitty was distracted, now, looking down at the hatpin in her lap. 'They are pretty things, are they not? Hatpins? I have a collection. This one was made to my own design. It is sharpened steel. This little button on the end is glass. Cool in the hand. Firm. I have many of them.'

Liam groaned, 'Help me, Kitty, please,' he murmured.

'What are your plans, exactly, Mrs Fitzsimmons?' Vita asked quietly. Her attention was fastened on the thin, sharp blade in Kitty's lap, which trembled and glinted in the lamplight. Kitty clenched her lace-gloved fist around its base to steady it. She smiled.

'I want a champion, of course. A world-beater. A fighter my Daddy can be proud of.' She turned confidingly to Vita, speaking close to her cheek, 'but they're hard to find. The men I chose were strong and well-trained, but they didn't have the true fight in them. They were soft in their hearts. The true fighter is hard and cold and ruthless to the core.'

'Like you, Kitty,' Liam said, his voice weaker now.

'Like this blade,' Kitty corrected him. She reached a trim boot to his shoulder and kicked, so that he fell with a moan to the straw. She then turned back to Vita. 'He will die, but I guess it will be slow. I must kill you now, but don't worry, I will put it in your eye. It will be quick.'

Vita saw only a jagged line, a firework flash.

A clatter of boots on the cobbles outside gave them a second's warning before the wooden stable door was thrown back and four or five police officers rushed in ahead of the nimble figure of Mr Derbyshire. Behind them, calling Vita's name and brandishing her umbrella, was Aunt Louisa.

63

Constable Williamson, one of Vita's First Aid classmates, having examined her eye, pronounced the cut to be small but solemnly applied an enormous bandage nonetheless.

Kitty had been seized and taken away. She had fought, biting and screaming with fury until they bound her. Liam was carried away to hospital, a watery circle of blood enlarging in his shirt.

'I am afraid of forgetting the details of all I saw and heard,' Vita told the constable. They were still in the stable waiting for Louisa and Derbyshire to return with a cab.

'A contemporaneous note, Miss, that is what we do in the police. Go home and write everything down exactly as you remember it. Don't leave any spaces and get someone to read and witness it immediately.'

'Thank you. I will do exactly that,' Vita said, 'I'm good at notes.'

'You're good at first aid, too, Miss, if I remember rightly,' the Constable said.

One of the other police officers came in. He was carrying

a portfolio. 'Is this yours, Miss? Your name is in it. We found it outside. It was dropped in the yard.'

'How did they get this?' Vita asked. She opened the portfolio with trembling fingers. As far as she could tell, the contents were intact. 'It must mean they took it from the house...Clara! They must have overpowered her!'

AT HOME THEY FOUND DR GOODMAN ALREADY ATTENDING to Clara. 'She is never going to be strong, Vita,' he told her. 'She is anxious to speak to you, but she must rest. Please try to calm her.'

Clara, pale and breathless, reached out to Vita as she entered the dimly-lit sick room. 'Vita, oh Vita, he stole the report! I could not prevent it! All our work for nothing.'

Vita took her friend's hand. 'You must calm yourself, Clara. I have it, but it is hardly needed now. They have arrested Mrs Fitzsimmons. She stabbed her man Liam before my eyes and confessed to killing Jack as well. I am told I must write everything down immediately and I shall, but you, Clara, must drink this warm milk and sleep.'

'What happened to your face, Vita ? Were you *beaten*?'

'A tiny cut and two sore cheeks, but nothing at all serious, Clara, I promise. Dr Goodman teaches his constables to bandage very generously. Now, please, Clara, rest.'

'What will happen to Liam, Dr Goodman?' Vita asked as she followed him downstairs. 'He stepped between me and that blade. He did not deserve it.'

'No more did you, or Clara.'

'Will he recover?'

'I cannot say. A fine blade penetrating vital organs is likely to cause catastrophic damage, but it might, somehow, have missed them. We can only wait.'

'Poor man. There was no pain. She stabbed him and he felt nothing.'

'It is infection one fears...'

'We will not talk of this now,' Aunt Louisa told them. They were beside the fire in the drawing room. She handed round small glasses of medicinal brandy.

'Kitty's man Liam said she stabbed Edward too. For *practice*, he said,' Vita looked at her Aunt and the doctor. 'She is mad, I suppose,' Vita said, 'she sounded mad.'

'Someone will have to decide exactly *how* mad,' Goodman said.

'To stab a man,' Vita said, 'to drive a hatpin into his skull...'

'...I think that's enough for one night,' Aunt Louisa said, firmly.

'I must write my statement,' Vita told her.

'Tonight? Are you not too fatigued?'

'I cannot sleep until it is done.'

'Then let me put some more coal on the fire so that you will at least stay warm.'

VITA'S STATEMENT, THOROUGH AND CLEAR, WAS READY BY the time she opened the door to the panting lad from the telegraph office the next morning. She had all but forgotten her message to New York. The reply said, 'RADWAY QUESTION STOP CONFIRMED TWO SMALL UNEXPLAINED WOUNDS NOTED IN POLICE REPORT STOP ONE TO NECK BENEATH LEFT EAR ONE TO LEFT EYE STOP MULHEARN'.

64

Professor Rusbridge arrived at ten o'clock and after the usual delay whilst he completed the descent of the carriage and the ascent of the stairs, he was installed, still slightly breathless, with a cup and saucer in his hand. He was all business.

'I believe your household has information which might be of some consequence in the post mortem case. It has naturally now, after recent events, taken on a sightly different complexion, in terms of its forensic significance. Ah yes, thank you Louisa. Two lumps, if you please. It has been a trying night. I was disturbed at 4 am.' He sipped his tea, his eyes closed briefly in appreciation. His raised little finger made Vita think suddenly of a piglet's tail and have to look away.

On consideration the Professor thought he would take a little bread and butter with his tea. His digestion, having been disturbed in the middle of the night, had left him unable to manage more than a mouthful of his college's breakfast of devilled kidneys. Vita went to fetch some.

'It shows admirable initiative, this careful re-examination

of the post-mortem evidence,' said the Professor. 'I am surprised that your nephew found the time, we work them very hard, you know. There is hardly time for *hobbies*.'

The ladies had prepared for this too. In fact they had decided to encourage, without actually deviating from the truth, the Professor's immediate assumption that the scientific work had been carried out by Edward. If their report was to have credibility and achieve its effects without delay, this was the price they had to pay.

'And which lucky gentleman's portrait are you engaged on at present, Louisa?' asked the Professor.

'I have just completed a portrait of Mr Aloysius Derbyshire, do you know him?'

'Derbyshire? Is he a John's man?'

'He is a fencing instructor.'

The Professor stopped chewing. 'You surprise me, Louisa. I thought your portrait studies were confined to distinguished members of the University.'

'Normally, yes, but Mr Derbyshire is a very celebrated swordsman. It made an entertaining change for me to paint a younger man, and an athlete.'

'Well, I never,' the Professor declared, with a moist chuckle, 'it will be chimney sweeps next!'

Louisa smiled graciously. 'It is the Master of Emmanuel College next in point of fact, and he would be very surprised to be called a chimneysweep.'

The Professor went back to his bread and butter. 'Ah well,' he said, 'I have work to do in college, I shall read your nephew's report this afternoon. I'm sure it is very interesting, though I cannot imagine what new discoveries are within. Brilliant students often try to teach their grandmothers how to suck eggs, as it were. I'm sure you agree, Louisa.'

Louisa briefly caught the suppressed agitation registering between Vita and Clara. 'I am afraid the report is urgently needed by the Coroner. We invited you here to read it before it is sent, and it must be sent promptly.' Aunt Louisa sounded mild and smiled amiably, pouring more tea as she spoke.

'Out of the question, I'm afraid. I have far too many demands on my time.'

'Then alas, the report will have to go as it is, without your oversight.'

'Its credibility will be much reduced. I am the examining pathologist in this case. I doubt it will carry much weight. It contains speculations by unqualified persons, as I understand it.'

'Yes, and that is why we were anxious for you to read the new findings,' Clara put in.

'You ladies are the typewriters of this report?' The Professor was puzzled.

'We are its authors,' Vita said.

'In the sense that...?'

'In the sense that we carried out a review of the evidence and established a new interpretation of some information that had been overlooked.'

The Professor turned his head slowly and looked for the first time at Vita and Clara. 'Carried out a review? What review? On whose authority?'

Louisa sprang from her chair and, taking the portfolio from the sideboard, leaned over the seated professor, placing it reverently in his lap.

'Perhaps, Bertie, if you just read it? Ladies, it would be easier if you withdrew while the Professor reads.'

Though sounding serene, Aunt Louisa's look towards them carried a strong command. They could do no other than obey, trailing out of the room and sitting first on the stairs and then later wandering into Aunt Louisa's studio, where they could hear if they were called.

They were not called. They waited, toying with pieces of

charcoal and looking out of the window at a blackbird tossing fallen leaves about. After less than an hour the front door slammed, and the Professor was gone.

'He is a busy man,' Louisa told them.

'You did not allow him to remove the report?'

'No. It is here. He recommends we submit it to the Coroner ourselves.'

'I should so have liked to discuss it with him!' Vita said, frustrated.

'He read it in silence.'

Clara picked up the report and leafed through it.

'He wrote one or two brief remarks in the margins, but I saw no extended writing,' Louisa told her.

'What did he write?' Vita asked.

'He appears to have changed two words, apparently he is correcting the spelling of one, and that is all I can see.'

'So nothing is crossed through or disagreed with?'

'Nothing, as far as I can see...oh!'

'What?' Vita asked, peering over her friend's shoulder.

'He has signed his name at the end!'

The younger women looked at one another in astonishment. Aunt Louisa was lifting tea cups onto a tray. 'Yes,' she said, 'he thought his signature would demonstrate his approval. It now carries the weight of his authority, which means it is certain to be accepted by the Coroner.'

'Did he...make any comment about our efforts?' Vita asked.

Aunt Louisa stopped piling saucers and came over to where Vita was standing. 'I do not think you should expect compliments from that quarter. You were, in a sense, correcting his work.'

'Well, adding to it,' Clara said, 'contributing additional observations, perhaps.'

'Indeed.' They all looked at the portfolio Clara held on

her knee, and at the large and elaborate signature on the final sheet.

'The signature is the highest compliment we could be given, I suppose.' Clara said.

'He will take all the credit!' Vita could not be as patient as her friend.

'Vita, dear, you need some sleep. You both do. I assure you I did speak up on your behalf. He will not forget what you have done.'

HE WILL NOT FORGET WHAT YOU HAVE DONE.

Vita, though unwilling to contradict her aunt there and then, felt fairly convinced that the Professor had, in fact, forgotten their work by the time his well-shone shoes had reached the pavement of Eden Street, but there was nothing to be done, so she and Clara, both suddenly exhausted, gave in and went to their beds.

65

Constable Williamson, the officer who had applied the six-foot bandage to Vita's eye wound, escorted Tabitha back to Eden Street personally. Though offered a cab, Tabitha chose to walk, having longed for daylight and fresh air for several days. The pair left the station by a back door and made their way over Parker's Piece. The sky was bright and it felt warm in the sunshine. Stiff, hunched and anxious at first, Tabitha took deep breaths of autumn-scented air, her stride lengthening and the colour returning to her cheeks.

'You are pleased to be going home, I expect,' said the Constable.

'Yes,' she said, pulling her shawl closer, 'but I have given my Mistress a lot of trouble.'

'Not by your own deeds, though. You were wrongly accused. And Mrs Fitzsimmons is mad, the doctors are bound to say so. She just picked on you. It was not your own doing.'

'I deceived Mrs Brocklehurst.'

'You only tried to do your best for the little one,' the police officer told her.

She looked across at him sharply, 'How do you know about that?'

'It's all been in the papers. Everybody knows about it now, and about the two young ladies and what they did to catch Mrs Fitzsimmons.'

'People should mind their own business, if you ask me,' said the maid, frowning. They walked a few steps in silence.

'Nobody in their right mind would think the worse of you for what you did,' he said.

Tabitha looked angrily up at him. 'I've been in a cell. People will remember that and forget the rest. No, I reckon they'll send me packing when I get back to Eden Street. I don't know what I shall do then. I shall have to go back to Cornwall.'

'I hope not,' said Constable Williamson, 'I was hoping to take you for another walk sometime.'

'What? The cheek of you!'

Tabitha hurried. For all that she was uncertain of the reception she would receive, she was eager to see her little niece. The Constable insisted they use the front door. Where exactly his police duty ended she could not say, but secretly she was glad of his tall, uniformed presence beside her.

'Ah, Tabitha,' Louisa said, opening the door in her paint-daubed apron. 'Welcome home. Monsieur and Hetty are in the kitchen. Go along down and make some tea for yourself and for this officer. Come and see me whenever you're ready. I'll be in my studio. Forgive me, I have a sitter, so I cannot stay to talk now. Vita will be glad you have returned, too. She is out at a lecture.'

Williamson watched the lady of the house disappear from view, then urged Tabitha over the threshold, 'Come on, I'm ready for some tea.'

Hetty - a different, clean, well-dressed and cheerful Hetty - made as little fuss about Tabitha's return as Louisa. She was standing on a chair wearing an oversized apron stirring something in a bowl. 'Look Tabby!' she said, 'Musher and me are making gingerbread men.'

Was there a formal conversation which resolved that Tabitha should stay? If there was, nobody remembered it.

Hetty was already so happily absorbed into the Goodman household that when Tabitha asked nervously what was to become of her, Louisa looked surprised.

'Can she not stay with the Goodmans? They are terribly fond of her.'

'But, Madam, I cannot expect them to keep her forever.'

'No, no, not forever,' Louisa had said, opening the latest copy of the Ladies' Journal and glancing through the contents, 'but for the time being at least. They are happy to have her. Monsieur sees her in the afternoons and teaches her cooking. She seems to be thriving. Does this arrangement not suit you?'

Tabitha blinked at her. 'Madam, what of her upkeep? Her board and lodging? I can pay a little from my wages, but I fell behind.'

Louisa was already being distracted by a fascinating article on medical treatments using electricity. 'The Goodmans would not dream of asking for money, Tabitha. I suggest we all return to our normal routine and allow the child to settle. There is plenty of time to consider Henrietta's future. Oh, and incidentally, I should like to paint her portrait, if you agree.'

'I told you it'd be alright,' Constable Williamson said, with a grin, when he and the maid were walking that Sunday. He had called without invitation, which was taking a liberty, but it was hard to say no. He had come in his best suit and polished his shoes.

66

There was a strict etiquette at the house in Eden Street surrounding the arrival of the post. Aunt Louisa insisted that all letters be delivered to her for distribution. Tabitha, but no-one else, was permitted to collect mail from the doormat and it was then brought on a tray with a letter knife at the ready.

'Ah. Something from your father,' Louisa said, passing the first envelope over the breakfast table to Vita, 'and this one is for me.'

Vita placed the envelope in front of her plate, then propped it against the marmalade; then shifted it to the right, against the butter dish. She made no move to open it.

Louisa, meanwhile, opened hers and read it rapidly before putting it aside and taking up her teacup again.

'I imagine Papa is reminding me that I am needed at the Parsonage and that I was to be here for only a few weeks,' Vita said. 'He would like me to take over the Sunday school. Miss Kinsham's arthritis is getting worse. He misses my help with his sermons and parish visits. He will probably be arranging his Advent services...'

'You might consider *opening* the letter, instead of speculating, dear.'

But Vita did not pick up the letter knife.

'It is true that I was only to be here for a few weeks. I was to be company for you, and to keep a distant eye on Edward and report back. All that is done.'

'And you wanted to see Cambridge for yourself...' Louisa suggested, taking a third letter from the tray and examining it front and back.

'I did. I was so curious about Edward's life here,' Vita took her own letter from its stand and laid it flat on the table beside her plate. She put her hand over the letter, as if to cover it. 'I knew it would not be something I could do myself, Aunt. I already understood about the fees and the entrance examination and so on. I knew it was not a possibility for me, with no proper education in Science. When I came, I thought I would just walk around the colleges and breathe it all in and that would be enough to make me see sense.'

'Well, you have achieved a lot more than that.'

Vita looked through her spread fingers at her father's letter. 'When I accompanied Clara back to Newton...'

'Yes?'

'When she took me on a tour of the college, I saw the young women there, Aunt, and they were just...so *ordinary*. They were walking about, carrying their books, going to the library, working in the labs, playing hockey...'

Aunt Louisa waited for the point, still holding the other envelope.

'Being a student was just normal, it was just what they chose to do. They were not extraordinary or wonderful or superlatively gifted - some may have been - but mostly they were just young women like me.'

'And you thought you could do it too?'

'Until then, I had thought it was out of reach, almost unimaginable, to study Science, to do it seriously, but there they were, doing just that, and laughing and enjoying themselves while they did it!' She looked up at her Aunt. 'It suddenly seemed real and possible. But it isn't possible of course, because there are scholarships and grants for a parson's son like Edward, but almost none for a parson's daughter, and besides I have had no formal training. I would never pass an examination.'

'Professor Rusbridge disagrees with you,' Louisa said.

Vita looked up at her aunt, surprised. 'Professor Rusbridge? What could he have to do with this?'

'He is an influential man, dear, as you know.'

'Yes, and Clara and I have annoyed him considerably. Bluestockings he called us!'

'You must be mistaken,' said her aunt, 'he appears in this letter to be recommending that you apply for a scholarship.'

'But there are no scholarships! None that could apply to someone in my position.'

'Ah well, he must be mistaken in that case. He says quite plainly here...' Louisa tapped the letter she had just read with her little spectacles, '...that there is something called the Mary Harding Fund. Perhaps you had better read for yourself.' She picked the letter up and fluttered it in Vita's direction.

Vita, rigid with sudden suspense, unfolded it with clumsy movements and read silently with her breath held, then burst out. 'Aunt! There is a fund! He will recommend me! Oh Aunt! I can apply to Newton. I can apply! Oh Aunt Louisa! I can apply!'

'Steady now Vita .'

'Oh Aunt, this is extraordinary. Why? Why has he done this?'

'He appreciated your work, dear, I suppose.'

'But he was furious.'

'Perhaps, but only briefly.'

'There is an entrance examination to be passed first, of course.'

'Of course.'

'I must get to work.' Vita was about to run for the door, when she looked down and caught sight of her father's letter again. 'But what will Papa say to this, I wonder?'

'Write a reply which explains everything. He wants what is best for you, Vita . I'm sure he will find someone else to help with his sermons and run the Sunday school.'

'Poor Papa, I seem so eager to stay away. It is only that I long to study. I don't know if I can make him understand. I am being selfish, perhaps, but I have not even dared to dream of an opportunity such as this.'

'He will understand, I feel sure of it, if you just tell him.'

'Yes. I will write. And Aunt, thank you.'

'I did little enough, dear.'

'You worked some sort of magic on the Professor, I suspect.'

'There was no magic, I can assure you. Although I did paint a particularly fine portrait of the man – as well as offering him a few choice cakes. Now run along and write to your Papa.'

THE THIRD LETTER, OPENED ONLY AFTER VITA'S ABRUPT departure, was an extravagantly ornate invitation to the Gala Opening of the Derbyshire Gymnasium and Physical Education Training Establishment. The evening was to include fencing displays, Indian club demonstrations, a ladies' health gymnastics routine and the unveiling of a specially commissioned portrait.

'The very cheek of the man!' Aunt Louisa said aloud, but she smiled at the embossed and lavishly-gilded card and later added it to the other invitations on the mantelpiece.

67

A polite young woman does not run in the street. She does not charge like a bolting racehorse along the pavements, narrowly avoiding passers-by, sidestepping dogs on leads and babies being pushed in perambulators, holding her hat to her head with one hand and grasping a letter and her skirt hem in the other. She most certainly does not call loudly to the postman when she sees that she has missed the 10 o'clock collection and he is already carrying his post bag away up the street.

It would be most irregular for her to pursue him and plead with him to add one more letter to his sack. There are probably regulations against that, but this postman ignored them and cheerfully took the letter, and the world as we know it did not end.

Perhaps restrained good manners in young women are not quite as important as we all thought.

A lecture on the anatomy of the hand was the next thing on Vita's agenda. It took place in the lecture hall on Old School Lane. Dr Westly, the anatomist, allowed women into his lecture room, so Clara was usually in the front row along with half a dozen others. But not today. Vita looked for her afterwards in a talk on methods of blood analysis, but she was not there either. She had recovered, and been back at Newton for more than a week. It was puzzling.

Vita thought of taking an omnibus to Newton to find her friend but had no money about her. She considered walking, but did not want to go without letting her aunt know, so went back to Eden Street instead.

'Keep your coat on. Clara is ill and she has asked that you visit her.' Aunt Louisa told her as she stepped through door.

'At Newton College?'

'No, she is in the hospital. It is her heart. You must go quickly.'

AT HER FRIEND'S BEDSIDE, VITA, SHOCKED BY CLARA'S pallor and weakness, could only take her hand. Clara turned her face to Vita and smiled a little.

'I am seriously ill, Vita, but do not worry. It is not unexpected.'

'The doctors here are very good,' Vita said, helplessly.

'Not good enough, though.'

'Oh Clara!'

Clara coughed, breathlessly, her shoulders hunching beneath the sheets. She had trouble speaking more but held up her hand for Vita to wait while she recovered sufficiently, then said, in a whisper, 'I want you to do what I cannot, Vita, I want you to complete your studies. I would feel so much better if I could think of you doing so.'

'There is a possibility now,' Vita said.

'I know. I heard. Please, Vita, *seize it*. I have a little money. Please, accept what I can offer you.' Clara's hand was cold in Vita's, and its grasp grew weaker.

'She must rest now, she tires easily,' a nurse in a starched white headdress gently told Vita.

'May I stay and hold her hand? She has no-one else here to be with her.'

'Of course.' The nurse motioned to a colleague and together they drew screens around the bed.

It was a long night. Vita remembered the dimmed lights of the ward, the muted comings and goings of doctors and nurses and the antiseptic smell for the rest of her life. Several times a doctor examined Clara, taking her pulse and listening to her heart with a stethoscope. She appeared to sleep and Vita dozed next to her, then woke with a start to see her friend clear-eyed and looking at her, smiling. 'I am glad you're here. Please tell my father I had company and was not distressed.'

'I will, of course.'

'You must be sure to study the heart, Vita, we do not know enough about it yet.'

'I will. I promise.'

'I am tired now.'

'Rest, Clara, you will feel better.'

Still with a slight smile on her lips, Clara closed her eyes. Her hand in Vita's grew chilled, her breathing lightened. A nurse came in and put a hand on Vita's shoulder.

'Your friend is slipping away now, my dear,' she told her.

'I will stay with her,' Vita whispered.

She did. The end was peaceful. For Clara the step between life and death seemed a small one. She breathed deeply for a while, and then it was done.

Without hurry or intrusion the nurses finally led Vita away. She sat for some time in the corridor, hollowed out by sleeplessness and emotions too large to be named or understood. She stared at the chequered pattern of the hall floor. The tall windows slowly lightened. Bare branches of the trees outside were lit by a winter's dawn.

Outside the hospital there were wet leaves on the pavement under her boots. She had forgotten wheeling the bicycle to the hospital, but there it was waiting against the railings. Clara's bicycle. Dawn was bringing the earliest workers out on the streets as Vita pushed the bicycle homeward. Early trams rattled in the distance, delivery carts began their rounds, lights were coming on in college windows. The city was waking around her. Somewhere nearby new bread scented the air as white-aproned bakers laid fresh loaves in their baskets. Wafts of frying bacon came from college kitchens. A day was beginning, but Clara would not see it; she would never see a day begin again.

Vita's steps were halted by the thought. She stood on Trumpington Street, the morning's activity unfolding around her, and wept. Then, unnoticed by deliverymen and hurrying maids, she climbed onto the bicycle, and jerky and unsteady at first, began to pedal herself home. It was a journey of veers and wobbles and several abrupt stops, but by the time she was in Eden Street she was a cyclist. Instead of stopping there, she continued through the town and pedalled a large circuit, braving cabs and carts, trams, horses, walkers, perambulators, dogs and all the hazards a real cyclist encounters. Vita thought of her friend with every turn of the pedals, the wind blowing the tears from her face.

When finally she reached home, Vita wept briefly in her aunt's arms before going to bed. It felt to her, when she woke later, as if her own life were now entirely different. Her room was the same, her notes piled on the table and her books stacked on the floor; the house was the same, she could hear someone sweeping stairs somewhere, and the smell of turpentine showed her aunt to be at work in the studio, but nothing was the same at all. She had a mission - and possibly the means to achieve it. She would dedicate her life's work to the memory of her friend.

68

A surprising number of guests accepted the invitation to the Derbyshire Gymnasium's Gala Opening. It offered a welcome escape from the grey chill of the season, as well as a buffet luncheon.

Vita, urged away from her books for a few hours, accompanied her aunt, but was so preoccupied with her studies in Science that she seemed only half present. As a guest of honour, Louisa was duty bound to attend. It was her own work that was due to be unveiled, even if she did have reservations about the location of the portrait, never having exhibited in a gymnasium before.

They spotted Edward in his white fencing clothes as soon as they entered. He was part of the entertainment. An épée display was on the programme, and he was mingling with the guests, showing them the equipment and describing the activities of the gymnasium in a proprietorial way.

'Those? They are Indian clubs, particularly useful for strengthening the upper arms and shoulders and very much favoured by ladies,' he was telling a fluttery pair, who begged immediately for a demonstration.

Derbyshire himself was similarly busy, leading curious groups around the hall, which was elegantly refurbished with a fine wooden floor and high beamed ceiling. Long ropes hung from the rafters along one side, and all the walls were lined with wooden climbing bars. There were vaulting horses and mats, rows of giant medicine balls and racks of clubs, sticks and poles for use in combat - all the most up-to-date equipment. An expert on the parallel bars was swinging himself around in one corner and another was drawing gasps of admiration performing handstands on a high beam nearby.

Along the far wall a refreshment table was weighed down by an elegant buffet, already so well attended that it was almost invisible behind the eager crowd pressing two and three deep towards the food. Aunt Louisa, when she passed that way, felt she recognised the style of the offerings, and then spotted Monsieur, in full whites and chef's toque in the background.

'Well, Monsieur Picard, is this your work?'

'It is Madame. Monsieur Derbyshire was most persuasive.'

Aunt Louisa raised her eyebrows as together they looked along the sumptuous display on the table.

'It is certainly magnificent,' she remarked, 'he has spared no expense.'

'He insisted upon the finest dishes as well as the best chef,' the Frenchman told her, with a little shrug.

Louisa said nothing for a moment, glancing towards the caviar and lobster coming under attack from diners to her right.

'And seafood...I thought you generally avoided serving seafood,' she remarked.

The chef looked very briefly at his shoes. He ran a hand over his apron and touched the very corner of his moustache.

'That is all in the past, Madame.'

'Perhaps you will soon be leaving Eden Street to work for someone more...generous,' she suggested.

The chef frowned and stood to attention.

'I do not forget what I owe you, Madame. I never forget. It will always be my pleasure to cook for you and for your family and guests. And if the little girl stays, for her also.'

'You mean Hetty?'

'Yes, *Henriette*. She is an agreeable child and one day she will be a good cook also.'

'Well, Monsieur Picard!' Louisa exclaimed, giving the chef a sidelong glance, 'I did not expect you to be so easily won over. You seem almost soft-hearted.'

The chef straightened a salad bowl on the food table and removed a serving dish that had already been cleared of salmon.

'I have observed that the child has a gift for cookery,' he said. 'It is rare. It should not be wasted. I say no more,' and with a small stiff bow he left to continue his duties.

Looking across the hall, Louisa could see her niece among a group who were trying stretching movements. It was the first time she had seen Vita do anything other than study for several weeks.

'Ah, Mrs Brocklehurst! How good of you to come to my little opening,' it was Aloysius Derbyshire, proud owner of the new gymnasium. He had escaped his many guests for a moment and joined Louisa, both taking in the whole scene.

'I had no idea your gymnasium would be so large and well-equipped,' Louisa said. 'Congratulations, Mr Derbyshire. If this crowd is any indication, it should be a great success.'

'Yes. All is set fair, so far,' he said, beaming around him. 'My services are in demand, and the gymnasium is already thriving. Has your nephew spoken to you yet?'

'Edward? About what?'

'Ah. I will allow him to speak to you first. Now, the portrait. What do you think of its position?'

They both looked across the echoing gymnasium and up at the veiled picture on the wall at the far end.

'It is certainly prominent,' Louisa said. 'Who will carry out the unveiling?'

'I have a special guest! He will pull the cord at the end of my speech. Here he is now.' Mr Derbyshire indicated a broad figure trying to make its way across the hall.

'Who is this gentleman? Should I know him?'

'It is the boxer, Sam Shepherd. He is to be one of our patrons and an occasional instructor. It is a great honour.'

⁂ 69 ⁂

Crowds were already surrounding Mr Shepherd, eager to shake the hand of the well-known boxer. He seemed delighted and a little disarmed by so warm a welcome, and was helpless to make any progress across the room. From across the hall he looked like a shire horse surrounded by eager pit ponies.

'I shall have to rescue him,' said Mr Derbyshire. 'If you will permit me to bring him over, I will show you both to your seats and the speeches can begin.' He was about to leave, but then hesitated. 'Mrs Brocklehurst, about your fees. May I call on you later? It will be too busy here tonight.'

'Of course,' she said.

It was not until after the ceremonies - the unveiling (to gasps of admiration) of the portrait, the speeches on the necessity of exercise for the maintenance of health in both body and mind; on the virtue of physical discipline, its good effects on character, longevity and intellect, all interspersed with demonstrations of every variety, from Cossack strength training to Turkish tumbling and Far Eastern exercises for balance and breathing - it was not until all this was over and the evening was drawing to a close that Edward finally managed to speak to his aunt.

'Well, it has been very interesting to see Mr Derbyshire's splendid new gymnasium, I must say it is most impressive,' Louisa said, 'I expect you will spend time here whenever you can, Edward.'

'I shall indeed,' he answered, 'Mr Derbyshire has offered to employ me here as a fencing instructor and general trainer.'

'Good heavens,' said his aunt, 'but Edward, what of your studies?'

'They have allowed me to degrade for a year. I need to recover my strength and my memory. It is slow, I am afraid. I cannot rely on my memory yet.'

'And your father?'

'He seems to have accepted that this is the right thing.' Edward smiled and pleased onlookers by adopting his fencing stance and touching a small boy on the nose with the buttoned tip of his sword.

Louisa looked proudly on. He was a fine figure. Ladies on all sides were hoping to catch her nephew's eye.

'Will you live with us at Eden Street?'

'No need. I shall live here, there is a small apartment at the back. I shall not abandon my studies, there will still be plenty of time for book work.'

'Have you told Vita ?'

'Not yet. I wanted you to hear first. Does my plan have your blessing?'

'It does, Edward. It is a wise decision. You will certainly not lack for female pupils, to judge from this evening. You must be careful not to let it turn your head.'

Vita was deep in conversation with Sam Shepherd when her aunt came over.

'How did you hear about her?' Vita was asking the boxer.

'It was in the newspapers. I was troubled by it,' he said.

'What troubled you, Mr Shepherd?' asked Louisa, joining them.

'I was full of doubts about what might become of the little girl,' he said, 'only I read about her and thought to myself, there's a poor little mite if ever I heard of one. Her aunt trying to do the best for her, but her not having any parents. I was orphaned at an early age myself. I know what it is to be passed from pillar to post, unwanted, like a raggedy parcel.'

'She is staying across the road with our neighbours, Mr Shepherd, she has not been passed carelessly around, has she Aunt?'

'No indeed,' said Louisa, 'far from it.'

'Would you allow me, would you kindly allow me to make a contribution to the child's upkeep?' the boxer asked. 'It would be a pleasure to me to know that a little of the money I have earned in the fighting trade would do someone good. I am a single man, I can afford a sum that would allow her some schooling.'

The ladies looked at the boxer in astonishment.

'She might have an education that would set her up in the future,' he went on, 'if you would allow it, of course.'

'You would have to speak to Tabitha. Come to Eden Street tomorrow and you shall meet her there. And Hetty too,' said Louisa.

'Is she a little Hetty? I have a sister called Hetty,' he said with a broad smile.

But the next day the boxer was beaten to Eden Street by Aloysius Derbyshire.

'I was hoping to make you a suggestion, ladies,' he told them.

'Regarding...?'

'Regarding the little girl.'

'You mean Hetty?'

'Yes!' He was sitting on the edge of his seat, filled with twitchy energy, paying no attention to the cup of tea in front of him.

'My, but the child is popular lately!' Louisa remarked.

'I should like, with your permission of course, I should like to pay for her education.'

Louisa and Vita both reacted with laughter, which was not at all what Mr Derbyshire was expecting.

'But why do you laugh?'

'Forgive us, Mr Derbyshire, it is just that you have been pipped at the post in your kind offer.'

'Really?'

'Yes. Mr Sam Shepherd has also very kindly offered to be the child's benefactor.'

'Sam Shepherd? Has he indeed?'

'You must speak to Tabitha. Oh, and Monsieur believes the child is a natural cook and has offered to teach her the skills of French cuisine.'

'My word. She has done well, when you consider what a grimy ragamuffin she was when I first saw her that day, poor little thing.'

'So it seems. Perhaps the best arrangement would be if you three gentlemen, that is to say yourself, Sam Shepherd and Monsieur, were to discuss the matter between yourselves before making a proposal to Tabitha as to the arrangements. She will be very shocked as it is. One joint proposal will be much easier for her to grasp than three different ones.'

'Very true,' Mr Derbyshire agreed. 'Oh, and incidentally, I must give you this with my earnest thanks. My clients adore your portrait. It is very vain of me to say so, but I adore it too! Truly, I feel it fills the whole gymnasium with its beauty, artistic energy and inspiration.'

'Oh good heavens,' said Louisa, 'if only all my sitters were as enthusiastic!'

'And here is your fee in full,' he added, handing her an envelope.

'...and so prompt in their settlement! I am quite overwhelmed!'

'Then you will allow me to pour you another cup of tea, I hope,' said the sportsman with a shy smile.

Both sipped their tea for a moment in happy contemplation of the future.

'Would you be offended, Mr Derbyshire, if I enquired as to the reasons for your enormous success as a fencing instructor...'

'...and *gymnasium proprietor*,' he added.

'...yes indeed. How is it that you are so celebrated and so much in demand?'

'There is no secret, Mrs Brocklehurst. I am simply extremely good at my profession, and extraordinarily hard-working. In my early days I attracted some very influential pupils - aristocratic gentlemen, mostly - a good word from Lord This or Sir That, and many others beat a path to my door. I treat them all alike. A streetsweeper is the equal of a Viscount in the gymnasium.'

'It sounds remarkably similar to portrait painting, Mr Derbyshire,' said Louisa, smiling at him over the rim of her teacup.

70

Miss Harding's room was Vita's dream of what a tutor's room in a Cambridge college might be. Its mullioned windows looked out across wide lawns to ancient pine trees; there was a huge desk, a few thousand books and a pair of worn but comfortable armchairs by the hearth. Miss Harding herself was rather younger than Vita had expected, she was business-like, plainly dressed, and completely at home.

'What is it that attracts you to the Natural Sciences, Miss Carew?' she asked, 'I hope you will not mind if I make a note of our conversation - I have several more candidates to see.' She took a notebook and a pen from the shelf nearby.

Vita had the odd sensation of her brain emptying. Every carefully prepared answer took wings and flew off towards the gardener raking leaves outside the window. Her mouth was dry. She could remember nothing.

'Come now, Vita, there is no need for anxiety,' Miss Harding had carried out many interviews, had indeed undergone one herself years before. She was sympathetic, but she also had five more promising young women to see that day.

'I saw a brain,' Vita finally blurted out. 'It was a human brain, it was in a tank and my friend and I...there was a post mortem and you see, he was murdered, that's what we thought. But she died. It was her heart.'

Miss Harding looked at the note she had attempted to make of this utterance and winced. 'Just take your time,' she said, in her gentlest voice.

Vita took a deep breath. 'My mother died,' she said, finally managing a more normal tone, 'I was nine years old when she became ill. My father had his parish, he was busy, my brother was away at school, so I was with her often. I saw the doctor, a good man, Dr Kilmartin, I watched him with her, but there was nothing he could do.'

'I'm sorry to hear that,' Miss Harding said.

'He was a young man and diligent, but Science simply had no answers for the disease my mother suffered. It was gradual. She lost her memory first, then her powers of speech. There was little he could do. He had an idea that the seat of the problem lay in her brain. Its functions were ceasing, but no treatment was known, and the progress of the disease was little understood. He talked to me, because I was always with her. He explained to me what his limitations were; he had no means of intervening.'

'So Medicine began to interest you at that time?'

'Nursing at first. I read a book and tried to follow the practical advice it gave. I helped the nurses who came. They thought I was foolish, I see now. I read that she needed certain nourishing foods and hunted high and low for them. I made broths and jellies, it probably made no difference, but I was trying to do my best for her. My brother was already interested in Science and I read his books when he was at home from school. I read about the central nervous system and its ailments and I asked Dr Kilmartin a lot of questions. I wanted to know how the disease worked and how it could be cured. And how other diseases could be cured. I read about smallpox and how it could be prevented, I read everything I could find.'

'And did you have any schooling?'

'A governess until I was twelve or so, but there was no school nearby. I was needed in the household anyway, after mother became ill. I read all my brother's books and Dr Kilmartin lent me more. He and his wife were very encouraging. They took me to lectures in Plymouth.'

'But no regular classes?'

'No. After mother passed away, I had more time to read and I began to help my father, he is a keen naturalist, with his observations and recordings. I developed a note-taking system - I still use it. When my brother came to Cambridge for his second year, I came with him. I have an aunt who lives here.' Vita paused and looked across at her interviewer.

'Go on,' Miss Harding said.

'There was an accident. A neighbour's child kicked by a horse in our street. I was nearby. I ran to help, but I did not know even the most elementary ways of assisting someone who was injured. I could shout for help and watch him die. Nothing more. It was too much to bear. I told his father I must learn. I needed to know what to do. I never wanted that feeling again. That helplessness. He sent me to a First Aid class and soon after that I began to attend lectures. Then I met Miss Shorto, and...'

'I know Miss Shorto well. You chose a fine teacher.'

'Yes. I have worked with her for almost a year now. I will never feel ready, but my brother recently showed me his entrance examination and I found I was able to answer many of the questions. Not absolutely all, there was a Physics question I was completely confused by, but the rest I thought I might be able at least to try.'

Miss Harding, bowed over her notes, allowed herself the

slightest smile. 'So you feel quite confident, then, about taking our entrance examination?'

Vita looked directly at Miss Harding. 'I was lucky enough to meet Clara Benn, you knew her, perhaps.'

'Yes, of course. We were very sad to lose her.'

'I was with Clara at the end, and she encouraged me even then. Right at the end of her life she urged me to go on with this. So, yes, I must take the examination, but no, I cannot say that I feel any sort of confidence about it.'

71

Miss Harding looked at the fire for a moment. 'Your academic ability has attracted the attention of Professor Rusbridge. He has written personally, recommending you most highly for a scholarship. He is not known as a supporter of women's education. You must have impressed him greatly.'

Vita briefly summarised her involvement in the pugilist's post mortem. 'It was really Clara who took the lead. It was her observations that first alerted us to the suspicious nature of Jack Fitzsimmons' death. I acted only as an assistant.'

'I am aware of the case, of course,' said Miss Harding, 'The two of you found crucial evidence. They charged his wife, I believe. Is there to be a court case?'

'She was not deemed fit to plead. She stabbed a man in front of me, and would have killed me too, I think. She is in an asylum now. It was a horrible affair.'

'Your actions showed admirable courage and determination. You will need such qualities if you are to study Natural Sciences. You know already that there is often opposition among the male undergraduates and teachers to the presence of women. They are openly hostile in some quarters. One needs...' Miss Harding broke off and straightened her back until she sat very upright in her chair, 'one needs a certain steeliness of nature to overcome it.'

'I may have lacked that once. I believe I have it now,' Vita said.

Miss Harding smiled more openly.

'Let me explain some of the practical matters,' she said, 'you will not, even if you successfully complete your studies here, be able to graduate. Women are not permitted to do so. You will receive a certificate and we are able to give you references, but you will not formally be a Bachelor of Science or have any letters after your name. Other universities do allow it now, you might want to consider London, for example.'

'I shall be dependent on a scholarship you offer, so only Newton will do. Besides, Clara was here. Perhaps it sounds peculiar, but I promised to finish her degree on her behalf. It is a very serious commitment, Miss Harding.'

'But there is no means of a young woman qualifying in Medicine at present. Not at Cambridge.'

'I know that from my brother.'

'There is a London School of Medicine for Women, I know many of the teachers there, but no equivalent in Cambridge. I am telling you all this, Miss Carew - Vita, so that you have a very clear understanding of what you would be undertaking. Frankly there are great limitations to a woman with a calling to study Science or Medicine, but there are opportunities as well. The teachers here are at least as passionate about their subject as at any other institution in the world. There is every encouragement to a young woman who is determined and hard-working. And also - I should not forget to mention this - we have a strong community at Newton, and a great deal of fun!'

On cue a group of young women in hockey boots crossed

the frosty lawn in the distance, calling, laughing and dribbling a ball from one to the other.

'It is daunting to begin with, I can tell you that much from personal experience, but if you are prepared to give your energies to it, the rewards are immense and long-lasting. There is still something of the pioneering spirit here, Miss Carew, we are among the earliest women to have these chances and our students aim to make the most of them.'

'I believe you have your own laboratories,' Vita said.

'Oh yes. Come, I have a few minutes before the next candidate, I'll show you round. The examination will be at half past one, so you have time for a tour and luncheon first.'

AFTERWARDS VITA REMEMBERED WALKING THROUGH Gothic arched doorways and along endless wood panelled corridors which seemed to spread in all directions. The college buildings seemed enormous. Each ground floor corridor was lined with rows of doors, a painted name plate marking each one. Wide staircases rose here and there, but it was a narrow one that twisted up a turret which they climbed to the laboratories in the attics. Work benches with rows of gas taps and high stools stood in rows under steeply pitched roofs. Shelves of glass jars, racks of test tubes and strangely shaped vessels lined the walls. The space, empty now, for the vacation, was lit by a row of dormer windows with long views over the gardens and the fenland landscape beyond.

'I could live here quite happily,' Vita said, as they stood in the doorway.

Miss Harding laughed. 'To be frank it is too hot in the summer and bitterly cold in the winter, so that would not be advisable, but if you do join us you will certainly spend a lot of time up here.'

72

When Miss Harding left her at the dining hall, Vita was faced with rows of huge empty tables and only one other diner seated far in the distance, a young woman with dark curly hair and a striking purple dress. One of her hands was generously bandaged.

'Oh do join me, please,' this lone figure called across. 'I thought I should have to eat alone. I was feeling most uncomfortable.'

Vita walked the length of the long room and sat opposite.

'All the portraits seemed to be scrutinising me and finding me wanting!' said her companion, 'I am Dorothea Monkton, by the way.'

Vita introduced herself in return. Several uniformed college servants appeared and began to serve luncheon. 'They are not so very fearsome,' Vita said, looking round at the portraits, 'most of them look quite kindly to me.'

'Not that one,' said Dorothea, raising her bandaged hand towards a large painting on the wall behind Vita, 'that is a truly formidable face. She disapproves of me, I know it.'

It was true that the dignified lady in the portrait did have a particularly penetrating eye. They laughed.

'Are you here for an entrance examination?' Dorothea asked.

'Yes. Natural Sciences. And you?'

'Terrifying isn't it?'

'Well, it would be, but it all seems so unreal.'

'Oh, not to me, this is something I've imagined for ages. My governess, Miss Tilbury, has told me so many stories. She was a student here herself. I am her great project.'

Both women were presented with plates of mutton stew and greens, and began to eat, but very soon Dorothea had to surrender her attempts to eat one-handed. 'Could I possibly ask you to cut my meat for me?' she asked Vita, 'I still cannot hold a knife and this mutton is quite resistant.'

'Of course.' Vita sliced her companion's meat into edible pieces. 'Have you hurt your hand badly?'

'It is only a scratch, but it is quite a large one and I was told to keep it covered. I was mauled by a lion, if you can believe it!'

Vita's knife and fork stopped in mid-air. 'By a lion? Wherever did this happen?'

'In Norwich. There was a travelling circus and I took my brothers to see the lions in their cages afterwards,' Dorothea said, between forkfuls. 'Lucien, who is five, reached out to one in its cage, and the beast suddenly lunged its great paw between the bars. I thought it would hurt him, so I grabbed his hand, and it caught me instead!'

'That is a marvellous story, I must say!' Vita said, laughing aloud, for it had been recounted in the most cheerful manner.

'I know,' Dorothea continued, 'it was a week ago and I have been telling it ever since. It's probably going to be the most interesting thing that ever happens to me. Meanwhile my hand is healing well. I shall no doubt have a small scar that will come in useful if I need to start a conversation!'

'Is it daunting, being someone's project?' Vita asked, returning to their earlier subject. 'You said your governess took a close interest in your studies.'

'Well, I certainly feel I must not let poor Miss Tilbury down, but one can only do one's best.'

'And your parents?'

'They are kindly, but rather perplexed by my wanting to study full time. They cannot see a purpose in it - not for a young woman. If I had told my mother I wished to travel to Cambridge to buy hats she would have been perfectly serene, but when I told her I was taking an entrance examination, she did not know what to say at all. She did nothing to prevent it, however.'

'And what is it you would like to study?' Vita asked.

A college servant came and removed their plates, replacing them with large bowls of what appeared to be treacle sponge and custard.

'Mathematics,' Dorothea said, 'I have been fanatical about it since I was a child. I should really like to spend every waking moment about it, but I have six younger brothers, so unless I come here the chances of that are not high.'

'Oh! You are a Mathematician?'

'I would certainly like to be. And you, Vita ? What is your ambition?'

'I would like to study Science and perhaps become a doctor,' Vita said. It was still strange, saying it aloud.

'Well,' Dorothea said, raising her glass of water and proposing a toast, 'here's to good luck! Cheers!'

'Cheers!'

A shaft of wintry sunlight angled softly across the dining hall. It sparkled in their water glasses and made even the sharp-eyed lady in the portrait seem a little less severe. Under her gaze they were soon led away in different directions to sit their examinations.

ACKNOWLEDGMENTS

I was greatly helped in writing this story by the letters and notes in the archives at Girton College, Cambridge. Thanks also to the library at UCLA Los Angeles for their welcome to a visiting stranger. The stories I heard directly from women scientists at Lucy Cavendish College, were also a great inspiration.

Thanks to the Crime Writers' Association for shortlisting this story for a Debut Dagger in 2019 and to Alison Joseph, who probably doesn't remember the casual remark that got the whole thing started!

Tricia McBride continues to be a great coach and supporter.

Chris and the whole family cheer me on.

ABOUT THE AUTHOR

Fran Smith lives near Cambridge, on the edge of the Fens in the UK.

This is her first crime novel but definitely not her last. Lots more stories about Violet Carew and the people in the house in Eden Street are planned.

She has a blog about books and writing called Granny-writesbooks. You can also sign up to her newsletter on www.fransmithwriting.co.uk.

She loves hearing from readers:

fran@fransmithwriting.co.uk

A quick review is always very welcome too.

Thank you, dear reader, for getting this far.

Best wishes,

Fran Smith

May 2020

BY THE SAME AUTHOR

Miracles happen every day, so why shouldn't the remote little convent survive?

Sister Boniface knows that the centuries-old convent of St. Winifreda has crumbling towers, a leaky roof, and a rat infestation, but to her and the other sisters, it's home. When the Bishop demands they be sent away so the land can be sold as a car park, Sister B will need more than prayer to keep the place going.

Only with the help of ex-offenders, migrant workers, and the convent's team of international nuns can she succeed in their quest to save, renew, restore, and revivify the sisterhood. Sister B must go far beyond her comfort zone to win out in a hilarious and holy struggle.

Told through a series of letters between convents, *Best Wishes Sister B* is the first instalment in a heartwarming and gently humorous series. Readers are saying the book is a peaceful yet powerful tale and a genuine guilty pleasure. Featuring beautifully-drawn characters, whimsical humour, and a dose of divine intervention, *Best Wishes Sister B* is a triumph of good souls over adversity.

If you like James Herriot, Gervase Phinn, or Call the Midwife, you'll love this enchanting visit to an English village so much that you'll never want to leave. Pick up this gentle, funny, feel-good novel today!

BY THE SAME AUTHOR

Are cake, kindness and unwavering optimism enough to save St Winifreda's?

The centuries-old convent is struggling to survive. Its new café, with irresistible cakes, is soon popular, but the ancient chapel is in bad repair and the management consultant from the Bishop's office dislikes the sisters' unbusinesslike approach. When someone makes off with their hard-won funds and the auditor is acting strangely, Sister Boniface has her suspicions. And when a mysterious prowler creeps into the convent on Christmas Eve at night, she must tackle him alone.

Then Emelda, their long-time correspondent in South America goes missing, apparently kidnapped by illegal loggers and Sister B is catapulted into public speaking, salsa dancing and internet celebrity in an attempt to raise funds to save her.

The indomitable and eccentric cast of characters you met in *Best Wishes, Sister B* continues to find quirky ways to get to grips with the realities of the 21st century in this sequel; a joyful celebration of the resourcefulness of a remote and eccentric English community.